We've let her know

We've let her know

(that you are interested)

Etienne Bijnens

ISBN: 978-0-6451431-1-9

Typeset Paperback Palentino Linotype 11 – 5.5x8.5 (13.97x20.32)
Printed and bound in the USA

Chapter 1

This exaggerated London rends the heart

1

Her name is Anna, and in her message, she lets me know that I sound interesting. She writes that she likes my profile, and though she doesn't appear to be my type, I am overjoyed.

Two days since I've subscribed to this dating app, my existence has been recognised. I feel like a newborn, yanked into this novel life, and all of a sudden, I can breathe.

She tells me that she also likes mountain climbing and waterskiing and asks me where I am from.

I think her message is tedious. I browse her profile, and it looks lousy. The pictures are blurred and only show her from a distance. I don't make an effort to read through it at all and decide not to reply.

But then I notice an attachment. There are another four pictures, and they are of far better quality. The first one shows her sitting on a bench together with some friends in a park. I think she looks pretty. The second one is of her and a dog whose face is so close to Anna's that it seems like it wants to lick her. On the third one, she sits next to a woman who looks like an older version of her. It could be her mother. And finally, the fourth picture makes me decide to reply. It shows a close-up of her face; her hair is blond and curled; she has the most endearing smile. Her right shoulder is casually turned forward, and with her left hand, she brushes through her wind-combed hair. It almost feels as if she is looking at me.

She is gorgeous.

I read her profile again, this time more in-depth. It seems that I have missed things the first time I looked, and I am starting to be intrigued by what she has written. I read her message again, and it sounds lovely.

My profile doesn't mention that I like mountain climbing. I have never done it. But one of my pictures shows me dangling from a rock, and even though twenty centimetres below is solid ground, the angle makes it look as if I am a regular free-climber.

I did mention the waterskiing part, but I haven't uploaded any pictures of me being towed behind a speedboat. A genetic blemish in my family line makes me look as if I am burdened with a beer belly. All my cousins have it. We can't get rid of it, and although (when I tense my muscles) it doesn't look too bad, it certainly doesn't establish a good first impression.

I could have let her believe that I live somewhere in the United Kingdom. The great thing about the internet is that you can pretend to be in any country in the world. But in my reply, I stick to the truth. I let her know that, while I am originally from Belgium and currently live in South Africa, my company will relocate me to London in two weeks from now.

If anything, it at least tells her that I have a job.

She replies a day later. She wants to know if September is summer or winter in South Africa. She comments on some of my pictures and asks if I am really six foot three. She says that she especially likes the one where I am milking a cow and thinks I am attractive. She asks if my eyes are blue or greyish-green, as it is hard to tell from the pictures I have uploaded. She wants to know if I happen to live in Cape Town and confesses that she loves that city and its people.

'Green,' I write back, and: 'Early summer-ish.' I further tell her that I live in Port Elisabeth and that (because she thinks I am attractive) she has won extra brownie points.

During the first couple of days, I don't spend too much time checking the dating app, and even though I did see her messages, I restrained myself from replying immediately.

I don't have to rush things, I tell myself. It's another twelve days before I fly to Heathrow, and it would be silly of me to jump straight from the plane into a relationship with some English girl that I have just met on the internet.

Three and a half years ago, when I first arrived in South Africa, I did a search on the local outlet of this internet dating website. I keyed in some features like pictures, height, distance, no children, and the like, and a lousy thirty-two girls were the result. None of those could tempt me to write a message. But this time, while probing through the United Kingdom's version and putting in a mere range of ten kilometres from Ealing-London, the site releases no less than nine-hundred and twenty-eight potential dates!

In one of her messages, Anna explains her reason for using blurred pictures. She believes that no one would select her profile if she hadn't put any on. At the same time, she didn't want people to recognise her. What if a colleague of hers stumbled upon this site, she wondered, does she then become the laughing stock of the office?

'This whole inbox messaging is silly,' she writes back the next day, and then her question comes: 'Would you like to chat on Skype?'

2

I am shocked.

A friend of mine has warned me about this. Anna might not be who she portrays herself to be. "There are many internet-based scams out there," my friend had said and revealed that he had experienced it first-hand when a pretty blond girl (who claimed to live somewhere in the north of England) had contacted him over a dating site.

In hindsight, he'd told me, he should have been a little bit more suspicious. Instead of writing the usual chitchat, she'd immediately given him a complete description of her family's background. Already in that first message, she'd told him that her mum and dad had passed away and that only her grandmother was still alive. On top of that, there were many English language mistakes, which was bizarre, especially for someone who claimed to have a university degree in geology.

It didn't take her long to tell him that she didn't want to endlessly write up and down over that dating app and that it would be far better to chat over Skype.

My friend agreed. He was, I guess, blinded by her looks. They started chatting. Within ten minutes, he learned that she worked for a large oil company and currently lived in Nigeria. But her contract had come to an end. She needed to return to the United Kingdom because her grandmother had been hospitalised in St Georges London.

They agreed to meet, but then things got complicated. While chatting over Skype, she told him that she had a problem. Her flight to London was booked, but the hotel she was staying in didn't want to let her go as it appeared her credit cards had been stolen, and she had no money to pay her bill. Of course, the next question she asked was—could he help her out? He simply had to deposit some money into a Nigerian bank account, and she would pay him back the moment they meet-up.

My friend, realising that this was a scam, immediately deleted all her details. But a week later, he was approached by another pretty girl: similar language mistakes and a request to chat over Skype. What followed was a detailed story about her being a fashion designer travelling through African countries to purchase exclusive fabrics, and, of course, one of those countries was—Nigeria.

Did Anna really say Skype!?
I decide to write back and ask her if WhatsApp would do? I mean, everyone talks on WhatsApp nowadays, right?

But when I explain that I'm not that often on Skype, her reply says that she dropped her phone in the sink and WhatsApp needs a working phone.

I reluctantly give her my Skype name and wonder if this is a red flag? While I half expect her to write that she has been kidnapped by warlords (that they have already wiped out all her friends and family and that they demand a ransom—or else), her Skype message appears. In pure Bugs Bunny style, she asks: 'What's up?'

'Hi Jennifer,' I reply hesitantly.

A yellow smiley-face emerges in the next line, quickly followed by: 'It's my flatmate's name.'

Question-mark.

12

Then Anna again: 'I'm using her computer and also her Skype account. Sorry, I am completely disorganised. I normally chat over WhatsApp, but my phone is absolutely dead.'

During the next half an hour, I learn that she recently moved house and that most of her stuff is still in cardboard boxes. She tells me she needs to get her life sorted out, which means: she needs to find a new job, a new flat and, well, in a way—a new boyfriend. She says that it doesn't necessarily need to be in that order, and another yellow smiley face full-stops her message.

From then on, Skype takes over my life. I regularly check if Anna is online. Most of the time, I write her a short message, nothing more than a 'how are you?' and wait for her to reply. This often arrives immediately, and then we start our chat which can take up to an hour or more. Sometimes I wait for her to contact me first. I don't want her to think that I am desperate or don't have a life?

At this stage, I actually don't.

I convert my precious sunny South African days into waiting. I wait for the morning to come. I wait for the day to finish. I wait for Anna to go online. And, I wait for the moment I can finally fly to London so I can meet up with her and jump straight from Heathrow into a relationship. But she doesn't need to know that.

However, the days pass and Anna and I spend our time chatting with each other. It feels like I am really getting to know her. She has three sisters who all live in England. She tries to visit them as often as she can and misses her little dog that stays with her parents in Leicester. She further doesn't like ironing, olives, visiting the zoo, cleaning the bathroom, peeling mushrooms, people who pull up while the traffic light is still orange and washing greasy frying pans in the sink.

On the other hand, she enjoys eating spicy food, all sorts of dried fruits, drinking coffee and listening to the alternative metal band Korn. In fact, she has plenty of time to listen to Korn now that she is in-between jobs and in-between flats. ('Or in-between boyfriends,' I reply.) But she is lucky that her ex-colleague is letting her stay at her place for a couple of weeks until she finds another flat.

I, on the other hand, let her know that I am an outdoorsy person. I like walking shoes and rainproof jackets, forests, mountains, the smell of pinewood in summer's dawn misty woodland lakes, the noise of crickets in the background and campfire sparks leaping into the open night sky while trying to become stars when they grow up.

In one of her messages, she says that she really likes me. She tells me that she enjoys chatting with me and that she often can't wait for me to come online.

She is already becoming a close friend, and four days before I fly to the UK, I decide to voice-call her.

She sounds wonderful. Her voice is soft, almost velvety, and she laughs the most endearing laugh. "When shall we meet?" she asks.

"As soon as I've landed," I reply.

"When will you land?"

"Saturday morning."

"Saturday it is then," she giggles.

I will leave South Africa Friday evening around nine to arrive at Heathrow a little bit after six in the morning. That same afternoon I will meet Anna in a coffee shop in Ealing-Broadway, West London. I have lived in South Africa for over four years, and although I have dated quite a few girls, it never truly felt right.

I can't believe the amount of time I have wasted.

3

After a two-hour delay, I land at Heathrow airport. I couldn't sleep on the plane, and so I watched all the movies that were showing. At times two or three at once, just to keep my mind off Anna, but I can't remember any of the titles.

I feel exhausted.

It's a quarter past eight in the morning when I finally spot my friend Brett at Arrivals. He has been waiting here since six and looks tired too. We give each other a brotherly hug. He asks me how my flight has been, and I reply that it was okay.

It is raining. Heathrow airport is only twelve miles from Ealing, but while we drive back to his place, traffic peaks, and he is getting late for work. He manages a small sales team for a real estate company, and since Saturday is the busiest day of the week, he has to be at his office at nine.

An hour later, he drops me at his house. He doesn't have to show me where his fridge, shower, toilet or TV is. I have been here before. After he hands me his keys, he rushes off. But forty minutes later, he's back. He has told his office that he has to show clients a flat.

"Tell me all about this girl you'll be meeting? Who is she? Where is she from? What does she do? Is she nice?" he grills and gasps, "I can't believe you have a date on the exact same day you land in London."

I show him the pictures on my phone. It makes him bite the knuckle of his thumb. "You are such a lucky man!" he says and slaps me playfully on my shoulder while he moans: "I feel betrayed. You're such a bastard. We were supposed to lead a bachelor's life in London. I've been waiting for you to come over, so we can go out on the piss every weekend and hunt for girls!" he whines, "But now you've messed that all up by landing yourself into a relationship the same day you arrive in the UK."

"I'm not sure if she'll even like me," I laugh.

"Don't bullshit me!" he roars, "Of course she'll like you."

"Anything could go wrong. Chatting over Skype is meaningless. She might take one look at me and think that she needs to get the hell out of that coffee shop as soon as she can."

"Rubbish," he says. "The moment she sees you, she'll fall head over heels in love with you."

He is always positive, always encouraging, and I appreciate that.

"I wish," I reply.

"And what about you?" he asks and laughs: "Do you like her?"

"Mm," I smile, "I haven't seen a girl that pretty in a long time, and I know it isn't all in the book's cover, but she seems to have a truly wonderful personality. She is sweet and interesting and lovely to talk to. If I had found a ring in Johannesburg airport," I jokingly say, "I would go on one knee and propose even before she sits down at my table."

"My goodness," he chuckles, "you're such a wimp!"

Then he's off again but promises me that he will try and drop by later. He tightens his tie and walks out.

Brett is as tall as me but bigger built. Years ago, he was selected to join the South African 'Springboks' Rugby College'. But for some reason, he decided not to pursue it as a career. He still plays rugby but never pushed through to top level.

If you ask me, I believe he was scared of getting hurt in much the same way as he's scared of getting hurt by girls. That's the reason why he wants us to lead a bachelor's life.

I once knew a young football player in Belgium who, already at the age of fifteen, showed true talent. One of the top clubs invited him to play a test game. A couple of weeks after that, I ran into him and asked him what the outcome had been. He told me that they'd let him play a complete game against another national team, and that was where he saw top-level football's true nature. The other players kicked, hit and spat him in the face every time the referee turned his back. It intimidated him, and he ended up playing the worst game of his life. He never joined that top team and now sells office supplies to small and medium-sized businesses.

Perhaps something similar happened to Brett in rugby and his love life. He got married at a young age and really loved his wife, but she fell in love with someone else, so they divorced. Even though this happened a year and a half ago, he's still not ready to dive into anything new. He keeps his dates at safe arm's length, nervous that they might kick, hit and spit him in the face every time the referee turns his back.

In a way, there's no difference between him, the young football player in Belgium and me. Brett might have expected us to hit London's nightlife, but I'm nervous too. I've arrived in a completely new country, and I don't know anyone. To end up being lonely in this gigantic city—is my biggest fear.

An hour later, Brett walks back into the flat and demands to see Anna's pictures again. "She's gorgeous," he groans and, for a second time, bites the knuckle of his thumb. "How on earth did you pull this off?"

"She actually contacted me," I tell him. "I didn't even have to lift a finger. In all honesty, I haven't messaged or winked at anyone else during the whole three weeks I've joined that dating app."

"Well," he sighs, "then I think this is all meant to be."

4

A couple of hours later, I'm off to meet Anna. All my clothes look suitcase-ironed, and I've borrowed a shirt from my friend. I am wearing jeans that I wore on the plane. I want to keep it casual.

I'm lousy at directions. Brett had to explain over and over where the coffee shop was. "You can't go wrong," he said, but I did.

When I eventually walk in, I look around. There are not that many people. I scrutinise every face and search for something familiar; signs of recognition: a smile, her waving her hand, her getting up and running over to greet me, her throwing her arms around my neck and kissing me madly. But no one pays me any attention.

The few girls who sit at a table on my right don't resemble Anna's pictures, nor do the guys or the dog underneath one of the chairs.

I take a seat at a small table in a corner. It's not too close to the door, but not too far either. I haven't prepared any topics for discussion. I don't expect us not to know what to talk about. I don't feel I need to worry about this. Everything will go smoothly—of that, I am sure.

I look at my watch. It's ten past two.

She is late. I cannot believe this. I have gone through all this effort, and she is late!

But then another thought surfaces: could it perhaps be possible that she won't come? Have I been stood up? I immediately brush the thought aside, but it doesn't stay away. Instead, it starts filling my mind. What if she doesn't come? What if she has lost interest and decided she couldn't be bothered to meet me?

I let another five minutes pass. It's a quarter past two. I tell myself that I will wait until half-past—and not a minute later.

But when half-past two arrives, I am still in the coffee shop. For the zillionth time, I look around, making absolutely sure that none of the girls is her, that the guys are guys, and the dog is indeed a dog.

Only at twenty to three my phone finally bleeps. It is a text message from Anna. She writes that she is genuinely sorry. She has just left the underground, which blocked the signal from her phone, and it will take her another twenty, perhaps thirty minutes before she'll arrive in Ealing. Do I mind, she asks?

'Absolutely not at all,' I text back.

Absolutely not at all my arse, I think.

I'm irritated, though, at the same time, I'm relieved that she's still coming. I send her another text. I tell her not to worry and lie that I am quite relaxed reading a book.

Her reply comes almost immediately, 'Thanks, you are sweet.'

Almost an hour after she's sent her last text message (an hour and forty-five minutes since I entered the coffee shop), I see her walking through the door. She comes straight to me and says, "I'm sorry, I'm so sorry. I've had a lot of bad luck with the tube, and I didn't realise Ealing was so far away."

I feel nauseous.

5

She definitely looks like her pictures: soft blond hair, almost angel-like, and she is beautiful. But there is something wrong. Something I was unable to spot during our weeks of emailing, chatting, phoning and exchanging photos. Up till now, I have only seen pictures of her face, and I realise this was a mistake.

I feel sick in my stomach.

It is not so much that she is shorter than I expected. Even her neck and shoulders look elegant and slim. But there is one thing which is entirely out of proportion ... —it's her butt.

I am shocked. I did not expect this. It's not that she is merely a tiny bit overweight and that a few walks in the park could trim any excess off. It goes far beyond that. Her backside is enormous, and her slender shoulders only accentuate the contrast. Calling her pear-shaped would be an insult to pears. On top of that, she wears a long, broad skirt, most likely to conceal this part of her figure, but it only makes it look wider.

I'm not prepared for this, and even more, I'm startled by my own reaction. It feels like I'm gasping for breath, and it has turned me speechless.

I see her hesitate for a moment, and then she grabs a chair to sit down. "Are you all right?" she asks.

I keep looking at her face. I am sweating. How on earth is this possible, I think? How can fate just slap me in the face like that? This wasn't supposed to happen.

"Yes," I eventually answer, forcing myself to act nonchalant. "How was your tube ride?"

Too late, I realise that this is quite a stupid question given the fact that she is almost an hour and forty-five minutes late and that she already told me it was terrible. But she grabs it as if it were a lifebuoy in mid-sea and starts telling me the complete story in detail.

Apparently, it was horrible! I hear the sounds of her storytelling, but I am not listening to the words. Instead, I am thinking about her butt and what to do. Her face is pretty, but I seem to be unable to get around her backside. Could she go to the gym; do some running or cycling? Would any of this help? I am not sure what to do.

Well, in a way, I am ... —I can't continue with this. I still try to tell myself that she is pretty, that I liked chatting with her and that I should give it a chance. But I don't want to listen to this. Instead, I scream in my head that I want out! I want to leave this coffee shop, and my earlier concern that she might not like me has turned into fear that she might.

She has stopped talking and looks at me. She smiles, and there is an awkward silence. It feels as if she has asked me a question and is waiting for me to reply.

"Your flight?" she smiles, "Was it good?"

"Yes, very good," I answer almost automatically, realising a bit too late that I should have grabbed the opportunity to tell her that I am exhausted. It could have prepared her for the fact that I will be leaving early. I quickly yawn and say, "Not really that good. I hardly slept and am very tired."

"I am sorry to hear that," she replies.

"I shouldn't have put our first date right after I flew in from South Africa," I continue. However, I am immediately conscious that I said 'first date', which could make her think that there will be others.

I have to admit that she is sweet, and I can't say that I don't like her, but there won't be a second date. I only want to be polite about it.

I wish it was the other way around and that she would yawn, stretch her arms above her head and tell me how drained she feels after such a long flight. No one likes rejection. It inflicts pain, and I don't want to hurt anyone, especially not angel-face Anna. But how do I tell her? How do I get up and leave? We've only been sitting here for fifteen minutes. Do I have to stay and chat for a decent hour or perhaps even two? I will certainly not take her out for dinner. I don't want to contribute food to a problem she already has.

But what if she asks me if we will see each other again?

For a second time, there is a silence between us, and she is looking at me. "Weren't you listening?" she asks.

"I'm sorry," I apologise. "I'm really tired."

"Would you like to go home and rest?" she suggests. "I do understand that you've had hardly any sleep, and you must be exhausted."

"No, absolutely not," I say, and again too late, I realise my mistake. I could have grabbed this opportunity to leave.

"Oh, good," she sighs, "because, after all my tube hassle, I would have hated for you to run off."

We both laugh at this, and I could hit myself on the head. Now I might even have to take her to dinner.

It is not that she is hard to talk to. Our conversation starts to flow. She asks me about my stay in South Africa and if my parents are happy that I am living much closer to Belgium. She tells me about her ex-colleague, who in fact was her boss, but since Jennifer resigned, Anna's job as a personal assistant was no longer required. "I would have been homeless if she hadn't offered me a place to stay," she laughs. "She is a very nice person."

After dinner, I no longer have to act: I am drained. I ask her if she doesn't mind me heading home, and she says she understands. I walk her to the tube station, and when we say goodbye, I give her a tiny peck on the cheek. It makes her blush. I don't say anything about meeting up, but neither does she. I guess this is one of the advantages of internet dating—both parties know exactly why they meet and what the risks are.

I fake another yawn, which makes her giggle and say, "Go home and get under the duvet." Then she walks towards the waiting train. She turns around one last time, waves and moments later, she is absorbed into the crowd of passengers.

I am shocked by his question. "Do I need to?" I hesitate. "I thought I'd just leave it where it is. We said goodbye at the tube station, and that's it."

"Hmmm," he says.

I finish off the carton of juice. It is after ten, and we both go to bed. It is a big house with three bedrooms and a nice sized living room. I quickly check the dating app before I crawl into bed. There is nothing from Anna, which, in a way, makes me feel relieved. I don't send her a message, and neither do I text her, but perhaps Brett is right, and I should do it tomorrow. It would only be decent of me to let her know.

I promise I will.

7

On Monday morning, I take an early tube from Ealing Broadway to Euston. From there, I continue my journey by train to my company's UK head office in Northampton. I spend the entire day with Human Resources. They guide me through the different procedures; let me sign documents that say I have received certain information. They give me a laptop, a mobile phone and a temporary car which I can use until my new one arrives.

They have put me up in a hotel not too far from the office and told me I can stay there until I've found a flat. I can work from home (or basically from the hotel), but nonetheless, I drive to the office every day. I rarely leave before seven or eight in the evening, and Monday, Tuesday and Wednesday fly by. I try to meet some of the colleagues I will be working with, but hardly any of them are there. They are all field-based, and I soon learn that they prefer to go to the office in Nottingham rather than to our head office in Northampton.

Nottingham, depending on traffic, is at least a three-hour drive from London. I don't want to move too far away from where Brett lives as I plan to spend most of my weekends at his place. Even if I move closer to Nottingham, my colleagues will hardly be there. Besides this, I need to be close to an airport with easy access to most European cities.

So, on Thursday, keeping all those reasons in the back of my mind, I take a drive to Leighton Buzzard. It's more or less halfway between London and Northampton.

I've browsed the internet while looking for flats, and a little cottage-like building jumped out. Judging from the pictures, it seemed very nice, but when I arrive, I notice it is actually a converted garage built next to the landlord's house. Still, it isn't too bad, but I am a little disappointed.

When I'm back in my hotel room, I sit on my bed for a while and think about my next steps. Tomorrow, I will drive my company car to London and stay the weekend at Brett's. Then another week will come. And another one. I plan to find a flat by the end of this month. I could push to stay a second month in the hotel, but the food isn't that great, and I already feel I need some proper structure in my life. I might as well go for the Leighton Buzzard's converted garage.

At some point in time, I should focus on my job. The company I work for believes that I am good at what I do, and perhaps I am. I started as a business development manager in Belgium. When the local sales team needed advice or when a customer was too big to handle, I was brought in to give my support. With an in-depth technical understanding and good commercial skills, I was thought to be more qualified to take a customer to a higher level of partnership.

However, now that I am playing on a European level, the job has slightly changed. I will be more involved with project management and the implementation of corporate strategies. Although some degree of business development will remain, my responsibilities are no longer limited to just one country. Aside from the UK, there is Ireland, France, Belgium, the Netherlands and, for some strange reason, Scandinavia.

I need to set up some meetings with my colleagues or at least let them know that I exist. I doubt that any of them are waiting for that. I could even decide to keep a low profile and hide for a couple of weeks, but surely Josue, my boss in Spain, might at some stage ask what I have been doing.

I better be able to give him some answers.

8

That same evening in the hotel, after I shower, my phone flashes.

Of course, it is Anna.

'Are you online?' she wants to know, and I can tell she sent her message about fifteen minutes ago.

I am not sure what to do. I could pretend I am not online. My Skype profile is set to private. This means no one can see when I am online or read their message, although she will know that it has been delivered to my phone.

I could simply not reply, pretending that I haven't noticed her contacting me, but I am torn by that nagging feeling of guilt which, I am sure, will disappear with time.

I should be nice to her, and I should make her feel good about herself. It's the least I can do.

'Hi there,' I type, 'I was in the shower. Are you still there?' When I press enter, I realise that letting Anna know that I was in the shower might have been a little too much information.

She replies immediately. 'Great to hear from you. How was your week?'

It has almost been a week indeed, and I am quite surprised to learn that time also flies when you are … well … —not really having fun.

'Pretty busy,' I reply. 'I finally managed to catch up on some sleep. What about you?'

I don't tell her that I think she is a genuinely wonderful person. I don't sandwich information by using words like; sweet

We've let her know

and interesting and lovely-to-talk-to, to eventually let her know that I feel it might —for whatever reason— not work out between the two of us. Let's face it, she might not even like me, and how ridiculously presumptuous would I sound by telling her that I think we would not be a good match. She most likely will laugh in my face and tell me she has no interest in me whatsoever and that she was just trying to be friendly by messaging me.

A few more questions and answers follow, and they all fit the 'how-was-your-week' category. After about ten minutes, I lie and tell her that I'm getting a call from someone else and that I need to go. She says goodbye and wishes me well, but the moment I think I am safe, her following message appears, 'We will have a barbecue soon. It would be great if you could come.'

You see what happens when you try to be nice to people!

I don't reply and log off.

I shouldn't feel bad about it, I tell myself. This is precisely what attracts me to the concept of internet dating. Everyone knows from the start what can be expected and what they are in it for. I am not responsible for other people's expectations and disappointments, or am I? In all fairness, the fact that I have not asked her on a second date is an answer in itself.

It works. This explanation eases my mind. At least for a moment. Then the guilt comes back. What if she is 'meant to be', I wonder. Would I then be the one who's slapping fate in the face? Let's assume that fate lets itself be slapped; how ungrateful would it make me?

I stare at my phone and find myself opening the dating app. All of this happens without thinking. When I click on the search page, I think: 'screw fate' and key in some features; like height, distance from Leighton Buzzard, no children, non-smoker and so on.

32

Within seconds, seven hundred and fifty girls appear to be within dating reach. I open a few of the profiles and scroll through the pictures. I even randomly read what some of the girls have written.

As it turns out, quite a lot of them would like to curl up on the sofa with a good glass of wine while watching a Netflix movie. It is almost as if they have copied each other's wording or have been on some internet dating course I still don't know the existence of.

Only after clicking through about fifteen profiles, I find someone who I could be interested in. The girl has uploaded seven pictures, and they (unlike the ones of Anna) show her in full length.

This is good. I will not make that mistake again.

I half-read through her profile but mainly focus on her looks. She is pretty, she has long blond hair and is quite tall. It seems she works as an accountant for a biscuit company and I decide to write her a message.

I stare at my phone for over five minutes before I start typing, 'Hi, how are you? I really like your profile and—...' But then I stop and realise that this is precisely what I can't do. I start again and tell her that I think we have things in common, to only backtrack and erase what I've written.

I'm sure that she gets approached by hundreds of guys who tell her that they like her profile and feel they have things in common. I need to be original, but that's harder than I thought. I require a fresh angle, a method that wakes her from the boredom of reading all the other letters. I have to prove that I've at least made an effort to read what she's written. When Anna contacted me, she mentioned that she also liked waterskiing and mountain climbing. I have to do the same and need to pick out things from her profile which I can casually mention in my message.

I take another look at her but can't seem to find anything worthwhile mentioning. I can tell her that I am Belgian and that I lived in South Africa, but it is precisely the type of information she should be able to read on my profile.

This is more difficult than I thought. It is almost like a job interview. My curriculum vitae is out there, but what do I write in the accompanying letter? I should give this more thought, though at the moment I'm too tired. I can't be bothered. It's already late, and all I wanted to do is contact at least one girl, so the coming weeks don't look too empty.

If only friends of friends know someone who knows someone and invite her to some house warming party. But this is London, a city where no one knows anyone to invite anywhere.

Despair overwhelms me. This is exactly why I wanted to meet someone before I arrived at Heathrow. I dread being alone, and I certainly don't want to be lonely.

Before I switch my phone off, I notice that the app creators have thought of an easy way out. There is a button, and if I click it, it will tell the girl that she has been noticed. It is called 'winking', and it saves me from being forced to write her witty messages. In fact, almost immediately after clicking it, I get a message that lets me know that they have let her know. To be more precise, it says, 'We have let her know that you are interested'.

It's as simple as that.

Of course, I'm interested. There is no mistake about it, and even the girl with long blond hair in seven photos shouldn't have any doubts. This is great. It certainly saves me a lot of trouble—no hurting my brain about being original and no worrying about being different from others.

I quickly flick to another profile. A girl with dark hair has uploaded three pictures. She writes that if happiness were a religion, she'd definitely be a churchgoer. I think this is quite funny, so I wink at her. Another profile shows an Irish girl. I skip through her text, pass over her hobbies and favourite things and wink. The next one is a brunette with lots of freckles, and after that, I let a girl with black hair know that I have noticed her.

Within ten minutes, I have winked at six profiles, and I didn't have to read or write anything. By the time I have clicked on eight profiles, I no longer open the second or the third picture and wink immediately. In less than fifteen minutes, I let more than twenty girls know that I am indeed absolutely and tremendously interested. By the time I turn my phone off, I feel I have achieved something. It didn't even take any effort.

It's a quarter past eleven, and I crawl into bed.

The following day, I wake up at six. Even before I go to the toilet, before I brush my teeth, take a shower or make myself my indispensable instant coffee, I switch my phone on and browse straight to the dating app. I check my inbox to see how many replies I've received.

Nothing!

No messages whatsoever.

This is impossible. Something must have gone wrong. On the other hand, it is still early. I can't really expect that those girls sit up till late at night, waiting for a wink from me to reply immediately.

I crawl back into bed and lie awake for over an hour. After that, I recheck my phone.

Still nothing.

I shower, get dressed, have breakfast downstairs in the hotel's restaurant, and when I arrive back at my room, I open my inbox for the third time.

Again nothing.

What is wrong with these girls?

9

It rains while I drive to the office. I have a meeting with two of my colleagues: Roger and Eric. They are both field-based in the north of England.

Roger is a senior account manager, and Eric, still very young, a technical application specialist. I need to learn from them what they have been doing with some large international customers.

Roger appears to keep his distance. He sighs and shows his displeasure with the fact that he had to drive all the way from Newcastle to meet me. He even says that he doesn't see the point since all is okay, and therefore there is no need to waste time.

Eric, on the other hand, is more eager to talk to me. He says he wants me to join him on some customer visits to learn and absorb all he possibly can. I answer that this is great. He only needs to let me know when and where, and I assure him that I will be there.

While my two colleagues dutifully explain how they go about their daily jobs, I surf the dating site only to become disappointed again. My inbox is still empty. I double-check whether my profile is still visible, and it is.

Almost three hours into our meeting, a third guy walks in. His name is Rodney, and although he has been living in the UK for about six years, he still has a solid South African accent. During our lunch break, he lets me know that, even though he misses his country, he has no plans to go back. "Too much crime," he sighs, "and the politicians are unable or unwilling to do something about it. South Africa will end up like Zimbabwe," he concludes.

I am not sure if I share his apocalyptic view, but for some reason, I immediately like the guy. He grew up in Garden Route's Mosselbay and went to a private school. He is married with a daughter and has been working for the company for about three years. He tells me he manages a young team of sales reps in the south of England. He lives in Slough, west of London, which is not far from Ealing, and he says I should come around for drinks one day.

I check my phone for a fifth time to find the app's inbox is still empty. I am starting to become frustrated. Not only with the way my dating life is progressing, but also with work.

My boss Josue has sent me a tremendous amount of emails, and they are all packed with hundreds of attachments. 'For Your Interest', he writes. Not even that: his message says, 'Hi L, FYI, Rgds, J'. In a way, I prefer his 'FYIs' to his lengthy emails even though I am not interested at all. The only 'FYI' I really want to receive is from the girls on the dating app, who seems to be completely unaware of my existence.

I think that must be it: they simply are not aware that I am still there because I haven't renewed my subscription. It's been over five weeks since I joined, and I suddenly remember that I only subscribed for one month.

This newly gained knowledge exhilarates me. I browse straight to the settings but notice that the tick-box with 'automatic renewal' has been checked. They have also taken another twenty-five pounds out of my account to allow me to continue receiving messages from girls.

What do they mean 'to continue'?

I have received squat-all and aside from that—how dare they! It's not as if they have asked me for permission. If I hadn't checked this today, they could have been taking money out of my bank account for the next thirty years!

My frustration turns into irritation. Though I am not entirely sure what I am most irritated with: the fact that I am still a member or that none of the twenty girls I winked at has given me any attention. The least those girls could do is let me know that they are not interested. They should appreciate that it has cost me time and effort to get in touch with them.

At five in the afternoon, I decide to pack up and drive back to the hotel. Roger and Eric left at three and Rodney, the South African, around four. But before I fold my laptop into its bag, I check my inbox one last time.

There it is, finally a message!

I feel like I have just solved the issues around nuclear fusion and would jump from my chair and dance on the hot desks if it weren't for all the people around me.

'Hi,' the message starts. 'I must say I feel refreshed with you stating exactly what I believe in; the importance of good friends and family. If you love a chat and a laugh, good food and wine, then I am looking forward to your reply.'

She does not mention the wink, but then I don't know the rules around that. I open her profile, and though I can't really remember what all the girls I winked at looked like, I am sure that none of them was fifty-three!

Hasn't she checked my age range? I feel insulted. Who on earth does she think she is? She doesn't even live within the kilometre range I have specified, not even in England for that matter.

But what do I do? Shall I write back and tell her that she surely must have made a mistake. Does she expect me to reply? Must I become a slave to everyone who writes me a message even when their profiles are so remotely removed from what I am searching for?

I think not!

I do have a life. I just changed jobs, moved country and continent and have about a trillion bloody 'FYI'-attachments to read. Surely, I cannot be expected to reply to every bit of internet interest someone shows me!

But on the positive side, receiving this message means that everything works. My subscription is active, and indeed, my pictures must be visible. So why on earth have none of those twenty girls shown any reaction to my wink?

How rude of them.

10

Friday late afternoon, I drive on the M1 towards Brett's house in Ealing-London. It rains relentlessly, and I end up in one massive traffic jam. In my four years in South Africa, I've not ever seen the number of cars that are now lined up in front of me. It looks like everyone on this planet wants to spend the weekend in London.

I punch in a couple of keys on my GPS SatNav, and it quickly comes up with an alternative route. It tells me that it will take me half an hour longer, but I might not arrive anywhere before Monday afternoon at the speed I am going.

My GPS SatNav (which I've christened 'Suzy') informs me that, after eight hundred meters, I need to follow the turnoff. It takes me more than half an hour to get there, but I feel like I have broken out of prison once I have. While everyone is still stuck, I leave the motorway behind to cruise effortlessly over English country roads until I have reached my destination.

However, I did not foresee all these traffic lights. Every hobbit village is packed with them. Did they buy them in bulk? Continental Europe has, over the years, been replacing their traffic lights with roundabouts, and they must have sold them off as second-hand to England. They have not only been put on crossroads but also on T-junctions, Y-junctions, intersections and forks. Besides that, each individual pedestrian has his own private traffic light, as do all dogs, cats and sparrows. Every five metres, another red light orders me to stop, and it takes an eternity before I am allowed to continue.

Everything repeats itself over and over: stop, drive five metres and stop again. Before the car in the front even slightly accelerates, the lights switch back to orange and red. It takes me another two hours before I can find my way back to the M1, where traffic has come to a complete standstill.

I will never arrive in Ealing!

Brett and I are supposed to go out tonight. I left Northampton at three in the afternoon. It is six now, and I am not even halfway.

On top of that, my phone rings. My car receives the call, and Brett speaks, "Hi Bro, where are you?"

"About forty kilometres away," I reply, "which should mean that, in theory, I will be at your place in forty minutes. But taking traffic into account, I might arrive Sunday before breakfast."

"We need to be at Kyra's party at eight," he reminds me.

"I won't even be five meters farther around eight," I sigh.

"Don't worry, bro," he says, "but I am afraid you need to find the place on your own. Would it be okay for you if I text you her address?"

"No problem," I reply.

11

Kyra is not very pretty, and she is not a blind date for me through a friend who knows a friend at a barbecue. She is one of Brett's friends. They went to the same school in Port Elizabeth. She seems to have a crush on him. She keeps inviting him to almost every event in London, but he hardly goes.

Brett doesn't like her, and though I've only met her once, I can't say that I like her either. I don't even feel like going, and we are merely doing the good deed and saying 'hi' and 'bye' because it is her birthday. That's all.

After sitting still in traffic for another half an hour, my speed picks up and finally, at ten past nine, I arrive in Ealing. I enter the empty house, have a quick shower, borrow some of Brett's clothes since the few I have, are at the hotel's laundrette, and I head for the nearest tube station.

When I reach Kyra's house, I am immediately welcomed by a gorgeous girl with long wavy black hair. She asks me where I am from with a most endearing accent, and I assume she is Spanish. After I tell her, she says, "Ah qui, Belgique," and lets me know that, although she grew up in Madrid, she went to university in Paris.

She is beautiful. She giggles a lot, and her laugh hides in her deep watery eyes. It tells me she is drunk. We chat until she says she needs to mingle. She gives me a kiss on my cheek and waves her hand like a butterfly waves its wings. She knocks over a small table when she turns around, spilling beer and beer bottles over the floor. But she doesn't seem to mind and strolls off while others rush to clean up the mess.

By now, Brett has seen me and signals me to come over. We give each other a brotherly hug. "How was traffic, bro?" he greets but doesn't wait for my reply and instead calls out to Kyra, who stands a bit farther.

She appears to be pleased to see me or at least pretends she is. "How nice of you to come," she smiles.

I wish her a happy birthday and give her three kisses on the cheek.

"Are you enjoying England?" she asks.

"He already went on a date with some hot chick," Brett inserts, and I kick him in the shin. "Why did you do that!" he cries out and jumps around like a fouled football player exaggerating his pain.

"Yes, I've heard," Kyra laughs, "and apparently, you don't like girls with fat bums."

I am embarrassed. Kyra herself is a little more than overweight, and her remark makes me go red in the face. If Brett believes that this will break the ice, it is only because the room temperature dramatically increased. Sweat slides down from my forehead, and I stutter before I manage to say, "Where are the drinks. I need something icy cold."

"I'll get you one," Kyra offers and disappears into the kitchen.

"I noticed that you've met Estella?" Brett says while he points in the direction of the Spanish girl with long wavy black hair.

"Yeah, man," I reply, "she's hot," and ask him if he happens to know whether she's single.

I watch her leaning against a bookshelf at the far end of the room, and with the music blaring, I'm sure that she couldn't have heard us, but all of a sudden, she turns around and looks in our direction. She gives us a warm smile and waves her butterfly wings in greeting. At the exact moment that I raise my arm, I see a girl with short blond hair on my right side doing the same. With her hand, she blows Estella a kiss which is almost immediately returned.

After that, the blond girl turns her attention to me and says, "I can assure you that Estella hasn't got a boyfriend." And pauses before she continues: "She and I have been an item for over a year."

"Bloody hell!" I gasp. And not knowing what else would be appropriate to say while crumbling under the weight of even more embarrassment, I stutter: "Well ... congratulations."

She smiles. With a Spanish accent, she says, "You're very cute."

Excellent, I think. Within fifteen minutes, I received two compliments from two lesbians compared to zero replies from twenty straight ones who explicitly advertised that they are available. Only ... —not to me.

Kyra asked me if I am enjoying England. At this stage, I'm not sure and feel that what remains for me to do is ... —getting drunk!

12

After a week, I still haven't received any replies from the twenty girls I winked at, and I am starting to believe that winking is not the way forward.

Perhaps my whole profile needs to be rewritten, and it could even be that the pictures I have uploaded need reviewing. They're all a bit too outdoorsy and might give the impression that I am merely Crocodile-Dundee-ing my way through life. I need to start thinking like a woman. I need to crawl into their minds and figure out what they believe is important.

I suspect they want security and financial stability.

It makes me delete the text that I've crossed the Sahara and sailed on a fabulous yacht while diving for shipwrecks. I erase that we barely escaped the eye of a Madagascar cyclone (the raging water, the monster swells), that our sails got ripped, the helm got broken and that we floated at a speed of eight knots sideways while directionless meandering on an infinite ocean.

It pains me to remove the words which illustrate that I've dived for diamonds in the Atlantic and spent three days in a Zimbabwean jail. Or that I was held at gunpoint in Mozambique, that I smuggled a car out of South Africa and hunted for a fake passport in Tanzania.

Though after rereading this, it doesn't surprise me I don't get any reactions.

I do leave in that I love nature, the sun, the sea, and enjoy eating out while sleeping in after a night on the town. I add that

45

I love cuddling up cosily underneath a duvet with a glass of red wine and a pizza while watching a good movie on Netflix. It appears that women find this extremely important.

I don't mind doing it, but writing this cliché almost makes me want to vomit. However, it is a necessary evil.

To further address their need for security. I mention that I work for a big multinational company, that I regularly fly to different continents and that I've got all the perks, the freedom of decision and a boss who lives far away in another country (and only writes me FYI emails). Finally, I let them know that I am a thinker, a joker, but not a player.

Brett has read my other profile and, after I showed him the updated version, says that he prefers the previous one. Then again, he thinks like a guy.

"There is one point you need to take into consideration," he says.

"What is that?"

"What type of girls will you be attracting? Wouldn't you rather go on a date with the ones who like that you are adventurous? How would you feel if a duvet-cuddling-wine-pizza-Netflix girl contacts you? Wouldn't you get bored dating her?"

"I'd rather go on a date. Period," I reply, "because at the speed I am going, no one will be contacting me for the next twenty-five light-years, and I will end up being the only single guy on this planet."

He points out that 'light-years' is the term for distance and not for time.

On Saturday, when Brett plays rugby in rainy weather, I take time to read through profiles.

I don't randomly wink as I did before. I only choose the ones I genuinely like. I am highly selective. A girl needs to come across as relaxed and comfortable within herself before I decide to contact her.

I have set out some strict cut-off points. I would prefer my future date to be unafraid, original, intelligent and somewhat able to pursue her dreams. She needs to have a fair dose of witty humour, and there needs to be some hint of adventure. If I can't read these things between the lines of her profiles, then I won't be bothered.

After having read through about fifty profiles, I end-up selecting four. It has taken me all day, and now I still need to write them a message as I am well aware of the lousy effect the wink button has.

One of the girls mentions that she enjoys wine-slash-food and likes to spend time in the kitchen experimenting on friends. It makes her sound like the female Hannibal Lecter, so I delete her from my list.

I decide that to speed things up, I need to have a system. I do not have the time or the energy to write a message to every single girl, so I create a standard one that still leaves room to mention things I will select from her profile.

I start my message by telling them that I like their profile and that it is the most appealing one I've read. I further let them know that a couple of things jumped out at me, and I mention them. This will give them the impression that I have read what they have written. I compliment them on their looks, and after that, I ask a couple of questions. I conclude my message by writing that I am in a rush and need to go. The reason, I say, is that I am in France for business, more specifically—in Paris. But at the same time, I tell them that this shouldn't give them the impression that I'm always busy and that I don't have time for anything else. I let them know that it is only for the next two weeks, and then dust should settle again. I also comment on the

Parisian-French accent, which I find hard to follow when everyone speaks at full speed.

Mentioning France and especially Paris, I think, could have some mellowing effect. It is, after all, a romantic city and I haven't met a girl who wouldn't like to go there. Associating myself with Paris and accordingly with romance might smoothen my path. Secondly, pointing out that I speak French, though I struggle a bit with certain accents, could come across as exotic.

By the time I have finished the template message and sent it off to the three remaining girls, it's six o'clock.

13

Brett arrives back from rugby, all muddy and soiled-up, and he carries a couple of pizzas with him. I've invited Rodney, my South African colleague from work who lives in Slough, and we've decided to go out on the piss tonight. Even though he is the only one married, his wife seems to be okay with it.

Half an hour later, his Peugeot company car pulls into the driveway. Brett has showered and changed, and we eat our pizzas. After that, we make our way to the nearest tube station heading for Fulham.

It's the first time Brett and Rodney meet, and almost immediately, they seem to hit it off. It doesn't take long for Brett to update Rodney on my London life. He tells him that I spend hours on the internet luring girls into my dating web, making it all sound awful. He further shares that I've had a date only minutes after I landed in Heathrow and that she had a big bum.

"It was out of proportion," I throw into my defence, all-in high-pitched tones.

The three of us finally arrive at one of the cocktail bars in Fulham. From across the street, Brett waves at the bouncers, and they signal him to come over. There is a queue outside, but the three big eastern European doormen shake Brett's hand and let us through.

In the weeks and months to come, I learn and copy his approach. No matter how much we are enjoying the party, we need to chat with the bouncers.

Although I didn't grow up with the concept in Belgium, England apparently requires doormen. Bars and pubs close early, even though the eleven o'clock curfew has been abolished. This causes the English to drink as much as possible in the shortest available time. Around closing time, everybody is collectively tossed onto the streets. Hardly anyone is sober, and before you know it, people assume superman capabilities and believe they are indestructible. Gangs are formed, fights break out, guys try to stab each other, girls are pulling hair, etc.

Queues are a different story altogether. When I was a kid, I saw a short comedy on TV which started with two people standing in line, only to be soon joined by a third, a fourth and a fifth person. It didn't take long before a string of people patiently waited and waited. The silence was slightly interrupted by a man who asked what everyone was queuing for. Even though no one knew, everybody simply stayed where they were.

That is the way I perceive England. When most of the times, the bars are not even half full, a long line of people outside gives the impression that it must be packed inside.

At times, I wonder why there are not more people looking at a queue and thinking, 'Oh no, I can't be bothered to stand there for half an hour in the freezing cold'.

But queueing is incorporated into the English DNA. It's not only at bars but also at coffee shops, post offices, fast food restaurants, museums for stamp collectors and, as I have already learned, at the second-hand bulk-bought traffic lights! There must be queues where you wait to be allowed access to another queue. I am sure that there are. It surprises me at times that online shopping in the UK has not incorporated a queuing system yet, though I'm confident it will come.

After we've ordered our first drink, Rodney asks, "Are you still on that dating rubbish?"

I admit that I am.

"How can this ever work?" he wants to know. "The way I understand it is that from day one, everyone receives all the information about you and based on that, they make their selection. It comes across as if they are walking through the aisles of a supermarket and throw in or out of their baskets what they do or don't like. It's a disease," he continues, "a disease of our time. This can't be good as it makes everyone expect too much. Don't you understand that this whole bullshit about the knight in shining armour and conquering a girl's heart while stealing her from the tribe next door and that kind of stuff is pure rubbish?"

He looks at Brett and me for a moment and then asks, "What is that song again by that country-singer who lives in Switzerland?"

"You mean Shania Twain," Brett says.

"Yes, her. She sings about all those guys she's dated and who never really met her standards. One thinks he is a rocket scientist, the other one carries a comb up his sleeve, the third one looks like Brad Pitt and so on. Eventually, she tells them all that, even though she thinks they are all right, none of them will keep her warm at night. So, you know what I think? I think she should buy an electric blanket."

"I'd keep her warm any time of day or night," Brett smiles.

"So would I," I agree.

"Well, that's not the point," he says. "The point is that she's too fussy! There is this other song by this Ashley-what's-her-name where she sings that she has broken off a relationship because the guy doesn't want to open the flipping car door for her. That's simply ridiculous."

"What's the song?" I ask.

"Ashley-something…, that blond chick with the cute ass—I don't know, but it appears that she is utterly unable to open her own freaking door. It reminds me of when I started dating my wife some years ago, and she expected me to open the lid of a coke-can every time we were in a pub. I thought, 'What the hell is wrong with you? Can't you do this yourself? You're not Forrest Gump and mentally or physically challenged or anything.' It wasn't like she wanted me to lift up a fifty-kilogram bag of cement. I could understand that. Guys are stronger built, so no arguing that, but a stupid can of coke! I tell you what: if I were a girl, I would be insulted if a guy rushed over to open the freaking car door for me. If I had any self-respect, I would not want to be treated as if I was disabled. Here they get all worked-up about feminism and being equal, but what a load of crap is that. They don't want to be treated equally, and in actual fact, they are even confused about what they truly want. They go looking for Arnold Schwarzenegger, JC Van Damme and Bruce-bloody-Lee, or a strong enough guy to take on a gang of twenty punks. But at the same time, they want him to be all cultural; visiting museums, reading poetry and do the dishes after cooking a culinary feast in the kitchen. How do you add those two things up? You know what I mean?" he asks, "It leaves me completely confused. Girls nowadays are expecting the impossible. Then you go out there and put yourself on those supermarket internet dating shelves to get compared with all those players who lie about their height and weight and put pictures on from the times they still had hair...! —Bullshit, that is what I call it."

Both Brett and I laugh.

"Together with all those built-up expectations, there is a lot of disappointment as well," Brett says.

"Exactly," Rodney concurs. "Statistics show that divorces started to increase when people began to choose their own partners. It is almost as if one starts doubting one's decisions from the moment it is made.'

"I know what you mean," Brett throws in: "it happens to me every time I go to a restaurant. The second I have given the waiter my order, I start listening to what the others have selected and, more than once, I think: bloody hell, I've made the wrong choice."

"That's my point!" Rodney continues. "Because of all the variety, choosing has become impossible. Secondly, there are loads of psychological studies showing that chances for divorce increase when you marry out of love. A lot of times, people fall in love with their own expectations."

"Man," Brett chuckles, "does your wife know you have all of these opinions? You better be careful," he says. While pointing at me, he adds: "because thingy here is hoping to write a book one day, and whatever you say can be used against you."

"Will be used against you," I correct.

"Oh yeah? Good that you mention it," Rodney says and looks at me. "But tell me, how does that work?" he asks. "Do you hide in your little attic and write down everything we've discussed tonight?"

"Not always," I say. "But sometimes I do."

"Well ...," he hesitates, "... do you think you will be mentioning the stuff I just said about my wife not being able to open her can of coke or about women not knowing what they want?"

"If I end up disappearing into my little attic, I might do just that."

He is quiet for a moment and then, almost stumbling over his words, says, "You see ... if Cindy ... if my wife would read that book ... I mean ... —how would it really work?"

"How would what work?"

"Well," he says, "would you be changing my name and all that?"

"Look at who's the hero outside the bedroom," Brett laughs. "At first, you're all brave, and then you crumble when you realise that your wife might find out you have a mind of your own."

"No, seriously, man," Rodney insists, "would you change my name?"

"Of course," I reply. "If you want me to, I'll do it."

"What would you call me?" he asks.

"What do you want to be called?"

He thinks about it for a while and then says, "Richard. I've always wanted to be a Richard."

"Then Richard it is," I say. "If you want me to, I can even change your background. I can write that you are from Cape Town instead of Mosselbay. I can say that you work for a construction company. I can rename your wife from Cindy into Adele and make the readers believe that you don't have a daughter, but a little boy who is a bastard."

"I don't really like the bastard thing," he says.

"Okay, what about that your son is born out of wedlock?"

"Much better," he replies.

"But what do I get in return?"

He is taken aback for a moment. "Oh, I didn't know it works like that."

"It does," I assure him.

"What do you want in return?"

"One night with Cindy."

"You mean Adele?"

"Adele," I say.

"You bloody bastard," he blurts out and starts laughing loudly. "You wouldn't stand a chance. She's way out of your league. Adele will smack the door in your face if she hasn't already slapped you, which would leave you with a bloody broken nose."

"I might as well try," I say.

"Go ahead and try," he encourages. "I even dare you to. But don't come crying when she's beaten the crap out of you."

14

I've been in the UK for a month, and Sunday evening, after spending my third weekend in London, I'm packing my bags to head back to my hotel in Northampton. I prefer driving at night when the traffic is not too bad, but I hate leaving the house.

Brett notices this. He suggests that I stay another night and drive up Monday evening.

"I have a meeting tomorrow afternoon," I let him know.

"Have you found a flat yet?" he asks.

"I might have to take the one in Leighton Buzzard."

He looks at me for a moment. "The garage?"

I nod. "It's close to the UK head office."

"Do you need to live in that area for your job? I thought your role was international and that you would be spending more time in aeroplanes than in your Northampton office. Finding your way to airports around Leighton Buzzard might prove to be even more difficult."

"I don't really need to live there," I admit. "Why?"

"It seems to me that you will be coming over to Ealing almost every weekend anyhow, so how would you feel about living here?"

It's a big house with a massive lounge, a fair-sized kitchen and three bedrooms which, aside from Brett's, are empty. There is a big international airport, just a stone's throw away on top of it all. There are no reasons not to live here.

"I'd be happy to," I say.

That same evening I still drive to the hotel. Aside from my clothes being there and the fact that I need to check out, my Monday afternoon meeting is at the office. But instead of feeling deflated, I'm excited about the prospects of my new future. I finally have a proper roof over my head, and I will be sharing it with someone I consider my brother.

Monday late afternoon, I return to Ealing, and that night Brett and I discuss our living arrangements. We decide to act like a little family. Everything is shared since we both feel that it would not be right to divide the fridge and freezer into two sections, with one part containing my stuff and the other part his. We will buy groceries together, and when I cook, he can do the dishes, and when he cooks, I can walk around the house, switching the smoke alarms off.

On paper, it looks great, and in reality, it works brilliantly, with some minor embellishments. Since I work from home, I cook most of our evening meals, and because we feel that doing the dishes every night interferes with, well ... —our desire to do them, we stock-pile them until we run out of pans, pots, plates and cutlery.

The latter seems to happen quite quickly. Therefore, we decided to drive to the nearest supermarket to buy additional pans, pots, plates and cutlery.

We quickly fall into a routine. Before Brett leaves his office (which is only a five-minute drive from the house), he phones me and asks whether we need anything from the shops; should he perhaps get some pizza? Every Saturday, we take a trip to Tesco's to stock up on the bigger groceries. It almost looks as if we are a couple. Our friends even joke about it, and to completely keep up with appearances, we start calling each other 'darling', or 'honey' and 'sweetheart'.

We also use each other's soap. It reminds me of an episode in the American series 'Friends' where Chandler innocently asks his flatmate what he washes first when he's in the shower. Joey replies that this would be his face. Chandler subsequently wants to know what Joey washes last, and the answer this time is—his arse. There is a moment of silence, but the hilarity kicks in when Joey realises where the soap has been before he washes his face. The answer, of course: Chandler's butt.

Everything goes well, and Brett and I never argue or even have the slightest difference of opinion. It all flows comfortably. One evening, after a drunken night on the town when we lie on Brett's bed, he confides that having me in the house has made his divorce trouble far easier to bear. He hardly talks about this, but it is evident that he was very much in love with his ex-wife. He probably never imagined that they would ever split up.

They came to London to earn extra money to make life back in South Africa a little easier. But then she changed her mind. Unexpectedly, she didn't want to go back to South Africa any longer. She preferred to spend their money and time watching Chelsea play football (a sport she never showed any interest in back home). Every Saturday evening, she went out with her male colleagues. On more than one occasion, she arrived back home wholly drunk. They started drifting apart, and there were even rumours that she had an affair with her boss.

Brett's life fell to pieces. He never planned for this, but he stayed strong and firmly believed that whatever happens to a person does not define him—what defines him is how he deals with it.

However, it burdens him that he is a divorcee. Even two years after they separated, he feels no need to be with anybody. He has become sceptical and believes that women cannot be trusted. He thinks that they will all turn around and put a knife into his back.

Me being here in Ealing apparently has helped him, and at the same time, it has helped me adapting to life in England and living in London.

That night, when we lie on his bed, he says, "You know what? If you were a girl, I would marry you straight away."

I laugh. "No way, man, I won't be the girl in this relationship." I take a look at him and say, "Aside from the fact that you are butt-ugly—if you'd grow long blond hair and some boobs, then yeah—I will marry you as well."

"What about this," he starts, "if you and I don't find anyone suitable to marry, then we move to some exotic island and stay bachelors for the rest of our lives."

From that moment onwards, we start calling this our fifty-year plan. The true meaning of it is—the hell with girls. We don't need them. We can be on our own, have fun, live our lives the way we want to without the burden, the hassle and the heartache around break-ups, rejections, and them cheating on us.

Why is it that people are so convinced they need someone else in their lives? Is it because it makes you feel complete? In his 'Symposium', Plato wrote that the gods first created us as beings with four arms, two heads and four legs. But when humans began to wonder how they could climb to heaven and replace the gods, Zeus came up with the idea to cut all human beings in half. The analogy relates that from then on, we were constantly searching for our other half.

Could that be the reason? Is it incorporated into our being that we need someone else to make us whole? Plato's story might have some truth in it, though I like David Moir's version more.

It's the one where Adam is feeling a little bit sorry for himself. Even though he lives in the blissful Garden of Eden, he is depressed because he is lonely and asks God to create him a mate. God understands Adam's point but would like to receive some specifics. What is it that he really wants? Adam replies that this newly created person should be his opposite, but also the same: a best friend, someone he can talk to and can be with. It should be someone who understands him, who supports him when he feels down and who he can truly relate to. He further adds that he wants her to be beautiful, desirable and to have respect for him at all times. He needs to be with someone he can trust. Further, if she can cook, iron, clean and not complain, that would be great. But most importantly, Adam wants to feel complete and never be lonely again.

When he finally stops talking, God is quiet for a very long time. Eventually, he says, "It is possible, Adam, but it will cost you an arm and a leg."

Adam is taken aback for a moment and thinks about what God wants in return. Finally, he looks up and asks, "What can I get for a rib?"

15

It is getting closer to December. I have been in the UK for a little over three months, and the weather is appalling. When I lived in South Africa, I missed the snow, but all England offers is a miserly drizzle and constant overcast greyness. It affects my mood.

Work is not really picking up either. A month ago, I had a meeting with the managing director of the UK and Ireland. After our talk, he agreed to send out a letter informing everyone who I am and what my role is. He told me that everybody is eager to work with me and that they are well aware of my reputation. He ends his praise by saying that the UK is honoured to have a guy like me in their midst. But I'm not sure what my reputation is.

I worked hard while I was in Belgium, but I am not planning to put that many long hours into the UK. I am no longer concerned about networking or about eternally trying to find value and win-wins. Before, I had to work closely together with a team of fewer than ten people. Still, in England alone, there are more than sixty individuals I need to liaise with. On top of that, Richard (formally known as Rodney) has let me know that about eight of them applied for my job. There might be some additional friction lingering around. I have asked him to give me their names. In that way, I can show some diplomacy and avoid stepping on anyone's toes.

In some way, I feel like that young football player who is all comfortable with the ball while playing for the local team.

Everyone cheers for me, and I can easily score goals. But then I'm invited to join the ranks of a bigger club, and all those new players are faster and quicker. In a way, I'm scared that they will kick, hit and spit every time the referee turns his back. Perhaps I will end up playing the worst game of my life. And even though the managing director assures me that he has heard of my reputation, it doesn't mean anything if the other players haven't.

Yesterday, the promised letter was sent out. It informed everyone that, though I will continue to report to the European head office, I will be based and working in the UK. My primary role, it said, is to give support in terms of implementing and embedding some of the critical global strategies. I have to carry out risk analysis and ensure the transfer of best practice from the international team to the United Kingdom and vice versa. The letter ended by asking everyone to join the writer in welcoming me into the team.

I am expecting phone calls from all sorts of colleagues who will be asking me what they can do to help. But nothing happens. Instead, I have to nag and pester people to get a meeting organised, and at times I think, why bother. I could actually keep a low profile and live an easy life. If nobody is waiting for me, then why should I wait for them?

When I feel guilty for not doing my fair share of work, I try and set up meetings in the Netherlands, France, Belgium and even Scandinavia. But mostly, I can't be bothered doing that either. Instead, I spend more and more time on the dating website.

When at times, I do make a half-hearted effort in the UK to try and persuade people to let me do my job, they actually make me feel as if I'm not needed. They tell me that they are, after all, the UK and that they have been going about their business for years without anyone's help. They really believe that they are on top of things. That they have nothing to learn from outsiders and certainly not from some small league football player who grew up in one of the tiniest countries in the world. Let's face it, they claim: the UK is not even part of Europe and on top of that— England is different!

Yeah, England is different, just like France, Germany, the Netherlands, Sweden, and even tiny little Belgium is. I really want to tell them that according to Charles S. Maier at Harvard University, they suffer from 'Imperial Syndrome'. To truly believe that their own situation is exceptional, that they cannot be called to account by any foreigners and that they obey some higher law! Trust me, the 'Imperial Syndrome' says: 'We are different.'

16

I am finally starting to receive quite a few reactions in terms of winks and dating messages. However, most of them are worthless. I have clearly specified the age span, which I allow to be up to ten years younger than myself—but not older. Still, messages arrive from women who are over fifty, over fifty-five and even over sixty years of age.

I have clearly mentioned on my profile that I like my dates to be from the London region or maximum within a fifty kilometres radius. Yet, women seem to interpret that Canada, Columbia and Ukraine are within that range. I am rarely contacted by girls who live within the specified area and do not immediately need to apply for government pensions. It makes me feel that most of them haven't even read my profile.

If that's the case, what's the point in having one at all?

The truth of the matter is that internet dating is pretty time-consuming, not so much in replying to girls who have contacted me, but in getting someone's attention. It feels that I have to compete with hundreds of other guys, and if I want a girl to put my message on top of her pile, then a fresh approach is necessary.

When I open a profile, the first thing I do is take a look at the pictures. When I like them, I move to step two, which is quickly scanning through their profile's text.

I am sure that girls are no different. They firstly look at my opening picture, which must invite them to browse through the other ones. Only when I meet their criteria, they will skim through my profile. Also, here I must have no illusions; I am sure they will not read everything. Nonetheless, this stage must not be neglected. A properly written profile might sway the doubters into doers.

For a third time, I feel the need to change my pictures and the wording. Again, it leaves me with more questions than answers. Do I put pictures on the site that shows me in sport-clothes and give the impression that I am a triathlon freak who is never home and can't enjoy the odd night out because he has to watch his carbohydrate intake? Or do I wear a suit that portrays my seriousness, but at the same time shows me as this urban yuppie who thinks his career is more important than his family? Do I write that I am Belgian and run the risk that girls might assume I can hardly speak their language? What if they only want to date English guys? Would I eliminate my chances by writing that I am fluent in Dutch, German and French?

And what about my job? Should that be important to me, or do I say that it merely pays my salary and that I work to live and not live to work? Won't that give them the impression that I am an undercover beach-bum with hardly more ambition than a two-toed sloth who spends his weekends flicking through sports channels on TV?

It's complicated.

I wouldn't mind doing some in-depth research and comparing other guys' profiles, but I am too scared that they might think I'm interested in them.

Further, it has become clear to me that I have been all too serious. I need to change my attitude and follow Richard's—or ex-Rodney's advice. I need to stop 'giving-a-fuck'.

Some weeks ago, when I ran late for one of our usual outings (this time at a South African pub), I saw what the effects were of a happy-go-lucky attitude. I had already met most of Brett's friends, and when I finally arrived, quite a few came over to greet me. Most of them were drunk and loudly cheered their hellos. Before I knew it, I was hauling two bottles of Castle Lager in one hand and another three bottles of Appletiser in the other. I hardly had the time to look around and see if there were any interesting girls. But when the dust finally settled, I could tell that this had its own effect. The game had changed, and the girls in the bar were looking at me.

When I pointed this out to Richard, he merely nodded and said, "You don't have to scan a bar when the bar scans you. You need to be confident, smile and pretend that you know someone, even when you don't. On top of this," he added, "there is one crucial sentence you need to keep in mind."

"What is it," I asked?

"Don't give a fuck! I have seen it so often," he explained. "You can immediately recognise the players; how they dress, how they walk into a bar, but more importantly: how they don't give a shit about any of the girl's feelings. They have no problem approaching a girl who is surrounded by ten other guys, but we do! You know why we are so nervous?" he asked, and before I could reply, he said, "It's because we care. At least tonight, you've seen it for yourself and got your answer: girls only look at you when you pretend they don't exist or when you don't give a fuck. If you keep telling yourself that you don't care, girls will drop at your feet like dead flies."

It is not that I want them to become dead flies. Though that evening, I decided to further explore this approach. When I finally looked around, I noticed girls openly checking me out. Some of them bluntly stared at me, others smiled, and one of them even waved. It felt to me that I could walk up to anyone, utter the most ridiculous pick-up line, and they would still be interested.

It was as if a veil had dropped: as if I could suddenly see who was single or at least available. There were no secrets anymore. They shouted with their eyes that they were ready and waiting for me to do something.

So, if this works in a bar, could it possibly work on a dating app?

17

Brett, Richard and I regularly go out of our way to befriend bouncers and bar personnel.

During one of those weekends, I am introduced to Richard's wife Adele (formally known as Cindy). It's her birthday, and we have all agreed to meet up at one of the cocktail bars in Putney.

As it's becoming my routine, I'm running late. I quickly shower, get dressed and grab the tube. I have become pretty good at giving the others the usual excuse: stalled at the office, delayed on the M1 motorway and finally forced to stop at thousands of traffic lights.

Despite the queue outside, the place is not that busy. I spend my compulsory five minutes talking to the East European bouncers. When I finally walk into the bar, I can tell that most of our friends are already drunk. They loudly cheer their 'hey Lyam, brother, bro and bru's'. And depending on their nationality, they ask me 'howzit?' or 'what's up?'. Some of them give me a hug, others wave, and the ones who are English, well … they simply avoid eye contact.

I see Richard and walk up to him. "Glad you could make it," he says, and while pointing to the gorgeous girl next to him, he asks, "Have you met my wife yet?"

"No, I haven't," I reply and shake her hand. "You must be Adele?" I joke.

"No, Cindy," she clarifies.

"I know," I smile. "Happy birthday, Cindy."

She turns to Richard and frowns, "Who the flip is Adele?"

Some new girls are working behind the bar, and when I order a couple of cocktails, I ask them what their names are. All three of us do the same, and whenever we walk over to them to order more drinks, we enquire where they are from, how long they have been in England, what they do, what they like or what their hobbies are.

Taking the time to make this small effort pays off when the bar is filled with packs of thirsty, queuing people. It's then when we wave from a distance and point at our glasses while specifying by the numbers of fingers held up how many we want. We get served before anyone else.

A couple of times during the evening, we walk out and talk to the three doormen. They are all shorter than Brett and me, and we tease them about that.

"How on earth can you guys be bouncers?" Brett laughs and jokingly reassures them that they must just ask him if they have a problem, and he will help them out. They kid back, guaranteeing him that each of them can easily take on half the bar. We all laugh and slap each other on the shoulder and repeat this almost on the hour.

We never give them money, but every time we arrive at a place we have been before, we are let in without having to stand in a queue.

"Where is Brett?" I ask Adele while pressing four cocktail glasses against my chest.

She points to the dance floor, and I spot him making all kind of unnatural moves next to a rather petite but very attractive girl with curly blond hair. She appears to be in her mid-twenties and is entirely absorbed by her own dance motions. It is almost as if the outside world does not exist for her.

"Who's she?" I ask.

Richard shrugs his shoulders, and Adele says, "She might know someone in our group. I think she's English."

"Is she single?" Richard asks his wife, who immediately slaps him on his shoulder. "I am only asking for him," he cries out defensively in high tones.

"You still need to tell me who this Adele is," she says while pretending to be angry.

"It seems that Brett is trying his best to find out whether she is single or not," I say.

For the bigger part of the evening, the girl with the blond curls hardly leaves the dance floor, and when she does, it is only to drink some water. Brett stays at her side most of the time. He has consumed enough alcohol not to be aware that she completely outshines him when she dances.

Every now and then, he walks over to me to tell me that he thinks she's great.

"What's her name?" I ask him, and though he has marked her as his territory, he shrugs his shoulders and says that he doesn't know.

"I am not sure if Brett is getting anywhere with her," Richard shouts in my ear, trying to top the music, "I can't help but noticing how she is looking at you."

"Rubbish," I reply, but at that exact moment, she throws me a fleeting glimpse.

I tell myself that I imagine this. It is clear the girl enjoys Brett's company as she laughs and cheers while he twists her around. Then again, there it is: for a second time, she briefly looks in my direction.

I try not to pay any attention to this. In fact, I am terrible at noticing whether a girl likes me or not. She practically needs to tie me to the bed and strip me naked before it might dawn on me that she could be interested.

It's getting late, and the bar announces that it's time for one last drink. Brett and I say goodbye to Richard and Adele, and as it turns out, the girl (who by now has told us her name is Fiona) does not live too far from Ealing. The three of us share a taxi, but while we are getting closer to home, Brett and his dancing queen have decided that they are still in a party mood. There is a Polish nightclub not too far from our Ealing house, and they are determined this will be their next stop.

The taxi driver drops me off at the house, and though both Fiona and Brett nag me to come along, I'm too tired. Over the last week and a half, I've been twice to Denmark and once to Spain and now I can only think of my bed. Aside from that, I don't want to be a third wheel. I insist that they go by themselves and say goodnight, but while I walk up the stairs, I wonder if I really saw a look of disappointment on Fiona's face.

Around about three-thirty in the morning, I'm woken up by clattering noises. Brett has returned from the nightclub and is trying to mix up some concentrated apple juice in the kitchen. I can hear his footsteps in the hallway approaching my room. My door opens, and he walks in. He looks tired and sighs while he takes a seat on the edge of my bed.

"Where's your sexy girlfriend?" I ask and smile.

"Oh man," he moans while he lays himself next to me. He stares at the ceiling for a moment and sighs, "She's fun, and she dances like I haven't seen anyone dance ever before, but I think she likes you."

"Don't be stupid. What makes you say that?" I ask.

"She kept asking me why you didn't come with us. She wanted to know how long you have been in London, what it is that you do, and at one stage, she even asked if you had a girlfriend."

71

"That's just normal conversation," I assure him. "It doesn't mean anything."

Nonetheless, I am flattered. She looks pretty young, perhaps even ten years younger than I am. It makes me realise that I need to change my selection criteria on the dating website. I could easily go ten to fifteen years younger than myself. I actually want to get out of bed and do it now. But Brett is still lying next to me, and in his drunken condition, he feels quite sorry for himself.

"You know what we should do?" I say, "We invite her to come over on Saturday, and we tell her to bring a friend. We can cook for them, and if her friend looks half decent, then I'll hit on her. How does that sound?"

The next day, Brett phones Fiona, and she lets him know that she and her friend will gladly accept our invitation.

On Saturday, they arrive right on time. Fiona, full of energy, kisses both Brett and me on the cheek. She looks even prettier than I remember. With her curly blond hair, all boyishly charming, and a twinkle in her bright blue eyes, she radiates pure fun.

Her friend doesn't look too bad, but compared to Fiona, she is no match. She seems to be a few years older, which makes me believe that Fiona has brought her along, especially for me.

Brett shouldn't have worried after all.

While we sit around the dining table, we soon find out that Fiona's friend is in the process of divorcing her husband. They all live in the same house, Fiona included, and the guy doesn't seem to be too impressed with their separation. On several occasions, the police were called in because neighbours were complaining about their rowdy fights.

When eventually Fiona's friend takes a pack of cigarettes out of her purse, I catch Brett's eye and slowly shake my head, letting him know that I won't hit on her. He nods that he understands.

While her friend smokes a cigarette outside in the garden, Fiona asks me about the books I'm reading. Some of them are spread throughout the living room, as I like to read several simultaneously. She picks them up and, it seems, she has even read a few of them. She knows most of the authors, and I take her to my room, where more books are stacked up in piles.

While she browses her finger over the covers, lip-reading the titles and pointing out to me which ones she has read and which ones she has heard of, I look at her. I can't help thinking that she is not only pretty but intelligent as well.

A few months ago, Brett and I had joined a speed-dating event. We'd entered with the idea to do it differently from anyone else. Instead of talking about ourselves, we decided to only talk about each other. Even when some girls told me that they were not interested in my friend and just wanted to hear about me, I replied that I could not do that.

It wasn't a great success, and we never went back, but today, while Fiona is in my bedroom, I find it extremely hard to only talk about Brett.

By the end of the evening, when the two girls have left, Brett exclaims, "You see; she was all over you!"

18

Richard is more black and white in his opinions, while Brett is far more diplomatic. Even when something appears to be a hundred per cent wrong, Brett still leaves space for justification. Richard, on the other hand, has no problem to bluntly say that something is dead wrong.

At times, one needs a black and white opinion to put things into perspective. This time it's Richard's opinion I need. Aside from not being a hundred per cent sure whether Fiona truly likes me, I need to find out what to do if she does.

I like taking the tube. I find it far more relaxing than driving my car through London. You're even offered real-live entertainment by watching people and what they do, which books they read and how they react when their phone loses connection once the tube goes underground.

Brett, on the other hand, hates the tube. He says he prefers driving while watching real live entertainment and seeing what people do in the privacy of their car, how they pick their noses and anxiously put their phones down when they see the police driving past.

Richard lives about twenty kilometres away from us. On good days, it only takes me half an hour to forty minutes to get there. And since I am almost as fast cycling this distance, I gear up in black lycra, put my helmet on and take my bicycle out of the shed.

I cut straight through Gunnersbury Park and head for the Chiswick roundabout. It is a beautiful day, and instead of following the Great West Road, I turn left and cycle the left-side of the Thames next to Kew Royal Botanical Gardens. After that, I go around Syron Park and join the Great West Road. It is a bit of a detour, but I love to cycle along the roughed path by the riverside.

When I finally arrive at Richard's place, I am all sweaty and wet. Adele opens the door and tells me he is not home. "You should have phoned," she smiles, and I can only agree with her.

"When will he be back?" I ask.

"Probably this evening." Then she raises her eyebrows while adding in a threatening, though joking tone, "He better be, or he will be in big trouble."

I can't help but think how Richard can be such a big mouth when among friends. He has very clear, outlined opinions about everything and everyone, especially about women. Though hearing Adele talk, I truly believe Richard is a real softy.

"Why don't you come in?" she invites, "I'll make you a cup of coffee."

Adele is beautiful. She has brown curly hair and is, even though pregnant, quite slim. She doesn't know that I know. Richard can't keep a secret and has told all of his friends that they expect a baby.

In that way, Richard and Brett are much the same. Brett can't keep a secret either. Look at how he felt the need to tell everyone about my first date with Anna. For that reason alone, I don't always tell him everything.

Adele switches the hot water kettle on and throws a spoon of instant coffee and some sugar in the two cups on the counter.

"Are you and Rodney ever planning to go back home?" I ask. (I am not sure if she knows that Brett and I have started calling Rodney Richard, so to avoid confusion, I rather stick to his former name.)

The question about 'going home' is commonly asked among South Africans. In a way, everyone pretends they won't go back because of crime, just like Richard had done when we first met in our company's office. Many South Africans claim that the country is well on its way to becoming a second Zimbabwe. But whenever they meet, they discuss the possibilities of going back and the subject is raised in the same way the English discuss the weather.

At times, I'm even asked this question when, in fact, I only lived there for less than five years. But my English accent is intensely coloured by the South African rolling 'r' that I almost sound as if I grew up there. Some even get irritated when I claim I'm Belgian as they think that I am denying my roots.

In many ways, I do feel that I should have been born on the African continent instead of in Europe. At times, I become South Africa's most prominent defender and deem that all those who constantly publicise the terrible things about their country (the crime, the politics, the unemployment and so on) are denying their roots and their realm. I argue that it is a big country, it covers more than half the size of Europe. And yes, crime is high, but what about the former war in Bosnia-Herzegovina, the situation in Spanish Basque, the IRA in Northern Ireland. All those conflicts might have come to an end now, but how many people died?

When I put South Africa's crime into this perspective, many tend to agree that it isn't 'that bad'. But the reality is that everyone in South Africa knows someone who got burgled, robbed, raped or killed. Still, South Africans talk about going back all the time.

Adele points to her stomach. This answers my question about when she and Richard will be returning home.

She says, "We're packing up and flying back when this one is born and therefore automatically has gained English nationality. You never know what will happen back home." She smiles, almost in a giggly kind of way and adds, "I'm sure Richard has told you about the baby."

"He has."

"He can't keep secrets," she laughs.

She asks me how my online dating is going, and this time it's my turn to laugh. I would giggle if it sounded a bit manlier.

"It has its ups and downs," I admit.

"Do you think it is the right way to find someone?"

"What other ways are there? London is a big city where no one speaks to anyone. The mentality of the people in this part of the world is to avoid all contact at all times. Everybody makes a reasonable effort to ignore each other, whether on the tube or when they stand neatly in a queue. There is no way to break through that barrier. If not for the internet, how in the world can I get in touch with anyone?"

"Perhaps you are right," she laughs, "but the English are not extinct, and so they must have ways to get in touch with each other as I am sure the internet hasn't always been around."

For a moment, she stares at the ceiling and then wonders out loud, "If I know of someone, would you be interested in going on a blind date?" Before she waits for me to reply, she continues, "There is my friend Maggie. She is still with her boyfriend, though, but things aren't going that well, and I suspect that she is looking for a way out."

I shake my head. I have been set up on blind dates before, and it never worked. I have been forced to sit at a friend's dinner table, strategically positioned opposite the girl they think could be my 'one-and-only'. Perhaps my friends have formed an

77

opinion about who I am, as they might have formed an opinion about who the girl is, and they try to add those two ideas up. As it often turned out: my friends became offended, even insulted after I whispered to them in the kitchen that the girl they invited might not really be my type. They even made me feel that they are doing me this massive favour and let me know that I shouldn't look a gift horse in the mouth. 'She has a great personality,' they argued in their defence without grasping the fact that it is not a girl's personality I want to take to bed.

For some reason, checking my phone app and writing messages to cyber-dates feels more exciting (or at least less threatening) than choking on roast duck with mashed potatoes because you can't believe what your friends were thinking when they invited her!

I'd rather block those good intentions off right from the start before having to sit through one of those experiences again.

"I really appreciate the thought, Cindy," I say to Adele, "But I can't do blind dates."

"Isn't it better than the internet?" she asks. "At least you can trust that someone can vouch for the girl. You never know what kind of baggage someone on the internet is carrying with them."

"Everyone has baggage after you have reached a certain age. When you don't have baggage, you haven't really travelled through life. Doesn't your friend Maggie have any baggage? There she is with this other guy, but things aren't going that smoothly, so she might be willing to meet up with someone over dinner. You, as her friend, might even think that Maggie is great and can be trusted, but will her boyfriend feel the same when he finds out?"

I drink my coffee, and we talk a bit more about living in London. What Richard hasn't told me is that they are financially struggling. They have recently bought a house but can barely make ends meet. Adele is already working two jobs, and they first need to pay off their debts before they can start thinking of going back home. They wanted to save money so they'd have a better start back in South Africa. That was the main reason why they came to the UK in the first place. But they've been here for over seven years and seem to have only sunk deeper and deeper in debt.

I finish my coffee and decide to head back to Ealing. When she walks me to the door, I give her a tiny kiss on the cheek. Then, before I climb back on my bicycle, I remember Richard's words after he'd asked me to change his name. I told him that I wanted one night with his wife as compensation, and he mocked me and said, 'Go ahead and try, I even dare you to.' So, I turn around, look at Adele and ask, "Do you want to have sex with me?"

"What!?" she exclaims and smiles hesitantly, "Would I want what!?"

I repeat the question, even though I am sure she has heard me.

She hesitates, looks me up and down as if she is considering it and then laughs, "Are you out of your flipping mind?"

I laugh as well and say, "Tell Rodney that I asked you the question."

This confuses her. "You mean: do not tell Rodney?"

"No, I want you to tell him."

I start cycling and hear Adele calling after me, "You know, you are quite a cute guy, and I would consider it if I wasn't married."

Later that evening, I get a phone call from Richard and even before the decorous 'howzit bru?' have been exchanged, he blurts out, "What the fuck did you ask my wife?" But I can hear a smile in his voice.

"You agreed that I could," I defensively say.

"I should come over and kick your butt."

I'm sure he could. He's a muscular guy. We both laugh, and he pauses for a couple of seconds before he, almost whispering, asks, "What was her reply?"

"She said yes, of course."

"Bloody hell, she said yes," Richard barks.

"She did. We even agreed on a day. Aren't you going up north next weekend?"

I know he is.

"Fuck-off man," he says, "I don't believe you."

"You know I am only joking, right?"

"I know, my friend," he says with a soft voice, "I know you wouldn't do this to me."

But there is a peculiar undertone in his voice which, at the time, I don't pick up. I am too occupied with my own internet dating craze. However, at a later stage, I'm reminded again of this conversation.

19

When winter has fully arrived and the weather has reached its utmost lowest, I am genuinely missing South Africa. I frequently fly to different countries, though mainly to give everyone else the impression that I am working. The truth is that I am neglecting my job. I spend days thinking about new dating strategies: how to make my profile better and increase my response rate. I mainly spend my evenings searching for profiles on the dating site and make a solid effort to reply to the girls who have contacted me.

My response rate has increased tremendously, even though quite a few of them come back saying that they are not interested. But I guess at least it means they react. I prefer this over girls who pretend I don't even exist.

What irritates me is when girls don't give me any reason for their rejection. I am even more insulted when they have used an automatically generated 'not-interested' message by simply pressing a button provided by the dating app.

I cannot believe that they can't make an effort and simply choose the easy way out. Do they not have any sense of decency? Rejection is never pleasant, but being rejected by a programme is, in a way, a slap in the face.

I want to write to these girls and expose their impolite behaviour. I want to draw their attention to a scene in the South African movie 'Tsotsi', where a man, called 'the Teacher', vividly outlines the definition for 'decency'. Okay, he did first kill the elderly guy on the train, but that's not the point. The fact is that effort should be rewarded with effort, and I'd like to tell them that they should curl up on the sofa with a good glass of wine and watch this bloody movie on Netflix. In that way, they can learn that it would have been only flipping decent to send me a more personal reply. It doesn't have to be a three-page message and merely something in the lines of: 'thank you for your interest and for taking the time and energy to write, though, in all honesty, I don't think we would be a good match.'

The lack of this makes my hard work evaporate into falsehood and leaves me with the feeling that I am nothing more than an ordinary stalker.

20

By the time I have lived in London for a full six months, the global account manager for one of our largest customers phones. He asks if I can manage their activities in Europe, the Middle East and Africa. He is from Texas, lives in Houston, and his colourful accent is often flanked by the typical American adjectives 'excellent', 'awesome', 'wonderful' and 'amazing'.

"Their international procurement manager is not a happy chappy," he explains. "They are not very impressed with us, and everything that could go wrong has been going wrong. Not only are our chemicals being questioned, but they also put quite a bit of pressure on us to introduce new ways to save water and energy."

After telling him that I am on board, he exclaims a loud 'great, awesome and wonderful'.

"The set-up is clear," he summarises: "design something new and make one of our biggest customers happy again."

For the last month and a half, I have been working extremely hard. By the time spring arrives, I've created an entirely new approach and optimised one of our customer's systems regarding time, water and energy savings. By now, this new approach is being introduced throughout Europe, and the rest of the world will quickly follow. Our man in Texas has one word for me: "Awesome!"

Aside from the technical and chemical aspects, it is equally essential that all our national account managers are delivering the same message. We need to become more like McDonald's, and every operating country should start providing the same ... well ... —hamburgers. We will fail if we do something great on the one side and something stupid on the other. How people behave is extremely important. Call it the weakest link and that kind of rubbish, but there is truth in it.

For that reason, I have started creating new reporting sheets and manage the salespeople who have direct responsibilities over this customer. I'm holding regular teleconferences and keep closely in touch with everyone.

With an improved customer-supplier relationship, my reputation within our company seems to be growing, which in turn gives me more lenience; which I use to do less and less and spend more time on the internet dating website.

But today, I am in Russia and Yuri, one of my colleagues drives me around. He is the national account manager for this big customer, and we are on our way to visit one of their sites not too far from Moscow.

While Yuri kamikazes his way through the city's traffic, he confides that he is worried he is not bringing in enough sales. He can manage existing customers quite well but feels he does not have what it takes to hunt for new prospects. A few days ago, his sales manager had a conversation with him, and he was told that he urgently needs to bring in new business. The words 'or else' were mentioned in that same sentence.

Yuri is worried that he cannot afford an 'or else'-scenario. He and his girlfriend have just bought a new flat and are thinking about having babies. There is absolutely no room for an 'or else'.

"What do I do?" he asks, and desperation hides in his voice. "How can I bring in new customers?"

"There are many different ways," I tell him, "but the summary of it is that it is a number's game. If you only visit one prospect per day and your success rate is ten per cent, it will take you ten days to get a new customer. But if you increase your visits to five per day, it will take you only two days."

Of course, there is much more to it, but his English is not very good. It would take me ages to explain that, aside from visiting as many prospects as possible, you further need to work on your message, how you sell your story and most importantly—identify who you will be approaching.

21

Back in London, I realise that the advice I have given the young Russian account manager could be equally helpful in my own dating world. I simply need to increase my efforts. There is no point in writing a few girls a message and waiting a couple of days for them to reply. I need to work harder and reach out to more girls per day.

Again, I change my profile and, combined with the 'number's game', I mix Richard's 'don't-give-a-fuck'-twist into my new approach. I don't only change my pictures and my profile's wording, but even the standard copy-paste message I created. Also, when someone replies or writes to me, I present them with the same 'don't-give-a-fuck' attitude and —…

It works!

By deliberately not trying to impress anyone, I am doing precisely the opposite. I receive more reactions than I ever did before.

I start my messages by writing a girl that I think she is 'the one' and that it is only polite to inform her. I further tell her that I was born at the age of five and that, since I have no time to waste, I think we should get married straight away. I am sure, I write, that there must be internet sites where you just scroll and click yourself into holy matrimony. Or where we can order our children online: perhaps even buy them in bulk so we can get a discount. If we decide we like each other at the end of the day, we could even meet up.

One girl asks me in her message if I write this to everyone. I reply that this would be physically impossible as there are an estimated three point six billion girls on this planet. Even if I write one email per second, I would still need over a hundred and fourteen years to finish the job, and this when I work twenty-four-seven.

In my main profile text, I practically give them guidelines for the steps they need to follow. I advise them to read my profile, agree that I'm interesting, reply, email a bit up and down, and meet with me so we can drink a cappuccino. Then, I continue, we keep seeing each other and lie to everyone about the fact we've met on an internet dating site. I further admit that it is pretty different from the days where one simply had to trek to the other tribe's territory, hit the chosen one on the head and carry her back into the home caves. At the end of my profile, I write that I wish we could become filthy rich, buy ourselves a yacht, sail the coastline of Mozambique, get hijacked by pirates, undergo extreme anxieties and get shot because no one paid the ransom!

The response is tremendous, far more than ever before. Richard was right! All those players are right! When you act towards girls as if you don't care, they start showing interest— no more mister nice guy. From now on, I will be the player. The rules have changed. There is no holy matrimony, no wedding rings. This is the start of my fifty-year plan and—I don't give a fuck.

My success rate on the dating site centuples! Reading and replying to emails has become a full day's job. I often have two dates per day: up to five dates during the weekends. I see eight to twelve girls per week, and it digs a hole into my finances as I am still of the opinion that the guy —at least on the first date— has to pick up the bill.

To avoid bankruptcy, I have become less flexible on where and at-what-time we meet. Especially the latter is essential to prevent constantly ending up having to pay for lunches or dinners. I try to centre it around coffee or tea time or even right after work, at around six o'clock in the evening when all the English go out for beers.

In the past, I would let the girls choose where to meet. I have always understood the risk that women take when they go on a blind date. As a guy, I don't really have to be worried about getting raped by some girl in a dark alley. In fact, I am still waiting for that to happen. With this in mind, I can appreciate that a girl would like to meet me in a place where she feels comfortable.

However, taking tubes to all the different Boroughs of twelve-million larger-urban-zone London is not only time consuming, but it empties my railroad Oyster-card in no time. So instead, I ask my dates to train, tram and tube in the direction of Ealing.

They don't seem to mind.

During the weekends, I prefer Covent Garden. There is a lovely little French bistro not too far from the tube station. You can eat there, but I especially like it because it offers a choice between coffee and a glass of wine.

At first, I opted for coffee shops, but Richard made a good point when he (in his typical no-nonsense style) asked me what on earth I was doing? "Why are you filling the girl up with caffeine?" he asked, "Instead of getting her all hyperactive, rather mellow her down with wine."

Even though I enjoy the constant excitement of meeting new girls, it is starting to become a drag after all those months. Nine out of ten girls are a genuine disappointment. I already know this after a few seconds and have coined it my 'two-second rule'.

In a way, it's frustrating. I contact a girl; she replies, and after writing two, or a maximum of three emails, I invite her on a date. A week or a week and a half later, I take the tube all the way to Covent Garden, where we meet. Then, within two seconds, I know whether I want to see her again or not.

As I said before: nine out of ten times, I am not interested, and when I am—she's not. To keep me sheltered from constant disappointment, I tell myself that I am not going on a date and only want to have an exciting afternoon. I pretend I have no ulterior motive other than to meet new people in a city where everybody is too afraid to look anyone in the eyes. If anything, it takes me out of the house!

By doing so, I'm becoming less frustrated by dates who uploaded pictures from before they tried to win a pie-eating contest or from fifteen years ago.

I have been told that guys lie about their height, and that astonishes me. Do they expect to get away with it? Surely the girl will find out the moment they meet. At the same time, does the girl, who has put a picture up from ten years ago, believe that I won't notice? Or does she expect that I don't mind because they hope that their personality all of a sudden will hide their wrinkles?

One girl had written in her profile that she was training for the London Marathon, but when we met up, I couldn't help but wonder if they had to roll her over the finish line! There was no other way she would have made it. A Russian girl, who looked like a supermodel in her arty-like black and white pictures, reminded me of one of those olympian guys who had a sex change to win medals for the USSR. A Brazilian girl, who arrived late and asked me if I was her date, received my very puzzled look and a confident, 'I'm sure I'm not,'-reply.

There are many more, though not worth mentioning. What bewilders me is: why do they lie? Did they assume that I would fall madly in love with them despite all of their misrepresentations?

I guess that quite a few of the people who join an internet dating site are addicted to romance. They expect that, by some form of magical dust, 'love-at-first-sight' will strike like lightning and that the person opposite them will look past the book's cover and into the essence of their very soul.

In real life, this never happens, and that is why two seconds are more than enough to know if I want to see her again or not.

Note from the author:

There is a surprise bonus chapter available for you. See how to get it at the end of this novel.

Etienne

Chapter 2

Chasing Ducks

1

I have been in London for about a year and a half, and one particular Sunday, early March, at around three in the afternoon, I stumble across the profile of a French girl.

At first, I am not overly impressed. She looks a bit chubby, but in an all-right kind of way: not too fat and not too skinny either. Her age is thirty-one, and at one-meter seventy-six, she is quite tall.

Of course, I am worried that her pictures might be her best ones, and she looks like a rugby player in real life.

I don't have anything against rugby players. I just don't want to date them.

When I am not entirely sure about someone's profile, I don't write a message and merely 'wink', and in the case of the French girl, I simply click that button. The dating app immediately returns its standard reply: 'We've let her know that you are interested'.

As said before, I am not entirely sure that I am interested and leave it to fate to decide on what might come next.

Within five minutes, a message appears in my inbox. The dating site has let me know that she has winked back. It means she is online. It also means that she has not taken the time to even read through my profile. But at least she likes my pictures.

I write her a short message, asking (since she is from France) how long she has been in the UK and whether she likes it here.

I get an immediate reply. She tells me she is in France at this very moment. In fact, she is visiting her parents in Bordeaux, but, to answer my question, her message says she has been living in London for over twelve years.

After this first contact, we continue using the apps' inbox messaging service, though we have added each other on WhatsApp by the end of the evening. At around half-past ten, I say goodnight and close her profile. I quickly reply to another couple of messages, inviting some girls on a date while deleting others. By eleven o'clock, I close the app and plan to go to bed.

But then my phone bleeps. A WhatsApp message has arrived, and it is from the French girl. She tells me her name is Celine and says that she is having a glass of wine with her family. She lets me know that her sister likes my profile.

While still in my 'I-don't-give-a-fuck'-mood, I tease her and — she teases back. We keep writing to each other for the next two hours.

Only a week later, Celine returns to London. In the meantime, we have exchanged hundreds—if not thousands—of messages.

I am trying my absolute best not to care.

I have told her that I work as a journalist for 'The Globe' during the day, but I wear a red cape and save the world at night. I've let her know that, in that aspect, I'm obviously perfect. I've further written that I fight lions and tigers when I feel bored, ride white sharks for fun and drink tons of phosphoric acid while chewing on coal for evening snacks just to piss China off. In my messages, I've let her know that I might solve those global warming issues everyone keeps talking about, though I have my doubts that people would really appreciate it. I've told her that I once straightened the Leaning Tower of Pisa. I thought I had done a good deed, but the Italians were upset because no tourist wanted to see a straight tower. It just shows how one can't do anything right in this world! I told her how this disappointed me and stopped me from putting an end to the problems in the Middle East.

She wrote back, agreeing how people can be heartless and don't appreciate good intentions anymore. It used to be different years ago, she said, in times when animals could talk, and good men were still around.

I replied that good men are still around, but that, because of theft, vandalism and knife crime, governments have taken us out of sight. It is a bit like Easter eggs, I continued; one needs to look pretty hard these days to find them.

I've told her a hundred more things, some of them bordering seriousness, but most of them pure nonsense. I've said that I am house trained, don't like carrots, and cook, though only water to make coffee. I've consciously avoided telling her that I am really starting to like her or that I could enjoy curling up on a sofa with a glass of wine while watching a movie on Netflix.

She also kept it light. She chirped back in a similar kind of 'no-caring'-way. She told me that her sister wants to marry me and asked me if I would be okay with that. I wrote back that she has to bring her sister along when we meet, so I can cherry-pick my future wife. She immediately asked me if this means I am finally inviting her on a date. I replied that I am, because: let's face it ... a thousand words ... well, pictures ... Chinese proverbs and that sort of stuff ....

2

Celine sits on the pavement and leans against the wall of an old English building. She looks exactly like her profile pictures. I'm relieved that she is not a converted Russian Olympian medal winner or a Brazilian girl who I don't even recognise after an hour of conversation. She is the girl I am supposed to meet.

She is beautiful. She's got short blond hair and sparkling eyes, a relaxing smile, and she comes across playful, almost joyful.

When she gets up, she greets me as if she has known me for years. She embraces me and softly kisses me on my cheeks. She says she knows a nice little place and asks me if I am okay going there.

I am. I would be okay with anything she suggests.

I instantly like everything about her; the way she walks next to me when we go and search for a place to sit, the twinkle in her eyes, her short blond hair, and the fact that she is tall. She wears effortless blue jeans with an uncomplicated shirt. She is not over or underdressed, but perfect. She appears relaxed, in an almost careless kind of way.

We enter a little backstreet restaurant that has only four little tables. The lady behind the bar gives us a warm, welcoming smile, and aside from her, there is no one else around. We sit down and drink wine and eat and chat. We laugh and talk about France, about Belgian chocolates and the fact that she has lived in Brussels for a bit over two years. She says she loved it. We talk about politics, the third world, the fourth world, and our changing climate. We discuss the eleventh of the eleventh of the eleventh, and (in some sort of chauvinistic way) she wants to know what I would do if my country came under attack. I joke and ask her if France has plans to invade Belgium?

"Are you still pissed off that Brussels is Europe's capital instead of Strasbourg?" I tease, but she is serious and asks again what I would do.

Perhaps it has to do with the fact that she is French, and maybe this is some sort of oath to La Republique.

I tell her that I never believed that anyone should die for a piece of land. It doesn't mean you take the coward's way out. But let's face it: ordinary people (though never part of the decision to fight anyone) always end up paying with their dear lives.

"Compare it to your Napoleon Bonaparte," I say. "He decided to conquer Russia, and all the borders he'd redrawn to make France bigger were of no real interest to the French farmers. In actual fact, if someone had asked them what they really wanted, they most likely would have said that they needed to get their potatoes from the field before the rains would rot them. For this, they required their sons to stay at home and work. The father, whose son was looted away to wage war against some freezing cold country, was two hands short to fight starvation."

"Sometimes you need to stand up," she objects. "You need to protect what is important to you."

But what is important to me, I wonder. Which borders in which country would I protect; South Africa or Belgium? Even if I had to choose one, I would still not fight.

"No politician can convince me to kill people because they feel there is a need to claim 'weapons-of-mass-destruction'," I say

Celine cannot agree. She cannot even understand my reasoning. She searches hard to find an argument to make me see things her way. Then suddenly, her eyes start twinkling again, and she says, "Take Hitler, for instance. What if you'd lived in those days? Would you not have picked up a gun to defend your country?"

"Hitler is the perfect example," I say. 'If more people had refused to just blindly follow their leader's hunger for expansion, there would not have been a war in the first place."

It makes her laugh, and kind of in an awkward way, she says, "I actually meant it the other way around—that you had to fight and defend Belgium, but I like your version better."

When the friendly smiling lady finally kicks us out at half-past twelve at night, we stroll around in a park close by. There is even a little pond with ducks and swans, and when Celine tells me that every swan in England belongs to the queen, I reply that I didn't know that, but that I reckon her bird-food bill must be tremendous.

We laugh and tease each other. We run after the ducks, chasing them out of their sleep, and they reluctantly fly into the darkness of the night, being really pissed off about this and loudly swearing their discontentment. We eventually seek out a little bench, and my mind becomes overloaded with thoughts. What do I do? Do I put my arm around her and kiss her? What happened to the 'I-don't-give-a-fuck'-rule? It gave in to fear, into 'I-do-care', and it has made me nervous.

Celine tells me that she has been in a relationship with an Australian guy for more than five years. She left him when she found out that he was cheating on her. I tell her that I was told by a psychic in South Africa that there would be some sort of an Australian link associated with my future partner. I never really paid attention to this, and I am not entirely sure what she actually meant. Perhaps she believed my future wife would be Australian or that I would end up living there.

"Perhaps you should go and find yourself an Australian girl," Celine teases.

I laugh, and after I put my jacket around her shoulders (all chivalrous and stuff), I leave my arm there. She rests her head against mine, and I lean in and kiss her. It is a sweet and soft kiss, and it all feels new to me.

We sit on the bench for a while, relaxed and without words. While it gets later, it gets colder. It is after three in the morning, and both of us need to work the next day. She finally says, "Let's go," and I agree. Then she puts her hand in her trousers' pocket, takes out her cigarettes and lights one.

For a moment, I am shocked. She was vague about this on her profile. The box (whether she smoked or not) had not been ticked, and when I'd asked her about it in one of my WhatsApp messages, she had said something about quitting.

My cousin quits every evening before he goes to bed, only to start the following day.

I would struggle to be with a girl who smokes. I have always been like that. Perhaps it has to do with the fact that my grandfather died of lung cancer and that my mom has cancer. Brett feels the same. We can walk into a pub and be mesmerised by the most beautiful girl sitting a bit farther on a bar stool. She can look like a goddess, making everything around her disappear into nothingness. And I might even think that whatever happens tonight, I will walk over and talk to her. But then, when her hand slides into her shoulder bag, and she pulls out a pack of cigarettes, my interest completely evaporates.

But strangely enough, when I see Celine inhaling the blue-grey smoke, I don't seem to have a problem with it. I don't feel repulsed. I even think it is charming.

She notices me looking at her. She smilingly apologises and clarifies that she hasn't smoked all evening. She says that I need to accept this. But straight after she's finished her cigarette, she grabs another one. This second one is becoming less charming. Again, she looks at me—almost guiltily and says: "Not one single cigarette for a whole evening!"

I am not that endeared any longer, but still, I don't seem to really mind.

We are waiting for a taxi, but there are not that many around at four o'clock in the morning. The tubes stopped around midnight, as have the busses.

Half an hour later, one lonely taxi cruises the empty street and stops in front of us. It is now twenty to five. Celine runs towards it, and halfway she stops. She looks at me and says, "Aren't you coming?"

I am surprised, but in the taxi, she clarifies that this is not 'spending-the-night' and that she simply felt sorry for me. "It would have been impossible for you to find another taxi," she explains. "I didn't want to leave you waiting there by yourself for the morning to come."

At her place, she lets me know the rules: I don't get to sleep with her. I might be in the same bedroom, perhaps even in the same bed. There could be kissing: most likely, there will be kissing and possibly some touching, but that shall be all.

3

In the morning, Celine and I get up early. She goes to work, and I take the tube back to Ealing.

I've only slept for two hours, and when I arrive at the house, Brett is all suited up and waiting for me. It is a quarter to nine, and he says that I have fifteen minutes to tell him everything. He knows about me sending all those messages. I've let him read almost all of them, and he wants to know what she looks like? Is she pretty? Did she resemble the pictures I have shown him?

"It obviously went well," he concludes, "otherwise you would have been home last night already. Did you have sex?" he asks. Without letting me answer his question, he says: "You surely must have had sex because you stayed the night."

I tell him everything: the duck-chasing, the sitting on the bench, the jacket around her shoulders, me kissing her, the taxi back home, and us sleeping in the same bed. I even tell him about our Napoleon conversation.

He says that he's glad I have finally met someone I genuinely like. When I tell him about her smoking, he simply shrugs his shoulders. "She might stop, and if she doesn't, well ... then you need to buy an ashtray."

Over the next few days, Celine and I send each other more messages on WhatsApp, but not as many as we did before. On Thursday evening, I decide to phone her.

She says she is happy to hear my voice and sounds like she is.

I tell her that Friday afternoon I need to visit a customer in Peterlee. It is a five-hour drive from London, and since I will be too tired to come back that same day, I will stay the night in a local hotel and only return to London on Saturday morning.

We agree to meet Saturday afternoon, but while I am in my car driving the long hours back from Peterlee, I receive a message from her. She lets me know that she is sorry.

Sorry for what?

The tiny blinking dots at the bottom of the WhatsApp programme tell me that she is still busy writing. Then the rest of her message arrives. It says that on Friday evening, she went on a date with someone else. The following line tells me that it was a tough decision she had to make and that she doesn't want to lead me on. It's not in her character to play two guys at the same time, and she ends wishing me all the best in dating, in life and in chasing ducks.

I phone her, but there is no reply. Half an hour later, I call her again, and it goes straight to voice mail.

I feel sick in my stomach.

I'm devastated. It is as if she has stabbed me right through my heart. But I can only blame myself: I've let my guard down. I have given up the rule of not giving a fuck, and I was offered nothing in return.

I am pissed off. I blame the concept of internet dating. I blame the competition, the thousands of profiles competing with everyone on some surrealistic level. I don't want to accept her verdict. I want to argue with her and ask her why she has decided after only one date? Why not after a couple of dates so she could see who I really am and then make a more informed decision? How on earth do I digest this rejection?

When I'm back home, Brett, dressed up for his rugby game, looks at me with sad eyes and asks: "How are you doing, Lyam?"

"I feel like shit," I admit.

"This might not mean anything to you now, but there are plenty more fish in the sea. And look at it this way; perhaps it's better to learn this after only one date. If she was a less decent person, she would have been dragging you along for a couple of months, and then you would have really fallen for her."

In a way, I agree with him, but it doesn't make me feel any better.

"I phone Richard," he says, "and the three of us are going out on the piss tonight. Trust me; it's all part of the healing process. We need to hunt for girls."

I would rather crawl into a corner and lick my wounds. I prefer to make myself disappear, to hide under my duvet with a glass of wine and watch a movie on Netflix.

When Richard arrives late that evening, I do end up going out with them. Still, the music is a little bit too loud, the people laugh a little bit too hard, and everyone is getting drunk a little too fast. I leave the party before it ends and go back home while it is still early.

While on the sofa, I check my phone and browse through the all too familiar pictures and profiles. This needs to be a new start, I think. I have to rebuild my guard; my 'I-don't-give-a-fuck'-rule and I begin to invite girls on dates.

Some reply almost immediately. It is Saturday evening, and what on earth are they doing home?

In no time, I have three girls lined up for next weekend and another two for Wednesday and Thursday. I am not sure whether I really like any of them, but one of the girls is from Finland, and her pictures show her on a sledge being pulled by about twelve huskies.

I like the idea of being out there in the freezing cold with no one else except some dogs to rely on.

4

Finish Taimi's hair doesn't really look blond, but instead ashy white. It is very thin, making it seem as if she has lost quite a bit of them.

After a couple of glasses of wine, I take her to a place Brett and I discovered a while ago. It's a little bit up-market, and everything is expensive, but unintentionally I stumbled into a way around that.

This dates back about half a year ago. One night, when Brett, Richard and I were browsing our way through the usual bars and pubs, we arrived at a trendy place in Marylebone, central London. It was packed with dancing people and in the middle of the bar was a wide staircase that led to a level that only VIP's could access. We, the plebs, were denied entry by one of the bouncers.

Halfway through the evening, Brett walked up to me and told me he just had an interesting conversation with a big Nigerian while at the lavatory. Brett likes to talk to everyone, especially when he is drunk. At times, he disappears for hours as he stops and chats with each person he runs into.

He especially enjoys talking with people who, regardless of their colour, are in one way or another African. He loves to ask them what on earth they are doing in the UK while their own country is so much sunnier. More than anything, he feels that he is part of that continent.

It reminds me of a scene in Edward Zwick's movie 'Blood Diamonds'. Leonardo DiCaprio, who plays the white Zimbabwean mercenary, Archer, meets up with his former commander Coetzee on a farm close to Cape Town. Archer says that he wants to leave Africa, and Coetzee looks at him, squats down, takes some of the red soil and says, 'That's red earth. It is in our skin.' He lets it slip through his fingers and adds, 'You will never leave this continent.'

So, when Brett had his chat at the lavatory, the big Nigerian almost disclosed his whole life story to him. He told Brett that he's been living in the UK for over six years. He works as a bouncer during the evenings while studying accountancy during the day. His girlfriend, so it seems, is French and apparently tiny and petite, but the big man believes things are not going too smoothly between the two of them. He suspects that she is having an affair, and it really upsets him.

A week later, when we returned to that bar, Brett pointed to a man who stood at the bottom of the stairway leading to the VIP section. "That's the Nigerian I spoke with last week," he said.

A muscular, black guy was holding the end of a red cord in his hands. He hooked it onto a golden pole whenever he needed to prevent someone access to the VIP section upstairs. The privileged ones received a big, warm smile while he unhooked the cord to let them pass.

After a couple of glasses of wine, I decided to have a little bit of fun. While I pretended to walk past the muscular Nigerian, I suddenly stopped and turned towards him. I acted puzzled and looked at him. He stared back, confused about my intentions and ready to hook the red cord into the golden pole to deny me access.

I leaned towards him and said that I actually have psychic abilities. I explained that they don't work on everybody, but that, weirdly enough, I was receiving solid vibes from him. He appeared to be slightly entertained, but while he smiled, his eyebrows lifted, and it was clear that he struggled to believe me.

"You're from Nigeria," I told him, "am I correct?"

It didn't even slightly impress him. It was hard to imagine this big, beefy guy as an accountant, but I let him know that I could see numbers and asked if there was a link between him and what I saw. I hesitated for a moment and then said, "Are you by any chance an accountant or something that has to do with accountancy?"

This got his attention. He looked at me with eyes wide open. He put his large hand on my shoulder and stuttered, "Man, how do you know that?"

"It seems that I have a particular connection with some people, and information just flows to me," I replied while shrugging my shoulders.

He was impressed. He told me that his name was John and asked me what else I could see.

I stared at the floor, and after a while, I looked up. "Your girlfriend is very slim," I said, "And pretty. What I don't understand is how a big guy like you doesn't crush a petite girl like her." He smiled for a moment, only to let his mouth drop open when I enquired, "Is she perhaps French?"

Again, he stuttered, hardly able to utter a sensible word. He slapped his big hand on my shoulder, then grabbed my neck and pulled me closer to press me against his mighty ribs. He appeared happy with what I had told him, but suddenly, his face became sad. He looked at me for a moment, and then he asked me what else I could tell him about her?

I realised that I had taken this a step too far. But instead of walking away, I nodded. "You think that she is cheating on you?" I asked.

The sadness on his face grew. "Is she?" he wanted to know.

I shrugged my shoulders and shook my head. I didn't want to tell him more lies. I'd done enough. But as so often happens, the wine decided differently. "She needs attention," I heard myself say, "and perhaps you've been neglecting her. Why don't you take her out for a nice meal and treat her like a princess?"

He nodded. He told me that he has been too busy, working nights and studying during the daytime. He was hardly home, he admitted, so of course, that can never be good.

For a second time, the big Nigerian grabbed me, pulled me into a tight embrace and nearly squeezed the air out of my lungs. When he finally let go, he unhooked the red cord from its golden pole, winked at me and said, "There is free food and free booze for you, my brother, anytime you want."

Half a year later, Taimi and I enter the bar; I take her straight to the stairway leading to the VIP section. John, the big Nigerian, sees me. As he has been doing every time since we met, he smiles and grabs my hand, pulls me close, and squeezes the air out of my lungs. "Good to see you, brother," he says and clips the red cord from its golden pole.

I look at Taimi and can tell that she is impressed.

Upstairs, when I return to her with drinks and two plates stacked with food, she yells in my ear, trying her best to out-shout the loud music, "Did you see those Chelsea football players with their wives!?"

When people turn around and look at us, I decide Taimi might not be the right girl for me.

5

I keep a list of the girls I've dated. I put their names in a Microsoft Excel sheet. I give them scores from one to ten on how attractive they are, how much I like them, how much they appear to like me, how clingy they are, and whether she or I am in control of our relationship.

For instance, Ellyn from Kinston Upon Thames receives a definite nine on looks. Her face is boyishly charming like Meg Ryan in the movie 'Sleepless in Seattle'. Her big eyes are so endearingly blue that a nine might not do her justice. But I never give tens. I like her. She is fun to be with and is not afraid to be adventurous. But she WhatsApps me almost every hour of the day. When I don't reply immediately, she politely inquires with another message if I have received the first one. On clinginess, she scores a nine as well. As the one nine cancels the other one out, she gets a zero for 'potential-dating-material'.

Aside from Ellyn, there is Cathy from Ipswich, Dianne from Woking, the blond girl in marketing and Jo-Jean from Canada (though her parents are Hong Kong Chinese). When I first met her, I misunderstood her name to be Eugene, and I wondered why she was given a boy's name. I liked Jo-Jean, but she moved to Italy and out of my life.

Other girls on the list are Janice, Leone, Pamela, German Hanna, Swedish Gabi, Susie, Polish Anna, Catherine, Murielle, Michelle from New Zealand, Welsh Carey, Lizzi from South Africa, Marjo, Helena from Greece, Joey from the US, Elizabeth, snobbish upper-class Clare, Elvira, Nathalie, Nicolle, Tamara, Canadian Kris, Trish from somewhere in Ireland, Barbs, Kate from I-don't-know-where, Anna, Nikki and Antoinette. I've created this list so I can try and better understand myself. There must be an explanation of why I am still single. Perhaps, by making an overview, I can recognise a pattern. I'm starting to think that it might have to do with me. Although I have to admit that some of these girls really shocked me when I got to know them a little better.

Carey from Wales told me she always wanted to be a ballet dancer, and at the age of eighteen, she'd flown to Latvia to train there for a year. Instead, she ended up having an affair with the husband of the family she was staying with. Since he was involved in some weird sex industry thing, she spent most of her weekends horizontally entertaining her landlord's clients. Carey, for some reason, blamed her dad (or her psychologist did), and after two weeks, she blamed me for the fact that she cheated on me with another online date.

Hanna from Germany was not that much different. She admitted straight from the beginning that the only reason she was looking for internet dates was to have sex with them. At times, she would take home three guys during the weekend, and when she and I met, we stayed in bed for almost a whole week. She told me that she was raped by her brother's best friend. No one in her family knew about this, and certainly not her brother. She said she really liked me and wanted us to have a serious relationship but confessed that this didn't necessarily mean we would be exclusive.

Almost every weekend (and during my busier period, twice per week), I take girls to the upstairs VIP lounge. They are all very impressed with the way John embraces me and how he unhooks the red cord from its golden pole.

So far, the list hasn't given me any insights and when one evening, a Chelsea football player walks over, slaps me on the shoulder and asks, "How are you doing, mate?" I realise that I have been coming here too often.

But I'm getting to know the big bouncer a little better. For one, John is not his real name. He adopted it as it's easier for the English to pronounce. His Nigerian name is Chimwuanya, and it means: 'my God's eye is open'. He told me he doesn't want to be called Chimwuanya any longer, and I suggested shortening it to Chimp. We both started laughing when we pictured people's shock while thinking it must come from the word chimpanzee. "Or what about Champ?" I asked him, "As in champion?" But he shook his head and said he would rather not be reminded of his Nigerian days.

I enjoy his company. I stay till closing time just to end the evening having a last drink with this big guy. On one of those days, I asked him if he liked living in England.

He sighed and said that he hates it here; the rain, the constant dull greyness, the people's cold distance, and his job as a bouncer. "But what can I do?" he asked.

I told him that I only lived in South Africa for five years. Whenever someone asks me when I am going back home, I don't think of Belgium. Instead, I think of sunshine, a more relaxed lifestyle and the ocean. I told him that I also struggle in London, that the rain gets to me and that I understand it must be worse for someone who was born on the African continent?"

Again, sadness drenched his expression. He hesitated, and eventually, he said, "I can't go back." Then he looked at me and waited.

He probably still believed I was a psychic, so I took a guess: "Political refugee?"

He shook his head. "I killed someone," he said. "I lived in Lagos with my girlfriend, and one day, she came back home crying, and her knees and elbows were all bruised. She told me that two guys had pulled up at the traffic lights. They'd made her stop, opened her car door, dragged her out and had thrown her onto the pavement. Then they got into her car and drove off. A typical carjacking scenario," he explained, "and there are many every day in Lagos, but I took it personally. I knew a couple of heavy-weights, and it didn't take me long to find out where her car was and where the carjackers lived. I grabbed my gun, went up to have a chat and ended up shooting three of them."

He looked at me and sighed. "I had to leave the country. It was not so much to run from the police or the government, but the guys I killed belonged to a dangerous gang. I crossed the border into Benin, worked the docks in Ghana's Accra for a while and when I had enough money, I gave it to the captain of a boat that sailed to Essex in England."

He stopped talking for a while and stared at the drink in front of him. "It was always the plan to get my girlfriend to join me once I had saved enough to buy her a ticket to London. But I'm unable to get in touch with her."

"What do you think happened," I quietly asked.

He shrugged his shoulders and looked at me. "You tell me," he said, "you are the psychic."

I stopped going to that bar for a while. Still, weeks later, when I took yet another girl to the upstairs VIP, John confided that things had been better between his French girlfriend Sophie and him. He laughed and said, "I followed your advice, my friend and took her to some restaurants. I gave her a bit more attention, and it made her smile again." He playfully punched his big fist against my shoulder. "Thanks, brother, you've saved my relationship."

From that day onwards, John told all my online dates what a great guy I was and when we had our quiet little drink at the bar, he gave me feedback. He often told me that I would be stupid not to go on a second date or that I was stupid to have gone on a first one. It was during one of those evenings that he said, "You are a player, man."

I was shocked. "No, I'm absolutely not," I replied and honestly believed that this was not the case. "A player is dishonest to the girls he dates and tries to get his way with her under false pretences," I defined. "I'm not like that. Straight from the beginning, I let the girl know where she stands and whether I like her or not. I never go on a second date if I don't think there is future potential."

He kept quiet and looked at me. It was then that I realised I had been lying—not only to the women but to myself. How many of them had I taken out for an evening, letting them think that I would phone them the next day, never to get in touch again? How many phone numbers had I received? How many of them had waited for me to call and invite them on a second or third date?

It is easy to be a guy because when you don't phone the girl, you often don't get hassled by her calls. I made myself believe that I had done the right thing by not trying to lure a girl into my bed, but I probably kept her waiting the next day for me to get in touch.

I did phone Finish Taimi two weeks after our first date. I asked her if she would like to take a drive with me to Southampton on the coast as I wanted to find out what it would take for me to do a Yachtmaster's course. I knew she liked boats, and in my mind, this was not a second date but merely two friends on an outing.

While we drove back to London, she asked me what my expectations were around us. I simply shrugged my shoulders and returned her own question: "What are yours?"

"The least I expect," she said, "is friendship."

In a way, this sounded quite all right, but when I dropped her off at her place, she suddenly kissed me on the mouth.

Surprised, I looked at her. "I thought you only wanted friendship?" I asked.

"The 'least' was friendship," she replied with a smile, "but anything else is more."

I never phoned her again, and I remembered complaining to Brett that a guy and a girl couldn't just be friends as one of the two always seemed to expect more.

Two weeks later, Taimi WhatsApp-ed me. She said that she felt a connection between us, but there was, unfortunately—no chemistry from my side.

What is the difference, I thought? What is a connection, and what is chemistry?

There are many pickup artists who, by using specific techniques, can raise the idea of chemistry or connection. Neil Strauss, a writer for The New York Times, went undercover and spent two years living among those players while using the pseudonym Style to protect his real-life identity. In his bestseller 'The Game', he points out that nearly every major city in the world has secretive seduction dens. There, men trade the most mind-bogglingly effective techniques to charm women. This is not fiction. These men really exist, and I am not one of them.

In that way, honestly—I simply couldn't be considered a player.

"Your kind is the worst," John said: "The players who think they have been honest and decent with the girls. They are the ones who let the girls go home thinking they've met marriage material."

Was he right? It is true that all the girls who went with me to the upstairs VIP had, in one way or another, been lied to?

But if so, that still doesn't make me a player.

I looked at the muscular bouncer, waiting for him to say that he was only pulling my leg, but instead, he just smiled his big, broad white-toothed smile.

6

It is my second summer in England, and it feels as if it hasn't stopped raining since I arrived from South Africa. I haven't been back to the upstairs VIP since the big bouncer accused me of being a player.

I am dateless on a Friday evening. Brett is at a work function, and Richard has been ordered by Adele to stay home. I am trying hard to concentrate on the movie I rented for tonight, but the story doesn't grab me. I switch the TV off, take my laptop and go online to have another look at my online dating profile.

I read through it and conclude that there should be more honesty. Aside from that, I should stop winking at just anyone. Fate does not hide in numbers, and I'm not some sales guy trying to get as many customers as possible.

I should never have changed my profile. My many dates haven't delivered the website's promise of love. A sales rep can indeed visit twenty customers per day, but if he hasn't done his homework and properly profiled them, he will not make a single sale.

It has become clear to me that I need to carefully select who I want to go out with. My objectives have changed. I am no longer focused on getting as many dates as possible. Instead, I only want one single date with a girl I really like. And, for her to really like me, I need to be very sincere in my profile.

For the zillionth time, I start rewriting my profile and tell everyone who wants to read it that happiness hides in details: in being content. Life should be more than simply sliding towards your pension, and breathing has to go further than only filling your lungs with air. In a relationship, interaction should exceed silly arguments about dirty socks under the sofa. When you pull on the same side of the rope, you don't make knots or have fights about insignificant things. I tell my potential dates that I believe every person should stay an individual and that three things make a relationship work: connect, commit and communicate.

I finally close off with a quote from Ellen DeGeneres. I want my audience to know that I'm not very religious. It says, 'In the beginning there was nothing, and God said, 'Let there be light!' And there was light. There was still nothing, but you could see it a whole lot better.'

If the girl who reads this doesn't feel that there is a connection, she better not write back.

In my quest for selecting the right one, I have developed new rules. One of them is that I might not necessarily seek out English girls. I have been living in the UK for a little under two years, and I can't seem to connect to the Brits.

It might be me. I even told my boss in Spain about it, and he gave me a philosophical answer. He said that everyone is different, but that at the same time, everyone is still the same. In soft-spoken English (and with a hint of an Antonio-Bandera's accent), he told me that last week he had to go to a funeral in Barcelona. Everyone was crying and hugging each other. It was heart-ripping. Women were hugging women, and men were embracing men. Tears rained on their dark-grey suites, and they all expressed their grief in long whaling sobs. But some years ago, he had to go to an English funeral, and though everyone was wearing grey and black suits, hardly anyone cried. Some of the women did, but most people looked at each other with straight faces, trying their best to hide their grief. People would bite their lips, but seldom would anyone shed a tear.

"The Spanish and the English are different," he concluded, "but they are also the same. The amount of grief within their heart is not less, but they merely express it differently."

After hearing that, I tried to change my perception, but still, it didn't get me anywhere. For my job, I have flown to most continents and one week with my colleagues in a foreign country turned us into friends for life. But not in England. Having lived for close to two years in London, I still don't seem to be able to break through their grey suits and look at the tears inside their hearts. That is why I decide not to select English girls any longer.

On top of this, I read the profiles more in-depth. I try to filter them through a sieve I call 'the rule of opposites'.

When I read in a profile that someone wants their ideal partner to be, for instance, extrovert, the rule of opposites implies that they are introvert. When they mention that they want their date to be outgoing, the rule of opposites tells me that they are couch potatoes. They need someone to drag them off their sofa's to have a more exciting or adventurous life.

I have come to realise that a lot of people are looking for something they are not. Like in Plato's story, they think they need someone else to complete them. Often, they look for the thing they feel is missing in their own lives.

By becoming stricter in my selection, I have reduced the number of dates from about ten per week to, well ... actually ... —none.

However, one girl is finally able to push through. Her profile lets me know that she is a nurse who grew up in South Africa. She is shorter than what I would typically go for, but she looks quite pretty with her long, curly black hair.

We write each other a few messages, but by the time I phone her to invite her on a date, she says that she can't do this. She hasn't been on this dating app for that long, and now she suddenly realises that it was a mistake.

"From what I have read on your profile and in your messages," she says, "I can tell that I like you, but this is all too weird. It would have been so much better if we'd accidentally run into each other in some pub."

"Then why not do that," I argue. "Let me know where you will be tonight, so I can accidentally run into you."

She giggles and admits that it is a great plan. She tells me that on Thursday, she might be visiting a pub on the corner of some street in Chiswick, and she might be sitting there at the bar having a glass of red wine with a friend. If I accidentally happen to be there, I could walk up to her and ask her for her name.

"But I already know your name."

"True," she sighs and says: "then just ask me if you can flirt with me."

But Thursday morning, a WhatsApp message from French Celine suddenly brightens my phone, and I accidentally forget to go anywhere that evening.

7

In her message, Celine asks me how I'm doing and I think long about whether I should reply or not. When I eventually do, it is brief and unelaborated. I merely return her question by asking how things are with her. I am cautious not to mention or enquire about the guy she'd met that specific Friday evening, a bit over three months ago. On the other hand, I am dying to find out if they are still together.

She lets me know she is doing fine. She reminds me that she works in advertising and tells me she has been swamped: long evenings and stuff. At times she stays up till past midnight to get a Swiss account interested in joining her company. It appears that she has been flying to Zurich on a more than regular basis.

She doesn't mention her boyfriend.

We write another couple of messages, and by the end of the day, I finally ask her how her dating life is. She replies that all is fine, and eventually, she lets me know that she is still with that guy.

So why on earth is she getting back in touch, I think? Especially now—now that I have almost erased her from my mind.

I decide to ask her. 'Why did you get back in touch with me?' I write and specify, 'I thought you were quite clear in your last message?'

She apologises and wants to know if I prefer not to have anything to do with her. She says she has been thinking about me quite a bit; about the queen's swans, the ducks and our conversation in that little restaurant. Eventually, her question comes: would I mind meeting up with her? Just for a coffee, she adds, no other intentions.

Again, I think long and hard about whether I should. I even ask Brett, and he, as always, opts for optimism.

"You've got nothing to lose, Lyam," he says. "You might as well go for a coffee. It is only coffee; you won't get pregnant. If it turns out that you still like her and she stays with the other guy, well, then ... tough luck. At least you know. If you no longer like her, then it's all for the best. But whatever happens, this will give you a chance to close this whole chapter and leave it behind."

I ask Richard as well, and he says, "Screw her, man! She's not worth your time. She stabbed you in the back by going out with this other bloke the day before you were meant to see her again. Didn't you have a great time with her? Didn't you have wonderful conversations? Didn't you kiss at the end of your date, held hands, stayed up till four in the morning? If by now she doesn't know what she's missing, then she never will."

My mind agrees with Richard, but my heart tells me to follow Brett's advice. I decide to meet Celine for coffee and choose the little French bistro for the occasion. I am sure that she will like it. I pick three o'clock in the afternoon: that means no lunch and no dinner.

When Saturday arrives, I take the tube to Covent Garden. I'm early, and I am nervous.

Fifteen minutes later, I see her entering the bistro, and she looks adorable. Her hair is still short, just like I remember. She has hardly changed, but then again, it has only been three months.

She sees me, and immediately a warm smile appears on her face. She wears a loose summery dress, and it makes her look even more desirable.

Though it feels to me that something has changed. It doesn't take me more than two seconds to realise that I am no longer infatuated with her. Despite everything, her endearing smile still warms my heart, but I no longer feel what I felt that night in the park.

She gives me a kiss on the cheek, takes her seat opposite me at the small round table and says, "It's wonderful to see you."

"It's good to see you too," I reply.

She brushes her hand over mine and asks, "What have you been up to?"

I lie and tell her that work has been keeping me very busy and that things are going well overall.

"Have you been meeting interesting people on the dating app?" she enquires.

"Not recently," I admit, "but then again, I'm not rushing into dates purely for the sake of dating."

I tell her that I have become highly selective. The girl I would like to meet should really jump off my computer's screen before I even think of sending her an email.

Celine says that she entirely agrees with this approach.

I don't ask her about her boyfriend. It doesn't really concern me, but that's not the only reason why I leave the subject closed. Even though I've made up my mind that I'm no longer taken by her, it still feels as if she has betrayed me. My ego is bruised, and discussing him would be stirring in this pot of treachery.

We drink our coffees and talk for a couple of hours. After that, we go for a walk around Covent Garden. We don't hold hands, and there are no swans or ducks to chase. We look at some clowns folding balloons into animals, at magicians making things disappear and at how a few comedians try hard to make their crowd laugh. We stop and listen to a busker singing Leo Sayer's 'Orchard Road'.

Celine still smokes and lights her third cigarette. While the man jingles his guitar, I wonder whether she and I should be staying in touch. It feels that internet dating is not set up to form friendships, but I like her, and I honestly wouldn't mind.

Eventually, when I tell her I need to go, I think I can see disappointment in her eyes.

"Do you think we can be friends?" Celine asks.

I smile and say, "Of course we can."

8

A couple of days later, I receive a message from Celine wherein she lets me know that she has broken up with her boyfriend. She writes that he wasn't really what she'd expected (and I wonder if anyone ever is). She mentions a party she is going to on Friday evening and wants to know if I would like to tag along. In-between brackets, she writes, 'just as friends,' and she concludes her sentence with a smiley face.

I don't mind. It gives me a chance to pull away from the drunken weekends Richard, Brett and I are having on a more than regular basis.

I reply that it's a great idea and add: 'just as friends.'

The party is not too far from Ealing, but it's pretty dull, and it doesn't take long before Celine and I take one look at each other and decide to go somewhere else.

"What about Netflix and curling up on the sofa at my place?" I ask her.

She looks slightly puzzled but then says: "Sounds like a plan," and smilingly adds: "But only if there will be pizza."

Brett is out, and the house is empty. Celine and I sit next to each other on the couch. We're channel-hopping the TV while waiting for the pizza to be delivered. After we have eaten, we watch Charlie Kaufman's cleverly written 'Adaptation'. The movie is directed by Spike Jonze and stars Nicolas Cage. I have seen it before, and this allows me to be distracted.

On occasion, I look at Celine and consider folding my arm around her shoulders to pull her closer, to kiss her forehead or even her lips. I think about what could have happened if she hadn't met that guy the day before we planned to go on a date? Would she be here as my girlfriend? Would I be madly in love with her, or would I be feeling what I am feeling now: that she could be a good friend, but nothing more?

But what about her? Does she want me to put my arm around her shoulders, to pull her closer, to kiss her forehead or even her lips? Is that her desire? And if we were boyfriend and girlfriend, would she then have broken up with me while writing a message to the other guy, telling him that I'm not really what she'd expected?

The movie hasn't finished yet, but Celine looks at her watch and says that if she still wants to catch the last tube home, it's time for her to leave.

"Why don't you stay the night?" I ask.

She looks confused.

"There is a spare bedroom, and it would be a pity to miss the end of the movie. You might as well stay and make breakfast for Brett and me."

She laughs. "Have you been plotting this from the start so I would make you guys breakfast?"

"Yep," I say, "That has been the scheme from the very beginning."

Early in the morning, I see my bedroom door slowly open. It's Brett who walks in. He tells me he has been to some house party and slept there till he became a bit soberer to take the earliest tube back to Ealing.

"How did it go last night?" he wants to know. "Did you and Celine end up kissing again?"

I laugh. "No, nothing happened, but the party we went to was dead, so we came down here and watched Netflix."

"Are you honestly trying to tell me that the two of you silly duck chasers have been sitting here watching movies and that nothing happened? Not even a kiss or holding hands? Come on, Lyam," he says, 'I don't believe you. You need to lie better than that."

Then sounds emerge from the kitchen. Pans and pots are rattling, and Brett looks puzzled. The rumble is quickly followed by footsteps in the hallway. Moments later, a soft knock on my bedroom door precedes Celine's voice, "Where do you keep the bacon, or don't you have any?"

Brett stares at me with eyes wide open. He puts his hand in front of his mouth to prevent him from bursting out laughing. I can barely manage to hold a straight voice when I reply, "If there's none in the freezer, then we're out."

When I hear her walking towards the kitchen, I call after her, "Celine, I was only joking last night. You don't have to make us breakfast."

"I know," she yells back and asks, "when will your flatmate be back?"

"He already is and is lying next to me in my bed."

Celine remains quiet, and I guess I need to give her a little more information, but Brett burst out—almost shouting within his whisper, "You sneaky fox. I knew it, I knew it, I knew it!"

9

Celine and I stay 'just friends', and at times I wonder why my feelings for her have lessened. Did she change, did I, or is it simply because she smokes? On the dating front, I stick to my last method. I stay highly selective and meticulously read through every profile. I only message a girl when I feel optimistic that there could be a connection. I no longer wink, and my messages have become less standardised and more personalised.

I have also stopped replying to just any message that finds its way to my inbox. Not a lot has changed. I keep receiving winks from women in their fifties or sixties or women who live in Columbia, Canada, and Taiwan and believe London is just a stone throw away.

I eventually decided not to meet up with the South African nurse, whether accidentally or not. I figured that if someone at the age of thirty is too nervous about going on an internet date, then she probably is too nervous for life.

But my overall hit rate is still high. I carry on with my 'I-don't-give-a-fuck'-attitude, and on top of this, I have added a new step. If I don't receive a response within two or three days, I send her a second message.

I call it (like in tennis) my 'second serve'. I think it's only decent for me to chase them for a reply. After all, reading through a girl's profile and writing her a personalised message is a lot of work, so I expect a reaction. Let's be honest: being this highly selective and, on top of that, not receiving any replies tremendously reduces my chances of me ever meeting someone, let alone getting married, or even worse—getting laid.

In my 'second serve', I invite the girl to have another look at my profile. I tell her that I realise this attempt might be futile, but since it is the internet, trees have not been chopped for paper, and ink has not been wasted. I further let her know that I'm waiting nervously for her to respond, crossing my fingers till they hurt and checking my inbox while on the lookout for their message. I tell her that I would cry myself to sleep if it wouldn't make my pillow soggy because, so I've been told, that will give me wrinkles.

The response is enormous. Almost all the girls who receive my second message write back and apologise for their rudeness in waiting so long to reply. Only a few let me know that they feel we might not be a good match and wish me all the luck in finding that 'special one'.

The girls who respond to my 'second serve' apologise and let me know how busy they have been. They try to make up for their delay in writing lengthy messages.

However, what I only start to realise over time is that I never get to meet any of the girls I've sent that short additional 'second serve' message. For some reasons, our follow-up emails die out, either because I or because they lose interest.

What if they never wanted to write to me in the first place?

Like me, they might base their decisions on some sort of instinct, which can't really be explained by any rational thinking process. Sometimes I browse through profiles, and a gut feeling tells me not to write even though there doesn't seem to be anything wrong with the girl. When I ignore this feeling and contact her anyhow, we seldom get to meet as our conversations at some point die a slow death.

When I think about it a bit more, I come to the conclusion that everything can be narrowed down to some standard relationship law, which is: 'effort equals interest'. It basically means that when you are willing to put in the effort, you are actually interested.

Perhaps you are too busy. Maybe you've been too swamped at work, or your friends take up all of your time, or you need to eat and sleep and, as a result, have no time so send a simple text message. But when this becomes your excuse, it only shows that you were not prepared to put that essential effort in.

When you really like someone, you will move heaven and earth to find a way to get in touch. If you don't, then let's face it: you are not genuinely fond of that person, and you'll create all sorts of reasons to justify your escape route.

Brett and I developed a name for this and call it the 'big-hand-syndrome'.

10

It all started when Brett received an email from his mother in South Africa. She wrote that she'd met a woman in Port Elisabeth whose daughter lives not too far from London.

As it turned out, the girl had just broken up with her boyfriend and was feeling a little out of place. Brett's mother (the unyielding match-maker) asked Brett if he'd mind getting in touch with her. He only had to take her out for a drink or to the movies, so she would feel less lonely.

Brett didn't mind. He wrote the girl an email and introduced himself. After she replied, he suggested they should meet.

They did.

He drove to Crawley, took her out for a drink and came back telling me how pretty, wonderful, adorable, brilliant and fabulous she was. Overjoyed, he related in exhausting detail what their conversations were about, how insightful, funny, deep and intense they were. No topic was taboo. He truly felt close to her, and more importantly—he felt as if he had known her for years.

On their second rendezvous, they kissed, and after that, they went from 'dating' and 'seeing each other' to becoming a couple. He introduced her to me, and she started visiting our house in Ealing on a more than regular basis.

However, not long after they'd first started going out, things deteriorated, and one evening, Brett confided that he was not that impressed with her any longer.

"What's your concern?" I asked him because all I could see was this tall, gorgeous, lovely smiling blond-haired girl who—on top of everything else—was great to talk to. Every time she came to the house, she helped out in the kitchen, was content with whatever movies we watched, ate pizza when we did, etc. "What an earth can possibly be wrong with her?" I asked.

He thought about it for a long time and finally, with a deep sigh, he replied: "She has big hands."

I couldn't believe what I heard.

"Big hands?" I repeated. "What about her looks, her personality and all the other things? Surely, you can't just throw that overboard for something trivial as big hands."

He looked at me ashamed, and eventually, he said, "I can't bear it any longer. When we go for a stroll, and she wants to hold hands, I shudder. I can't do it. It bothers me, and I become irritated with everything else: the way she smiles, how she acts and the things she wants to talk about."

"You used to have such great conversations?" I protested.

"I know," he replied, "but they only annoy me now. Aside from that, she is pale white. She has this constant factor-fifty-sun-block on her face, even here in England where the sun never shines. She says that she wants to look great when she is old, but what's the point when you look ugly while you're young? She's white like … like …," he dithered.

"Like Snow White and the seven dwarfs?"

"In a way, yes—but without the dwarfs."

"And just as good looking."

"But with big hands," he added.

"You can't say that this makes her ugly, though," I objected.

"No, but I don't think she is that pretty anymore. On top of that, the sex isn't that great any longer."

"And all because of her big hands?"

"Exactly."

"So, when did she start growing them?" I asked.

He looked at me, puzzled.

"Well, surely, she didn't have big hands when you first met her, so when did they become bigger?"

He laughed.

In a way, he had always known that it wasn't about her big hands, but for some reason, he simply started liking her less. He didn't mind them when they'd first met, as he didn't mind her toneless complexion. But after spending some time with her, he decided that she wasn't really what he'd hoped for, and he merely tried to find a rational explanation.

Big hands became the answer.

It made me wonder if he'd ever truly liked her. Was he only infatuated by what he had dreamed up? Because, after all, she was a cure for his loneliness in much the same way as he was for hers. Even before they'd met, he might have already decided that he wanted to be impressed with her. She wasn't only South African but had grown up in his beloved hometown. So, the main question was ... —had she actually changed during those few months or was she never pretty, wonderful, adorable, brilliant and fabulous? Had she indeed grown bigger hands?

Had Celine grown bigger hands as well?

11

No matter how I try to avoid it, I am starting to become really busy at work. More and more flights to other European cities are lining up, forcing me to spend three or even four days per week away from home.

Texan Donald thinks it's all great and awesome as his global customer appears to be rather pleased with the results of my work. We're saving them loads of water, energy and time. In his Southern States accent, he tells me everything is wonderful, but he is married, and I'm still dateless as I hardly have time to chat up girls.

My internet dating has been put into its lowest gear. I try to adhere to my 'two-messages' rule, but it's not possible. By the time I arrive back in London, I have sent most girls four, five and even up to ten messages. Because of my busy schedule, it has become increasingly hard to go on dates, especially during the week. And before I finally get to meet someone, either she or I have lost interest.

Perhaps it's true that when it goes well on the one front, it goes wrong on the other. If I'm failing to find a proper relationship because I'm starting to become more successful at work, I might have to resign.

I'm sure Texan Donald would not say 'great, awesome and wonderful' when he finds out.

I'm in regular contact with Celine, and she is becoming a good friend. At times I still wonder if there could be anything more than being 'just friends', but the fact that she smokes bothers me. In some ways, smoking has made her hands grown bigger, and I no longer think it's charming.

Brett, contrary to me, has become less busy. The property market has reached its lowest in years, and he hasn't made his bonus for a couple of months in a row. Since most of his salary is dependent on this, he has fallen back to a basic income and is financially struggling. On top of this, his costs are high. He drives a new Volkswagen Touareg Four-Wheel-Drive, and his BMW motorbike is parked in the garage. The rent we pay is not too high, but he says he urgently needs to review his social spending. He tells me he can't do the big-nights-on-the-town any longer, and I happily agree with him.

I am starting to feel that I've overdosed on London's nightlife. I want to slow down and don't mind staying at home every now and then. Instead of going out, we can have friends over for drinks or organise barbecues, where everyone brings their own food. That might save us some money.

Brett agrees, but still, I see him hesitate.

"What's wrong?" I ask.

He takes his time before he warily lets me know what he has been thinking of. "There is this third bedroom," he starts but pauses before he continues. Eventually, he says, "How would you feel about renting it out? It could easily give us an extra five hundred pounds per month."

I love the fact that it's just the two of us in the house. We live here as a family, like two brothers. But I understand that this third bedroom, in his mind, has become a cost.

"Fine with me," I reply.

"I appreciate it," he says, "but let's have this rule: if either of us does not get along with the new tenant, then he or she will be kicked out without discussion."

Half an hour later, we have browsed the internet site Gumtree and written our announcement: 'Spacious three-bedroom house in Ealing is looking for a third tenant. Two great guys are already staying there.'

A couple of days later, we receive our first response. The applicant lets us know that she's in her fifties and asks if there will be a lot of noise. We wait another four days till the weekend arrives, but no one else contacts us about the room. The elderly lady remains our only candidate.

Then, unexpectedly, Fiona (the girl Brett and I met at Adele's birthday party) phones to ask what our plans are for the weekend. It appears that her friend has offered to cook for us.

While I'm speaking with her, she complains about her friend and her ex-husband's endless bickering and says that it has become impossible to live there. The two children are constantly running around, her friend only wants to party all night, and at times it feels like twenty-five people are living in the house.

I look at Brett, and I whisper to him that we have found our new flatmate. He gazes at me confused but smiles when I ask Fiona if she wants to move in with us.

When Brett lets our only applicant know that, after lengthy deliberations, we decided to go with someone else, the elderly lady amiably says that she is convinced it must have been a tough decision for us.

12

Two weeks later, Fiona moves in. She immediately pays the deposit, and our little family has an additional member. At least, that is what Brett and I think, but we quickly learn that Fiona wants to stay her own person. She cooks her own meals and doesn't join us when we have our lunches and dinners together. She even has her own fridge.

Aside from that, all is going well, and I soon find out that Fiona has joined the same internet dating app like the one I am on. "How else can you meet someone in London?" she defensively says when I ask her about it.

"I didn't think it would be an issue for the English to meet other people," I object.

Fiona and I spend our evenings browsing many different profiles and show each other what our potential dates look like or what they message us. It doesn't take long before Brett shows an interest and decides to give it a try.

Every evening after dinner, the three of us scroll through the dating profiles on our phones, trying to cash in on future happiness. Brett takes the long sofa and Fiona the short one while I sit on the hard, wooden bench at the dining table. The only sound that can be heard is the clicking noise of our phones while we write our messages. We don't speak, and whenever we spot someone attractive or receive an amusing comment, we forward it to each other. Sometimes we ask for advice on whether they are good looking enough, funny enough, down-to-earth enough, cool enough or responsible enough to write back. It even happens that Brett and I swap profiles around while commenting: 'this could be for you, bro,' as if girls (like shirts and ties) are things that can be lent out among friends.

Brett's response rate is lower than mine. I believe he has uploaded the wrong pictures of himself. One of them shows him at a party while yelling his head off and holding three beers in his two hands. Another one is of him smoking a Turkish water pipe.

"Girls don't want to see this," I tell him. "They don't wait in front of their computers hoping to receive an email from a guy who brags about getting drunk and smokes funny stuff with his mates."

He agrees and makes some changes, but still, an overflow of reactions stay out. It is clear that it annoys him.

When, after dinner, we compare the number of responses received, I often find three, four and even five times more in my inbox than him.

There has always been a healthy competition between the two of us, whether waterskiing, snow skiing, running of hills and getting phone numbers from girls. The reason I don't play rugby is that he is so much better at it. And the reason why he wants to stop searching for girls on the internet is that he feels he is not getting anywhere.

I can't help but notice how he follows a similar pattern when I first joined this dating site. He starts with reading the profiles in detail, then becomes bored and fast-forwards to the main bits. Soon after that, he loses interest and then he merely looks at the pictures. In his final stage, he only clicks the 'wink' button. Without even opening any of the profiles, he tells twenty, thirty and even forty girls per evening that he is interested.

Like me (and like so many others), he has turned online dating into a lottery game. He uses it as a slot machine and snatches the handle down to make the three wheels spin. He winks and winks and winks, but while the machine promises love, it endlessly keeps on presenting non-matching fruits.

Two weeks later, a girl from Ukraine writes in poor English that she really likes his profile. After an hour of chatting, she asks him for money, and Brett becomes even more disillusioned.

13

Fiona receives ten to twenty times more winks and messages than Brett and me combined but is less outspoken about who has contacted her. We suspect that she is actually going on a date when she tells us she is out for drinks with friends. However, she doesn't want to admit to it.

In a way, we get along, though Brett still claims Fiona likes me more than him. "Look at how she singles you out when the three of us are having a conversation. It's almost as if I don't exist," he moans. "Whenever I'm in the kitchen, I hear you guys chatting away, and when I'm back in the living room, she's all quiet and reserved."

"Are you jealous?" I joke.

I start paying more attention to how she interacts with both of us. Only now I realise that she is no longer sitting on the short sofa but right next to me at the dining table when we surf the match-making app.

She says it puzzles her that a guy like me needs to go on the internet to find a date. She claims she is sure that I simply have to walk into a pub, and ten girls would be willing to come home with me.

"Yeah, right," I say to her, "I am a guy, not a girl."

"What do you mean by that?" she asks.

"For a guy to have sex, he must pursue a girl, flatter her, take her out for meals, buy her drinks and flowers, open the car door (or a can of coke for that matter) and wait days, if not weeks before anything happens. For a girl to have sex, she simply needs to show up."

"Isn't it obvious?" Brett whispers, when both of us are in the kitchen doing the dishes: "She is all over you." He foolishly mimics her voice, pretending to be her while rubbing his body against mine, saying: "Oooh, you are soooo nice, and you can get any girl in any pub, you big lover boy."

With her curly blond hair and a constant twinkle in her blue eyes, she looks very attractive. I recall when she and her friend visited our house and how she browsed her fingers over the covers of the books I've read while lip-reading the titles and telling me which ones she knows and which ones she doesn't. I remember looking at her and thinking that I liked her, that she is pretty and intelligent.

Could I date Fiona, I wonder?

At times I can have long and lengthy conversations with her, but for some reason, I can't help but think that she is not my type.

Why not? I ask myself. What is wrong with her, or is there something wrong with me?

In a way, I have told myself that it's because she is English and that I would like to return and live in South Africa one day. A West-European girl would not be able to deal with the hazards over there. Firstly, she needs to want to go and secondly, when she does, she needs to want to stay. If anything minor happens, like a car-jacking or a burglary at gunpoint, she will surely take the first flight back home. And then what?

On the other hand, I could be lying to myself. I went on a date with Celine, who, after all, is French. I have dated other girls who grew up in Western European countries. Am I just trying to find excuses?

What would Richard say?

Richard would say that if you're not convinced, you're not convinced. So, I keep it at that: she is simply not my type.

However, I assure myself: this doesn't mean that I can't flirt with her. Right?

I look at Fiona and finally say, "If it's true that I can pick up any girl in any pub, why haven't I picked you up yet?"

"Well," she boldly says, "why haven't you?"

A couple of days later, I'm about to head out to meet Celine and some of her friends at a South African pub in Fulham. I turn to Fiona and say: "You know, it's pretty cold tonight, and if there's one thing I hate, it's climbing into a cold bed when I return home. So why don't you crawl in there and wait for me till I'm back."

She laughs and says, "Yes, I might just do that."

But when I return home, there is no one in my bed, and the following day, while I question her about it over breakfast, she says, "I didn't think you were serious."

A week later, when Brett is out, Fiona and I are watching TV. We're both sitting on different sofas, and she wears her nightie. Without there being anything funny on TV, she starts giggling.

I look at her and ask, "What's wrong?"

"You won't believe how horny I am," she says. "I haven't been with a guy since my last boyfriend."

I am not sure how to react to this. I laugh awkwardly and tell her to go to her room and play with herself.

"That's not the same," she moans.

I leave it at that, and though I try to focus on whatever is on TV, I am too distracted.

Is there a chance that Fiona could become my 'friend-with-benefits'? Or will she be expecting more? I don't want a relationship, I tell myself, or at least—I don't want a relationship with her.

Again, I try to concentrate on the programme on TV, but quickly lose interest. I look around the room and can't help but notice how dirty everything has become. Before Fiona moved in, our fifty-year plan lifestyle was not a very neat concept. In a way, it didn't bother us, but when Brett and I realised that a girl was moving in, we took the weekend off to clean the whole house. We spent most of our time scraping the limestone layer and soap residues from the shower window. Even our bedrooms underwent proper metamorphic changes. We located the vacuum cleaner, which was strategically hidden underneath some camping chairs, a tent and other outdoor stuff. By the time we'd finished, the house seemed almost new.

When I look around to distract myself, I can see how cobwebs have been gathering dust in the ceiling corners and how everything has become dirty again.

With my left hand, I pat the cushions on the sofa next to me to see if a cloud of dust would rise from them, but instead, the patting makes Fiona look at me. She smiles, gets up from her sofa and climbs on my lap.

"I thought you'd never invite me over," she says and starts kissing me.

14

I don't stop her. At first, it's gentle, almost hesitant, but soon it becomes more passionate. I pick her up and carry her to my room, where I drop her on my bed. We start kissing again and eventually have sex. She stays the whole night, and it feels good to fall asleep while someone is lying next to you. I can wrap my entire arm around her — she is that tiny.

When I wake up and open my eyes, I see Fiona staring at me with a big smile on her face. The first thought that jumps into my mind is, 'oh my fuck, what have I done'.

"How are you?" she quietly asks.

Stupid, I think, but instead, I smile.

"I don't want to rush things," she says, "but how do you see this?"

"How do I see what?"

"On the risk of sounding pushy: are we a couple?"

I look away, sigh profoundly and remain silent for a while. After that, I look her in the eye and say, "No, Fiona, we're not." I see her face muscles tensing, and I try to explain, "I'm not ready for a relationship."

She is visibly disappointed. "Don't you find me attractive?" she wants to know.

"Yes, I do. It has nothing to do with that. I'm just at this stage in my life where I can't be bothered to be in a relationship. I'm free and want to keep it that way."

"Then why are you spending time on that bloody dating app?" she asks.

I shrug my shoulders.

"And why did you have sex with me?"

She sounds upset.

"Because you were horny," I reply, "and I thought you wanted this to be non-committal as much as I did."

"Well, for your information," she calmly says, "I don't want this to be non-committal. It appears to me that we simply have to pretend nothing ever happened between the two of us. I would appreciate it very much if you would be a gentleman and don't tell Brett about our mistake."

"I won't tell him," I promise.

She gets up, walks out, and the last thing I hear is her slamming the door of her room.

I stay in my bed for another hour. After that, I get up and walk over to Brett's room.

"What was that slamming the door all about?" he wants to know.

"I had sex with Fiona last night," I say while I sit on his bed.

"Oh my goodness," he says, "you shouldn't have gone there."

"I know, and now she wants a relationship."

"This will become messy," he sighs.

Later that day, Fiona apologises for slamming the door and lets me know that I need to understand I can't expect to have sex with her ever again.

I apologise as well and tell her that I understand.

At first, I am relieved that this all went so smoothly, though Celine assures me during our phone conversation that I shouldn't count my chickens before they hatch.

"From what you've told me," Celine clarifies, "she doesn't strike me to be the type of girl who easily gives up."

From that day on, everything becomes very complicated. Whenever Brett is not present, Fiona keeps asking me why we can't be together. "We have the potential to be wonderful," she claims.

One day she is all sweet and caring, bringing me a glass of wine and making me coffee or hot chocolate before I go to bed. On other days, she stays in her room throughout the evening or loudly stamps her feet while walking through the hallway and slamming her bedroom door. She regularly tries to kiss me, and when I stop her and remind her about her rule not to have sex, she says, "It's only kissing. Don't get too excited about it."

But one night, I wake up with a fright when I notice that Fiona has crawled into my bed and has put her arms around me. She is naked and starts kissing me on my lips and my body. "Have sex with me," she whispers, "have sex with me now."

"I can't," I say. "It wouldn't be the right thing to do, and you'll feel stupid in the morning."

"I already feel stupid," she angrily shouts and leaves my room while stamping her feet in the hallway and slamming her door.

The drama goes on for weeks. She makes me coffee and hot chocolate, stamps her feet and slams the doors. She crawls into my bed in the middle of the night, and the following day she accuses me of having led her on. I struggle to fall asleep as I expect her to enter my room at any given moment. When I finally do sleep, I have nightmares of girls in their nighties standing next to my bed while staring at me.

One evening, Celine comes to the house when we have a barbecue and spends the night in my bedroom. Fiona thinks we are sleeping together. Trying to prevent anything from happening, she stays up till the early morning hours while singing and screaming and slamming doors. The next day, she is all-loving again. She sits next to me at the dining table, showing me profiles of guys she is about to go on a date with and asks me whether I think they would be suitable for her.

When, after a few days, she tries to kiss me again, I push her away and become angry. I tell her that she needs to stop this silliness or move out of the house.

She gets up, slams the doors and disappears into her room for almost a week.

From then on, we are no longer on speaking terms.

15

Celine asks me if I am familiar with the term 'bunny boiler' and says we need to get her out of the house before accidents happen. She explains that the phrase comes from a scene out of the movie 'Fatal Attraction', wherein a woman (while seeking retribution for rejection) ends up boiling the rabbit of her ex-lover's daughter.

I look it up on the internet. Directed by Adrian Lyne, it stars Michael Douglas in the role of a married man. He has a weekend affair with a woman, played by Glenn Close, who can't accept that what happened was not more than a fling. She becomes obsessed with him, and it doesn't take long for the woman's mental instability to surface.

Celine claims that it doesn't make a difference whether I have rabbits or not.

That same evening, Brett and I discuss the pickle I find myself in and that we need to do something about it.

"I am afraid I need to pull my veto-card on her," I say, reminding him of our little agreement that if we don't get along with the new tenant, he or she will be kicked out without discussion.

Brett agrees that she needs to go. "The situation has become intolerable. It's not your fault," he assures me. "Anything could happen between a male and a female flatmate. It could even be

145

considered normal, but what isn't normal is the way she is dealing with rejection."

That evening, when Fiona comes back from work hauling half a dozen wine bottles into her room, we tell her that we need to talk.

Brett looks at me, and I look at him. She looks confused. I prefer him to tell her, but realise that it is my responsibility. I hesitate; clear my throat and say, "Fiona, we have decided to give you your notice."

"What!" she exclaims.

"We want you to move out," I spell out.

"This is not fair," she gasps, "I have my rights. You can't just throw me out like that." For a moment, she stares at the floor, but when she looks up, she says, "I won't go! I will stay where I am. I've been paying my rent perfectly on time at the end of each month, and I am a good tenant."

"A good tenant!?" I shriek. "You've turned this house into a regular Greek tragedy!" While I speak, I become more and more agitated. "You crawl into my bed in the middle of the night and have your little fits. Almost every evening, I need to go through lengthy sessions to explain why, on this flipping earth, I don't want to be with you. Is that your definition of a good tenant? It is my definition of a stalker. People have been arrested for less. You know what you are, Fiona?" I scream while deciding to practice my new gained knowledge in English expressions: "You're a bunny boiler!"

"I'll stop," she promises. "I will completely leave you alone."

I look at Brett for a moment. I calm down and sigh, "Sorry, but by the end of the month, you need to pack up and go."

"I won't," she stubbornly says. She gets up from the sofa, walks into her bedroom and slams her door.

After that, she is quiet and remains quiet for the rest of the week, leaving Brett and I fretting about whether she will move out or not. It makes it difficult for us to start looking for a new tenant.

Fiona's silence feels disruptive, but it doesn't take long for her to up the drama. She starts bringing home different guys who all stay the night and smoke in the house and drop their ashes everywhere and leave the living room a mess. At night she screams her orgasms, which are so loud we are sure they are faked.

Brett and I grind our teeth.

Richard says that if she hasn't moved out by the end of this month, we need to throw her stuff outside on the street. He even offers to bring in some mates and beat the shit out of everyone who does anything wrong.

Celine says: "I told you so!"

Bern and I keep telling ourselves that it's only for another three weeks—

Another two weeks—

Another week—

And another couple of days.

And then she leaves. She packs up without saying a word, but when we check her room, we notice that she has broken the mattress holders and smashed the inside of her wall unit.

After that, Brett and I decide not to look for a new tenant, and we're back to just the two of us.

Chapter 3

In fear of heartache

1

After three years in Londen, my dating subscription automatically renews itself month after month. Another rainy summer is coming to its end, and I miss South Africa.

I'd imagined my life to be different. I'd imagined London to be different, and I'd imagined myself not being single anymore.

Perhaps I've acted too hastily when I discarded Anna for having a large backside. What if she was my fate, put on my path by Plato's gods?

What if not Anna, but another girl I met was my destiny? Did I then act too impetuously by dismissing them after a mere two seconds of chatting? Is that why I'm being punished with loneliness? If I am to blame for my own misery, then maybe I should have been more patient and put in the effort. After all, being in a relationship is hard work.

At least I can find some diversion in my job. I spend most of my time managing that one large customer and things are going well. Yesterday, after quickly stopping in Paris, I arrived in Ljukwjbljijana (sorry … I always seem to get it wrong … let me try again) Ljubljana in Slovenia.

I am in my hotel room, and today, I log on to the dating app for the first time in six months. My main intention is to end my subscription.

As usual, there are a few messages in my inbox, though not that many. It seems that when you don't put in the effort, the dating world punishes you by turning its back on you. However, there is one message which draws my attention. It is from a girl who calls herself 'Mystery'.

She is in her early thirties, and her pictures are not too bad. With her dark hair, slim figure, and one meter and seventy-three centimetres height, she meets all my requirements. She has written me a long message that spans a little over three pages. Her tone is intelligent, almost edging towards sarcasm.

Overall, I find her funny, and some of her humour even leans towards a form of absurdity.

'Is that really your best feature?' she asks and refers to the dating site's request to name the part of your body you think is most striking. In my 'I-don't-give-a-fuck'-mode, I selected—feet.

In no time, I have read through it all, and though there is a moment of hesitation (after all, I decided to stop this nonsense), I feel excited at the same time.

I write back and use her style of shifting between seriousness and flippancy, between realism and absurdness. I reply that (while I am not working as a journalist for 'The Globe') I use my spare time to earn extra money as a foot model. But one day, while in Mozambique, I'd cut my right foot on some coral. It got heavily infected, puss sprung out and left a massive wound. At that stage, someone told me that I would never win a foot competition again, though it got better by taking penicillin.

I don't reach three pages, but it is not a short reply either. After I press 'send", I take a shower, and by the time I check my phone, I notice a response from her in my inbox. It makes me happy to see that she doesn't play the 'waiting-game', whereby people (in order not to come across too desperate) wait one or two days before getting back to you. Secondly, this is the 'effort-equals-interest' I have been looking for.

She writes that she knows all about coral as she has a Master in Marine Science. She is working towards her PhD in Marine Biology, studying coral disease and other factors that affect coral survival in captivity. She says that she is glad to read my feet have recovered and shares that she once had a septic foot after swimming. It also took a while to heal.

I decide to reward her promptness by writing back immediately. I leave the foot subject for what it is but mention that I am in Slovenia's Ljukwjbljijana. I tell her that I love this country and that I am staying in a beautiful hotel.

While I'm in the downstairs restaurant, her message brightens my inbox. This time she asks me how many stars the hotel has, and I reply that I don't know. It is not dark enough to tell.

By the evening, we have written each other over ten messages, and in her last one, she enquires how many more she has to send before I invite her on a date.

2

A week later, we are scheduled to meet at Trafalgar Square. It is Friday evening, and it's my first date in almost an eternity. I have told her that I will be wearing a brown suede jacket over blue jeans and that I will be waiting for her under Nelson's Column. She should have no problem recognising me.

She has given me her phone number (just in case), but I haven't rung her yet. The reason is, I think that I am nervous. I have been date-less for too long, and this time I don't want anything to put me off. This time, I want to keep an open mind and go without forming any prejudice.

I am half an hour early and continuously walk in circles around the granite column. Not even the four bronze lions can reassure me, and by the time it is six o'clock, I am still by myself.

After that, it turns to five past six—

Then ten past six—

At a quarter past six, she still hasn't arrived.

It makes me think of my very first date with Anna. She was almost an hour and forty-five minutes late because she got stuck in the underground. I wonder if she is still in-between jobs and in-between flats or in-between boyfriends.

Surely not after three years!

All of a sudden, I feel a hand on my back, and a voice says, "You must be my date." A face leans over my left shoulder.

I turn around and give her a big smile, which she immediately returns. "Caitlin?" I ask.

"Yes," she replies. "Or did you expect me to look different from my picture like you do?" She laughs while she says this.

"I don't look different from my pictures," I defensively say.

"Your hair is not black," she giggles, "but grey."

"It is not grey," I react in high-pitched tones.

"All right, not completely grey, but certainly salt and pepper."

"There is no 'salt-and-pepper'-check-box on the app," I try.

"Yes, there is," she teases, "and this just tells me that you lied. What else did you lie about?"

We both laugh and finally shake hands. I kiss her on the cheeks, and she apologises for being late. "Tubes and Underground and all that," she says.

With her striking face and great smile, she looks magnificent and comes across as marvellously easygoing. She grabs the sleeve of my jacket and leads me through the crowd towards a nearby pub. Although it is cold, we take a seat outside. Without any hesitation, she has taken it upon herself to walk to the bar and order some drinks. When she comes back with two pints of Leffe, she smiles and says, "I've done my research on Belgium."

I am charmed by her wit, fascinated by her quick and intelligent reactions. An hour slips past without me noticing it. It is after seven, and we decide to go to a restaurant nearby.

On the way, I tell her that I am still in shock about her 'black hair' remark. "This means I'm forced to change my profile," I joke.

"Aren't you going to take it off now that you've met me," she chirps back.

When, during dinner, one of my green beans falls off my plate, and I (hoping that she hasn't seen it) quickly pick it up, she sighs: "Not only a liar, but no table manners either. Will I ever be able to take you anywhere?"

I feel comfortable being with her. She is easy to talk to, and it is almost as if I have known her for a very long time. When I tell her that I have lived in South Africa, she reacts ecstatic and lets me know that she has to go to Durban for her PhD in Marine Biology in half a year. She says she will stay there for three months and hints that I could introduce her to the country.

"I thought you were joking about studying coral diseases," I say.

"Why would I joke about that?"

"Because of me pulling your leg about that foot-model thing and cutting myself."

"Another lie?" she mockingly asks while acting all upset. "Don't tell me you are not a journalist for 'The Globe' either!"

She is vague about where she lives at the moment. She tells me that she moves around from one city on the English coastline to another. It all forms part of her research, she explains.

"Why coral?" I ask her in an attempt to be more serious.

"Because I've always wanted to live in Australia," she replies. "You know—the Great Barrier Reef and stuff."

As the evening progresses, I wonder if she likes me. There have been some clear signs that she does. For one, she has invited me to travel with her to South Africa. Secondly, she has implied that I could take my dating profile off and thirdly, she hinted that she would want to take me to other places as long as my table manners improve.

But then again, Caitlin is English, and the English try very hard not to be too direct. Because of this, they have even changed their language. English words do not always mean what the dictionary explains. 'Interesting', for example, doesn't necessarily mean 'arousing curiosity'. It often implies that something is 'weird', or 'strange' or anything but 'curious'.

Caitlin sits opposite me in the restaurant, and we have finished our meal. We talk a little longer over a glass of wine, and when I discreetly look at my watch, I am shocked to learn that it is already half-past eleven.

"Are you in a rush?" she teasingly asks.

I feel a little uncomfortable admitting that I might be missing my last tube if I stay any longer. But there is a twinkle in her eyes when she, somewhat mischievously, says that she doesn't need to go anywhere.

I look at her for a moment and realise that she is not just trying to be polite. "In that case," I reply: "I don't need to go anywhere either."

I wait for her to go to the ladies and quickly wave the waiter over to ask for the bill. I prefer to have it settled before she comes back. I just want to avoid silly arguments about who should pay, and in that way, she doesn't have to pretend to take out her purse while hesitatingly asking, 'Are you sure?'

The 'who-should-pay-what'-issue is complicated. Some girls insist on chipping in and perceive a guy picking up the tab as male-dominance. They might not even want to go on a second date if he insists on paying.

I have a female friend in Toronto who I met on a yacht while sailing from South African's Durban to the north of Mozambique. She is the opposite. She will not even look at the bill. I asked her when guys have to pay, she replied, "Till I feel it's time for me to contribute."

"How long can that take?"

"Months."

"And what if the girl earns more than the guy does?"

"Irrelevant," she said. "A girl needs to feel that a guy can take care of her or at least that he has the willingness to do this."

"Then, where the flip has equality gone?" Richard asked me when I raised the topic with him. "How can they claim they want the same rights, the same responsibilities and the same salaries as guys? When it comes to an engagement ring, do girls realise it is a symbol of suppression, the shackles of slavery? It is, after all, the man who rings and, in that way, controls his woman, and yet women wear it proudly!"

To avoid this type of conflict is why I wait until my date has to get up. Girls always need to go to the bathroom before they leave a restaurant.

When Caitlin returns, she protests for a moment but then suggests we have a drink somewhere else and this time on her.

After we leave the restaurant, we go back to Nelson's Column and climb on top of one of the bronze lions. We talk about silly little nothings until it is too late for busses and tubes to take me home. Only a few taxis pick up the odd traveller, and I am really getting tired.

When Caitlin finally informs me that she stays in Southend-on-Sea, I realise why she said that she doesn't need to go anywhere. It is because she simply can't go anywhere. Anywhere is flipping two hours from where we are!

But I can't leave her by herself, and I still haven't kissed her, so I either have to stay here and talk throughout the night or the both of us take a taxi to my place.

She looks at me suspiciously after I suggest the latter.

"Don't worry," I say and start laughing, "there is a spare bedroom."

3

Caitlin never slept in the spare bedroom. After she left early in the morning (taking a tube and then a train back to Southend-on-Sea), Brett, as usual, tiptoes into my bedroom and wants to know how things went.

"This time, it feels different," I tell him, but I cannot explain how or why. Only that it does. "It has been a long time since I've met someone that I feel a connection with."

"Do you think this could be it?" he wants to know. "Could she be 'the one'?"

"If there is such a thing as 'the one', then yes—she might be it."

Monday evening, Caitlin phones and after we've spent about an hour talking, she asks me how difficult it would be for me to jump into my car and drive to her place.

The time predicts peak traffic, and it would take me hours to merely cross through the centre of London. Taking the M25 around the city won't be any faster either. There is a reason why they call it 'the biggest car park in the world'.

Nonetheless, I answer that it wouldn't be difficult at all and that I will leave straight away.

Minutes later, I am stuck in traffic for what seems to be an eternity. Still, all my frustration and annoyance evaporates when I see Caitlin three hours later. I stay the night and the next night, and we joke and laugh, and everything feels exceptionally comfortable.

This is the way it should be, and I can't believe my luck. Perhaps Plato was right after all: the gods did cut all humans in half, but I am whole again. There is no doubt about it. Caitlin surely is my other half. At long last, I think, I am in a real relationship. It has been a little over three years since I left sunny South Africa for rainy London; three years since I met Anna. From the moment I landed at Heathrow, I have been stumbling from one disappointment to another. I deserve this breakthrough (I more than deserve it). I am only a little bowled over that it has taken this long, but I can finally say that my internet-dating days are over.

When I arrive back at the Ealing house, the first thing I will do is take my profile off that site. I will delete all the messages I have sent and received over the years. There must be hundreds of them, but I am glad to say that those days belong to the past, and I can't help but feel exhilarated.

4

I intend to spend the weekend in Belgium as I have an early Monday morning meeting in Brussels. I grab my computer and fling some clothes into my travel suitcase. Tonight, and tomorrow night, I will be staying over at Caitlin's to continue my journey to Folkestone's Chunnel on Friday afternoon.

We've been together for close to two weeks and have spent almost every second day together. This required me to drive from Southend-on-Sea to Ealing and back. I guess I've covered more kilometres during the last ten days than I did during the previous year.

The room Caitlin inhabits belongs to the University she is doing her PhD with. She needs to stay there for a couple more months. After that, she will first visit Scotland and then she will move to Plymouth in the south of England. That will be, depending on traffic, four or perhaps even five hours from London. But I don't care, simply because effort equals interest.

When I arrive at her place, she runs to my car and gives me a long hug. "Sorry that I am wearing the same clothes all the time," she apologises, "but living-out-of-suitcases limits my collection, so please don't pay any attention to it."

I wouldn't have noticed it if she hadn't told me (guys, in general, don't). I especially don't see it because all these details are cloaked by my infatuation.

I smile at her and say: "If I die looking at you, it's because you take my breath away."

She rolls her eyes and laughs, "You stole that from that song 'No Air'. What's the singer's name again?"

"Jordin Sparks."

"Correct," she says.

We go to a restaurant that night, and when I look at her eyes sparkling in the dimmed candlelight, an overall sense of togetherness engulfs me. I touch her hand, and she smiles at me. I cannot remember happiness to me more delightful; perfection to be more complete. She is the most wonderful person I've ever met. She is lovely, sweet and fascinating to talk to. If I had a ring on me, I would kneel and propose even before she takes her first sip from her glass of wine.

After we've eaten, we stroll hand in hand alongside the Marine Parade. I try to impress her by balancing on top of a wall that surrounds one of the beaches while praying that I don't break an ankle or, worse ... —my neck.

When we arrive back at her room, she receives a phone call from her ex-husband. They have been separated for over a year. I hear her say again and again, "No, Mark, don't come over."

At first, she is polite, saying please and virtually begging him to stay where he is. As he keeps insisting, she becomes more adamant: "Mark, I'm telling you, do not get in your car and drive over here. It's a two-hour journey, and I will not let you in. Do you understand me!?"

When she finally puts the phone down, she explains that they were married for three years. In her mind, they are completely over, but he seems to have difficulties accepting this decision. She tells me that Mark is a genuinely great guy but that she couldn't see a future with him. She realised this when he wanted children. The thought suffocated her. Not so much the part about having children, but about having them with him. It made her realise that he was not the right guy for her. Perhaps, she reflects, they were too young, too stupid to think things through before they got married. But now he is hurting, and in a way, it makes her upset as she feels responsible for his pain.

"If only Mark could see it the way I do," she sighs, "then he would realise that we should never have married in the first place."

I'm in awe of the compassion and patience she shows him. I can see that his pain weighs on her, making me realise what a truly genuine and kind-hearted person Caitlin is.

The following day, I continue my travel to Folkestone. I drive my car on the railway wagon, which will carry me through the tunnel that connects England with France. Twenty-five minutes later, I leave Calais and continue over Dunkerque to Belgium. Throughout the whole journey, I keep thinking of her. It is as if I am addicted.

Not long after I have arrived at my mum's in Belgium, my phone rings and it is Caitlin. We talk for an hour, all laughing and giggling, and I promise I will phone her later tonight. But when I do, there is no answer. I try on four different occasions, but she does not pick up. I tell myself that her phone battery must be flat and that I should not worry. Undoubtedly, there will be some valid reason.

Only the next day, late in the evening, I finally get to speak with her. However, the conversation is short. There is hardly any laughing and giggling, and when I put the phone down, I tell myself not to feel too weird about it. It is only normal that we don't have hour-long chats every time we speak to each other. She must be busy studying—or something along those lines.

We don't phone on Sunday or Monday, and when I drive over to her place on Tuesday, I notice that she is still wearing the same clothes.

My concerns, which gathered in my head over the weekend, quickly disappear when she hugs and kisses me. Again, I stay the night in her tiny university room, and Wednesday morning, I drag myself through London's early rush hour back to Ealing.

That same evening, I receive a long text message from a number I don't recognise. While I start reading it, I realise it is from Caitlin's ex-husband Mark. He opens by telling me that 'technically' Caitlin is still his wife as they are separated but not divorced.

While I continue reading, a knot ties in my stomach, and I start sweating. His text lets me know that he and Caitlin spent the weekend together and that they had sex. He further informs me that this is the type of person Caitlin is: she does not respect relationships. Before they got married, he writes, she cheated on him with two of her colleagues and even had the audacity to invite them to their wedding. He lets me know that Caitlin had run off with a complete stranger during one of their holidays in Morocco and ended up giving him a blowjob. The text further mentions that Caitlin has a track history of cheating on all the guys she has been with. Mark feels it is only fitting for me to know what I am getting myself into. He ends his message by wishing me good luck.

By the time I put down my phone, I am in shock. I don't know what to do. I tell myself that all of this is not true and that it is just the doing of some guy in pain who tries to take his revenge by making up stories. One often tries to hurt the people one loves.

But what if there is truth in what Mark has written? What if the things he said about Morocco and about her cheating on him with other guys were lies, but not that Caitlin has spent the weekend with him? However, what if that is a lie, but not that she went off and gave a stranger a blowjob? Or did he lie that she invited those two colleagues to her wedding?

If any of these things are true or if only one of them is true—would that make me look at Caitlin differently?

I need to confront her. She has the right to defend herself.

I phone her, and she answers immediately. She says she is happy to hear my voice, but I don't waste time on endearments and instead read Mark's text.

She is quiet for a long time. Finally, she asks, "Where are you now?"

"In Ealing," I reply.

"Don't go anywhere," I hear her say, "I will come over straight away."

I put the phone down. It will take Caitlin probably two hours to make it to Ealing. My mind is working overtime. Why does this need to happen? I don't deserve this. I absolutely do not deserve this. Why can't there be uncomplicated, everlasting happiness? Why all the baggage, the snags, the hitches and the sorrow? Perhaps it is true that a person who doesn't have any baggage has not travelled through life, but why does it need to be a container full and can't it simply be hand luggage?

I phone Brett at his office and tell him what happened. While he listens, he remains silent, and even after I stop talking, he doesn't speak for a while.

I could have phoned Richard, but I already know that he would advise me to run for the hills and leave Caitlin while still in one piece. The main reason why I phone Brett is that I am not ready to leave her. He always tries to find the middle way and put things into perspective. That is precisely what I need right now.

I hear him taking a deep breath, and eventually, he says, "You were right to phone her, and it's good that she's coming over. It shows she cares. But there is one thing you need to keep in mind, Lyam."

"What is that?" I quietly ask with my heart pounding in my throat.

"If this ex-husband is so repulsed by Caitlin, then why does he spend the weekend with her, and why does he try to scare you off by sending you that text message? If Caitlin is really such a bad person, why does he want her back?"

This is true, I think after I've put down the phone. He does want Caitlin back, and perhaps everything in that text message is a lie. Maybe she never cheated on anybody, not even with the guy in Morocco or with her two colleagues from work. Perhaps she didn't even spend the weekend at her ex-husband's place, and all Mark wrote was fabricated bullshit!

But still, what would Richard have to say about this?

Even before the thought finishes in my head, the pounding of my heart swells in my throat, and my hope disappears because I know what Richard would say. Richard would say, 'then why the fuck is she rushing over to your place?'

Perhaps I have to phone Mark and ask him for an explanation?

He doesn't sound surprised when he answers his phone or me asking him why he sent this text.

"Because you ought to know," he replies. He clarifies that Caitlin had phoned to ask him if he could take a look at her computer. She drove over to his place, and after two glasses of wine, he suddenly was allowed to look at much more than just her computer. She eventually stayed the whole weekend, and Mark says it was as if they had never been separated.

He tells me about Caitlin's other escapades, about how she and her friends phoned each other almost daily to exchange stories on how they cheated on their husbands.

"I am sure you will end up meeting those friends," he says. "Caitlin will tell you all about their secret lives as she seems to get a kick out of telling those stories. But I wonder how their husbands will react when I tell them what happened," he concludes.

Mark wants me to believe he is doing this all for me: as if he doesn't want me to get hurt and is trying his best to spare me what he had to go through himself. I listen more than I talk, but at the end of the conversation, I ask him why, if she is such a bad person, he wants her back?

This startles him. He is silent for a long time, and then, in a soft voice, he says, "You're right, mate, I shouldn't want her back."

After that, he thanks me and says that I have opened his eyes.

5

Caitlin looks as if she has been running. She is out of breath when she arrives at the house. She stares at me, waits for me to react, and I can see tensed anxiety on her face.

I invite her in, and upstairs she takes a seat on the arm of the small sofa.

"So," I finally say, too scared of my own question and of what her answer might be: "what would you like to say about this text?"

She buries her head in her hands, and I think she is crying. Her eyes are still dry when she looks up, but her face almost seems deformed by fear. She is no longer as pretty as I believed her to be over the last two and a half weeks.

Eventually, she takes a deep breath and sights. "Yes, I did go to Mark because I had a problem with my computer and ... something happened that—well..., —shouldn't have happened. But only once," she quickly adds. "We only had sex once."

"Did you stay the night?" I ask her.

"No," she says.

"Caitlin, let me ask you again: did you stay the night?"

She looks at me in shock. She turns her eyes away and whispers, "Yes—I did."

"Did you stay the weekend?"

"Of course not," she replies.

"I phoned Mark," I say.

"You did what!?" she exclaims. "You phoned him!? How could you do such a thing?"

"I wanted an explanation, and he told me you stayed the whole weekend. He said you had sex on several occasions."

"That's a lie!" she yells.

"What is a lie?" I ask, "That you stayed the whole weekend or that you had sex more than once?"

"We only had sex once," she says.

"Did you stay the whole weekend?" I ask you again.

"—Yes." Her voice is so soft I can hardly hear her, but it quickly changes; it becomes livelier: almost defensive. "He had to repair my computer," she says, "and it was quite a big problem. He couldn't do it in just a couple of hours, so I had to stay until he'd fixed it."

I don't know what to think and stare out in front of me.

"I don't want to lose you," she whispers. "I'm really scared. Can't you see I'm trembling? Do you perhaps want me to phone Mark, so he can confirm we only had sex once?"

I am not sure if this will make it better. Does it even matter how many times she cheated on me? How do I digest this? It is too soon in our relationship—or is the timing of no importance either?

"I'll phone him," she says, and I notice her keying in some numbers in her phone. After she waits for him to pick up, I hear her yell, "Mark, what did you tell him? How many times did we have sex?" I can't hear his reply, but she argues, "That is not sex, Mark and I want you to tell him!"

She holds out her phone, waiting for me to take it so I can speak to her ex-husband.

I don't look at her. I can't think. I don't want to speak to him any more than I want to speak to her. I'm scared—scared that all of this is really happening.

I see her switching her phone off and tossing it onto the sofa. She keeps staring at me.

"What about the others?" I ask: "The affairs you had with your colleagues before you got married?"

She rolls her eyes and sighs. "What about them?"

"You invited them to your wedding?"

She looks surprised. "What else could I do?" she asks. "They were my colleagues! How could I have invited the whole department and not them? The others would have started wondering why."

"You were more concerned about what your colleagues thought than about the feelings of your husband?"

"The feelings of my husband!?" she exclaims. "Do you know what he did on our wedding day? Did he happen to tell you that?" She waits for me to reply, but I keep quiet. "My wedding day was supposed to be the happiest day of my life," she says, "but he came to me early in the morning while I was still getting dressed and threatened to tell the wives of those two colleagues that I've had an affair with their husbands. That is what he did. Can you believe it!?" she shouts. "It ruined my whole day. I was completely in tears! You can take a look at my wedding pictures: I am not smiling in any of them."

I want to ask her if she ever considered how Mark's wedding day must have been ruined? But am I really supposed to defend a guy who is trying to damage my relationship?

On the other hand, who has damaged it—he or Caitlin?

"What about the guy in Morocco?" I ask.

"Morocco!? What did he tell you about that?" She is visibly shaken. She takes a deep breath and then starts explaining: "I thought that the guy was going to rape me. I went for a ride with him on his scooter. Then he pulled up somewhere on a beach and started kissing me and grabbing my boobs. I really believed that he was going to rape me. Honestly, I swear! So, I told him that I had my period and that we couldn't do anything, and the only way to calm him down was to give him a hand job."

"A handjob or a blowjob?"

"What the fuck does that matter!?" she yells. "He was going to rape me, and doesn't that count for anything!?"

"Perhaps it does, Caitlin. And perhaps you really did save your own life that day, but why did you choose to go with a stranger on a scooter?"

"Not that this is any of your business," she yells, "because I don't see how this is related to our situation. Mark had invited two of his mates to join us on our holiday, and he was spending all of his time with them, playing golf all day and stuff. I just wanted to piss him off; make him jealous or something."

"Piss him off by having sex with another guy?"

"It wasn't sex," she yells. "It was only a blowjob."

"Isn't that sex?"

"No, it isn't!"

"And you are telling me that you and Mark only had sex once last weekend? What exactly is your definition of sex, Caitlin?"

She holds her head in her hand and starts crying, but I am not sure if her tears are real. I feel cold. I do want to be with her, but how do I deal with this? Can I step over it? Even when you glue all the pieces of a broken vase back together, won't you keep staring at the cracks? Will those cracks start living their own life and dominate our relationship? Will I ever be able to see the beauty of the vase again?

"I haven't really cheated on you," she says through her tears. "He is still my husband. You and I have only been dating for a little longer than two weeks, and all the others," she continues, "have nothing to do with us. That's all in the past."

I don't know if I can accept this.

"Did you truly think we were completely exclusive after that short time?" she whispers, almost mockingly.

"I did," I say, whispering as well. "At least I thought that much after we'd spent all those nights together."

"But we hadn't made any commitments towards each other. We hadn't had the conversation."

She keeps quiet.

"Can I ask you something?" I ask.

She nods.

"Do you think you haven't done anything wrong?"

She hesitates for a moment. Then she shakes her head and says, "I haven't cheated on you if that is what you want to know. We were only dating, and Mark is still my husband."

"Then why did you keep it a secret from me. Why did you not tell me that you were staying at his place when you phoned me while I was in Belgium. And why did you panic and rush all the way down here if you think you'd done nothing wrong?"

She rolls her eyes, and this irritates me even more.

"I am willing to accept that those two colleagues and even the guy in Morocco were part of your past and that it isn't any of my business—at least not directly. But I disagree that you haven't done anything wrong," I say. "How can you claim that you are allowed to have sex with other people because we have only been dating for a short time? Do you really believe that? And what about you going all Bill-Clinton on me by saying that a blowjob is not sex. Should a husband think nothing is wrong after his wife has given a blowjob to her whole department? Would he honestly be able to accept that she never had sex with anyone?"

I wait for her to reply, but she keeps staring at the carpet.

"Caitlin," I insist, "look me in the eyes and say that you believe that you haven't done anything wrong."

She looks up, stares into my eyes and says: "I haven't cheated on you. We were only dating."

"Are you telling me that I have the right to go out tonight and have sex with another girl?" I ask.

"Not now," she says, "because we've had the exclusivity-conversation."

"So, what you are saying is that if Mark hadn't text me, I would have been allowed to take any girl out for dinner, kiss her, bring her back to my room and sleep with her? Simply because we hadn't discussed it in full and failed to use some magic words that identify where we truly stand?"

She doesn't say anything.

"Have you done nothing wrong, Caitlin?"

She sighs while rolling her eyes at me and slowly says: "I have not cheated on you. We were not exclusive at that time, and he is my husband."

"If you can't see that you have," I reply, "then I don't think we should be together."

"What!?" she exclaims.

"I think you should go," I say.

She looks away and stands up from the sofa's arm. I follow her down the stairs to the front door. She walks out without saying anything, and I close the door behind her.

6

I walk to my room and lie on the bed. I stare at the ceiling and try really hard not to think about anything, but it's impossible. I wanted this to work and truly believed this time it was different. I feel numb and just want to sleep for days and weeks until all of this has turned into some vague memory.

I need a distraction. I am thinking of reactivating my internet dating subscription. The sooner I get past this, the better. But I do nothing and stay on my bed.

An hour goes by, and then the doorbell rings. It's Caitlin. She has been crying. Her eyes are wet and red, and she tells me that she walked up and down the street and thought about what we've discussed. She says that she agrees with me, that she was wrong to spend the night with Mark, and apologises.

Can I forgive her, she wants to know?

I take her in my arms and kiss her. I am glad that she is back, and I decide to deal with the cracks in the vase after we have glued it together.

We go upstairs and lie on the bed. We just hold each other and don't speak. Half an hour before Brett comes home, she gets up and leaves. She correctly assumes that I have already told him everything and says she can't deal with him judging her.

After Caitlin has left, I leave the house as well. I don't want to talk to Brett as I already know what he will say. He will tell me to give it time and that I need to be patient as only the future will show if I can trust her.

That is also what my heart advises me to do, and I absolutely want to listen to this. On the other hand, I don't want to cheat myself out of reality either. My mind doesn't agree with my heart, but its message is distorted by emotions.

Richard could bring perspective and kick some hard sense into me. Perhaps I need his opinion more than I need soft consolation.

When I arrive at his house, he opens the door. Adele is not home, and I am glad that I don't have to talk to her. We sit down, and I tell him about Caitlin's ex-husband's text message and about her spending the weekend with him. I tell him about her two colleagues, about her wedding and the guy in Morocco.

I expect Richard to bark at me, to tell me that I am a fool and that I should leave her right here and now. I expect him to say things like: 'wake up and smell the bacon' or, 'you're walking into your own misery with your eyes open' and even, 'once a cheat, always a cheat'. I expect him to take a long look at me and decide that I am setting myself up for hardship and grief, but he remains quiet.

Too quiet.

I wait while he stares out in front of me.

Finally, he looks at me and softly says: "When Adele and I got together—," he hesitates for a moment and continues, "—I can't prove it, but I believe something similar happened to us. We only dated for a couple of weeks when she had to go and do something at her ex-boyfriend's place. I think she spent the night with him."

"Shit Richard," I say. "Sorry, man, I didn't know."

"I'm not a hundred per cent sure," he sighs, "but all those little details have been bugging me over the years. You know— those little lies. First, she says she only stayed for an hour, then it turned out to be the whole day and after that, the evening. She claims that she did not spend the night, but why the lies in the first place? It was a long time ago, over seven years, but one day I will find out and get to the bottom of this."

"What then?" I ask, "What will you do when you know?"

"I would not be able to accept it," he says and shakes his head. "If I find out that she spent the night with him, I'll leave her."

"Leave her?" I ask. "After all those years? You have a child, and another one is on its way. What if you find out in ten or fifteen years, will you still leave her?"

"Yes," he says, "I wouldn't be able to live with it." He looks at me and says, "But you're different."

"In what way?" I ask.

"You always seem to go for the nutters." He hesitates for a moment, then takes a deep breath and says, "Do me one favour, Lyam. Don't start fooling yourself."

"What do you mean," I ask.

"In my opinion, she has cheated on you and don't let anyone tell you differently. There are no half truths, and there are no half lies. She either did, or she didn't. So, tell me, brother, which one is it?"

I shrug my shoulders.

He sighs, "If you really want to work through all of this, then you need to accept it first. Don't deny it. Don't pretend or make yourself believe that she hasn't done anything wrong. Don't tolerate that he is 'technically' still her husband or that the two of you haven't been together for that long and that you are only dating. If you tolerate that kind of nonsense, then you won't get anywhere. It is like stealing. Whether you have stolen a loaf of bread or a million pounds, you are still a thief."

When I drive back to Ealing, Richard's story fills my mind. He told me that if he finds out that Adele cheated on him, he wouldn't be able to live with the knowledge. I wonder if I can live with knowing what Caitlin has done, or will I be spending most of my time staring at the cracks? And what if there is truth in the saying 'once a cheat, always a cheat'? Will Caitlin, one day, drive off with another guy on some exotic island, or will she invite her escapees to our wedding because she is worried about what others might think?

In the book 'The Clinton Tapes', former president of the USA, Bill Clinton, admitted to journalist Taylor Branch that Monica Lewinsky was a moment of weakness. His mother had died, he'd explained; a friend had committed suicide, and investigations were mounting against him and Hillary. He felt sorry for himself and simply 'cracked'.

Is that what might happen? Will I just need to wait for that moment of weakness for Caitlin to climb onto the next scooter that drives along?

But there is another thing that bothers me. Richard said that I always seem to go for the nutters. "Every time you have issues," he'd explained. "You only fall in love with the crazy ones. What is that all about?" he'd asked. "Why can't you simply be with a normal girl? What is wrong with Celine, for instance? I tell you what is wrong with her … —nothing. That's the problem," he'd concluded, "there is absolutely nothing wrong with her or any of the other girls who have shown interest in you. But you don't feel attracted to them purely because they're just too normal."

Is this true, I wonder. Am I only interested in girls who have too much baggage?

I am deep in thought when all of a sudden, my phone rings. It is from Brett. "Where are you, bro?" he bellows, "I have been phoning you over and over. It's eight o'clock, and I am sitting here with dinner."

In a way, I think it is funny. Someone is waiting with dinner and worriedly phoning me to find out where I am. Only, it is a 'he' and not a 'she'.

If Brett had long blond hair and boobs ... then ... well ...! Oh, and of course, if his cooking was better.

7

December arrives, and it is cold. I don't want to stay in this country. I don't want to live in London. I have no reason to believe that next year will be better than this one.

Caitlin and I do our best, but things have changed. We argue more than we should for people who have only been in a relationship for a couple of months. It is as if some seal has been broken, and we fight about everything. Every minor detail can be a reason to have a go at each other: the movie we watched, the movie we haven't watched, the fact that she hasn't closed the cap on my shampoo, that I haven't rinsed out the shower when I stay over, that I've put too much salt on the food, not enough sugar in her tea or what restaurant we've gone or haven't gone to.

We even fought about hypothetically winning the lottery and what we would do with the money. My answer (to give some of it to friends and family) caused a near break-up. She said she disagrees with giving money to friends and family because, once people find out that we have won, relationships change. We should not tell anyone, she maintained, and we argued throughout the night, not realising the whole discussion was pointless.

During one weekend, when Brett was out having drinks with Richard, we watched the movie 'Eternal Sunshine of the Spotless Mind'. It is scripted by Charlie Kaufman and directed by Michel Gondry. Kate Winslet plays the role of Clementine, who, after a nasty fight with her boyfriend, decides to undergo a procedure that erases all the memories of their relationship. Upon discovering this, Joel, played by Jim Carrey, is devastated and decides to do the same. But while his memories are slowly being erased, Joel sees them playing in his mind and realises that there were also happier times. He desperately tries to fight against the memory loss, but the procedure relentlessly continues despite his efforts. Of course, closer to the end, both realise the true value of their relationship, and everything ends happily ever after.

I wonder if Caitlin and I argue this much because we love each other. After all, love equals suffering.

But Caitlin and I even disagree here. She says that it is too soon to know, let alone talk about whether we love each other. You can't experience feelings of love for someone you've only been with for a couple of months.

"But what about a mother," I ask her, "would she not immediately love her newborn baby?"

"Of course, but only because she has carried it around for nine months."

"And what about the father?"

"That is different," she claims.

"And a kitten—would you not love a kitten from the first day you've bought it?"

She says she would, but it is different as well.

"Do you perhaps have an issue with the word love?" I ask, "because, if that's the case, then we could simply replace it with another word."

I look around the living room and glance at all the different items which fill it: the TV, the big wooden table, my laptop, some plants, a mirror against the wall and the two long sofas.

"That's it," I say, "we can use the word couch." I wait for her to react, but she keeps quiet. "Do you couch me, Caitlin?" I ask, but there is no response.

We do have happy moments. She has an absurd kind of humour that I can very much appreciate. At times, when we go for a walk in Richmond Park, and the late October chill makes us stroll closely together, she pretends to be a cat and pushes her head into my hands, so I'll pet it. Or she pretends to be a dog and runs towards the grazing deer who suddenly look at her all confused. It makes me laugh, and during those moments, I feel fortunate to be with her. But on other days, I wish a machine truly existed which could erase one's memory.

Of course, when I tell Caitlin this, we start arguing about that. She says that suffering is part of life and that you shouldn't simply ignore things.

She might be correct, but that's not the point. I'm sure that if I had said that suffering is part of life and one should not erase one's memories, she would have stressed the opposite.

In the back of my mind, I hear Richard say, "You're attracted to her because she is a nutter! If she were normal, you would have left her long ago."

Perhaps (like Jim Carrey in 'Eternal Sunshine of the Spotless Mind') I cling too strongly to the good moments. I am worried that they will be erased together with all the bad ones the moment I decide to leave Caitlin.

When we are rational, both of us can't understand how two intelligent people like us cannot work through this. How can we let ourselves become agitated by those tiny little details? How can they grow this big so quickly? It should be impossible that some hypothetical conversation about winning the lottery can bring any couple on the verge of breaking up.

But the moment we're having a fight, we forget that we are two intelligent people and little details rapidly snowball into avalanches. Whether the topic is caps on the shampoo, salt on our food, sugar in our tea or winning the lottery, I always seem to be able to drag the fact that she slept with her ex-husband into it. On top of that, she no longer agrees that she has done anything wrong. She has u-turned from apologising and asking whether I can forgive her, to claiming that we were merely dating. She insists that we never had the commitment-conversation and that, to be precise, Mark was still her husband.

In actual fact, she asserted she was cheating on him with me and asked me if I am too stupid to understand this.

At times I wonder if I am too stupid. Am I really that out of touch with reality? Are people who are dating allowed to have sex with anyone they want?

When I speak to either Brett or Richard about this, they both give me their straightforward opinion, which can be summarised as — 'screw that!"

They feel that when you're in a relationship—you're in it, regardless of the terminology you use.

"But when does a relationship start?" I ask. "Is it after the first dinner, after the first kiss or after you've spent the night together? Or do you need to have a conversation about it first?"

It starts when it starts, they say. There is no room for confusion; when you like someone, it begins after the first kiss— or even after the first dinner. When you mess around, you never truly appreciated her in the first place, and you are simply lying to yourself.

Only when Richard repeats what he has previously told me (that I should not fool myself, that there are no levels in honesty), I understand what our fights are about. The details of our arguments are irrelevant; whether she and I have the same opinion or not is beside the point. The significance of all our disagreements simply exists in the cracks of the vase. I'm unable to see past them. It has been glued back together, but I can no longer see the vase's beauty. Every quarrel starts and ends with me trying to repair those cracks. But instead of using polish or plaster, I go about it with hammer and chisel—ending up making them only bigger and bigger.

At times, I haunt the ghosts of past relationships and try to pinpoint the moment that I should have made a clean break— that I should have walked away to never look back. In almost all of them, I can isolate the moment where we'd passed our expiration date: a time that can be identified as a point of no return.

With Caitlin, there are hundreds.

It is not that I'm unable to break up with her or that she cannot break up with me. By now, we have both done it a thousand times. We only seem to be unable to stay apart. She has turned me into a smoker who vows every evening to quit, only to light another cigarette the following day.

I wish a machine that could erase your memory existed and that I, just like in Kaufman's 'Eternal Sunshine of the Spotless Mind', could use it and move forward. The difference is that I'm not sure which memory I want to delete: the knowledge that Caitlin slept with her ex-husband or the fact that I've met her and liked her.

Even though Caitlin's online dating name was 'Mystery', in fear of heartache, I live in misery.

8

Celine and Peter got back together, and while we've never invited him, she is becoming our standard guest for all our parties, barbeques and Netflix evenings.

On most occasions, she stays the night, and our spare bedroom is slowly filling up with more and more of her stuff. At times, she stays the whole weekend and once or twice, she stayed with us for an entire week. If it wasn't for her having to fly to Zurich, Switzerland, I believe she would never leave.

She seems to like our house more than her own place, which probably has to do with her flatmate confessing that he has feelings for her.

Celine thinks it is all becoming a bit weird. She used to leave her bedroom door half-open, and now she locks it. She also feels awkward walking from the bathroom to her bedroom with only a towel wrapped around her. It never crossed her mind not to do this, but now she thinks he could be spying on her.

"I always believe he was gay," she says one evening when we're in the living room getting ready to watch a movie.

"Aren't you overreacting?" Brett wants to know. "It isn't as if he has said he wants to murder you. The poor guy merely has feelings for you, that's all."

"It isn't just that," Celine says. "He buys me flowers and chocolates. He writes me poems and leaves them on the kitchen counter or on my end of the sofa. One day, when I arrived home early, there was a single rose laying on my pillow and next to it a small handwritten letter telling me again how much he's thinking of me. He shouldn't have gone in my bedroom?" she says. "What else has he been going through?"

"Most likely your undies?" Brett chuckles.

"Yes," I agree. "You better check that you are not missing one or two."

"He might be wearing them as we speak," Brett adds.

"You guys are disgusting," Celine says, visibly upset. "It's a breach of my privacy," she continues, "I'm petrified."

Celine stays for over two weeks and only leaves because she has to fly to Switzerland.

While she is gone, Brett asks: "What about Celine?"

His question surprises me. He makes it sound as if there is something wrong.

"What about her?" I ask defensively: "Please don't let this become a Richard-type conversation where you tell me that Celine is much better than Caitlin, who's a nut-case and that the only thing wrong with Celine is that there's nothing wrong."

He smiles, which worries me even more to the point where I am becoming irritated. I already know that Celine is pretty, tall, witty and fun to be with and that Brett thinks she likes me. However, I am with Caitlin, and no matter how unhealthy our relationship at times might be, I still ... well ... — ... couch her.

Have Brett and Richard been talking about this, I wonder? Did they suddenly decide they need to cure me? Is this a one-man intervention?

I admit that I've had quite a couple of doomed relationships in the past and that there are plenty of ex-girlfriends who can be branded as nutters. Richard has not been the only one who claims that I tend to go for the crazy ones. Brett's dad —Byron— always told me that I am a sucker for punishment, and perhaps he's right. Maybe I am emotionally short-circuited!

I met Byron about eleven years ago. I was twenty-three and had taken a year off to travel overland from the north to the south of Africa. By the time I'd reached South Africa, I was running out of money and was looking for work so I could stay longer.

I'd just left a farm near South Africa's most southerly tip Aghullas and sat down next to the N2 to hitchhike my way to Port Elizabeth. A big greyish-blue Audi pulled over, and a man, who introduced himself as Byron, told me he would only be going as far as George. After about two hundred kilometres, he not only offered me a job but also a little flat to stay in and even the use of his company's pick-up truck. He told me that I could stay as long as I wanted.

He practically adopted me into his family. I joined him on hunting, deep-sea fishing and camping trips. Almost every weekend, he pulled up at my flat to take me waterskiing. While he taught his oldest son Brett to go from two skis onto one slalom-ski, he taught me.

Both Brett and I tried to outperform each other. I would often fall and hit the water at a speed of up to sixty kilometres per hour. The concrete-like surface almost knocked me out, and though my muscles and bones were battered and bruised, I stubbornly got up and tried to do an ever bigger slalom-spray.

That was the moment Byron decided I was addicted to pain. In his mind, I'd already been labelled crazy. After all: what normal person would pick up his backpack and travel Africa overland! When, years later, I repeated the journey a second and even a third time, Byron no longer had any doubts.

In a way, I blame Brett. He is a great storyteller, and at times he adds too much colour to them. He has been feeding his dad stories about us travelling through the Belgian Ardennes or the Swiss Alps. Wading through a river turned into 'swimming' across. Cracking through the ice is bent into almost dying of hypothermia. Picking a fight with a short guy in a pub is twisted into battling a hulk-like Hercules.

No wonder his dad believes I have a tendency to dive head-straight into brick walls and that something can't be good when it isn't bad.

When Brett asked, 'what about Celine?' I expect him to remind me of what not only Richard but also his dad thinks. I wait for him to advise me to leave the Carey's, the Hanna's, the Fiona's and the Caitlin's alone because there is, after all, lovely and more importantly ... —normal Celine.

I don't want to have this conversation, and while my irritation grows, I wait for him to explain himself.

"What about her?" I anxiously enquire.

He hesitates for a moment and then says, "Why doesn't she move in?"

I am flabbergasted.

"Move into our Ealing house?" I ask, making sure I understand him correctly.

"Why not? She's obviously unhappy with the situation at her own flat, and aside from that, she's here almost every weekend. We might as well look at the reality. She's taking up the spare bedroom, and all of her stuff is here even when she isn't. For heaven's sake," he laughs, "she has even brought her own duvet and pillows because the ones we have weren't soft enough. On top of that, we both like her, so she might as well be paying rent."

"Yes," I joke, "Make money out of her because we think she's nice."

"You know what I mean," he grunts.

"And what about Caitlin?" I sigh. "She's already pretty sensitive whenever I drop Celine's name into a conversation."

"Exactly," he says, raising his eyebrows while slowly repeating my question: "What — about — Caitlin!"

9

When Celine comes back from Switzerland late Friday evening, Brett sits her down and tells her we all need to have a chat. She looks worried. She turns to me and then at him.

"What's the matter?" she asks, "Did I do something wrong?"

We both laugh.

"No, absolutely not," Brett reassures her, "We're only wondering how you'd feel about moving in?

"I thought you'd never ask," she jokes. "Haven't I given you enough hints by dragging even my duvet over here and completely hogging your spare room?"

After the weekend, Celine phones her flatmate and gives her notice. He's not very pleased with the news and starts crying on the phone. He asks her if she thinks they don't belong together. He promises that he will make her happy.

It eventually takes six carloads to get all of Celine's stuff to our flat, twelve times driving up and down through murderous traffic from Ealing to North London and back. We started at eight in the morning, and by seven in the evening, our torture has finally come to an end. There is only one treatment to alleviate our trauma, and that is—pizza and Netflix.

The three of us curl up on the big sofa. Celine sits in the middle, Brett and I on the sides. We're streaming Garry Marshall's 'Pretty Woman', starring Richard Gere and Julia Roberts.

Before we press the play button, I look at Celine and say (while modifying Vivian's words), "In case I forget to tell you later, I really enjoyed you being our flatmate."

From that day onwards, we call ourselves the 'tripod'. Unlike Fiona, Celine is more than happy to share groceries, eat together and live as if we are a little family. She doesn't cook and hardly does the dishes, but Brett and I don't mind.

One day, after having lived with us for close to two months, she walks into the kitchen and comes and stands next to me. "Are you and Brett happy with me being here?" she asks and adds, "Because if there's anything—anything at all that you want me to be aware of, you need to tell me."

I dread these conversations. They're always tricky. I plan to steer around it, but she notices my hesitation and insists: "Please!"

"Well, Celine," I say, "you are wonderful. You are by far the best flatmate we've ever had, and we love you."

"What comes before the but is bullshit," she mocks. "Come on, spit it out."

"No, it is nothing," I say.

"Tell me," she insists.

"Only a tiny, little thing. Nothing important."

"What is it!?"

"Really a detail," I maintain.

'What!?"

"Well, it wouldn't really hurt if you do the cooking once in a while."

She's upset.

Her smile disappears, and her eyes lose their sparkle. Without saying a word, she walks out of the kitchen.

Half an hour later, she comes back. She puts her hand on my arm and looks at me with big, teary eyes. "It's because I'm intimidated," she finally says. "You and Brett are excellent cooks, and I'm scared that you won't like what I make."

I boisterously laugh. "Rubbish Celine," I say. "Brett and I eat everything. If you had to put ketchup on sand, we'd munch it down. You've got nothing to worry about. We consider ourselves food disposals."

She giggles. "Okay," she says, "what if we compromise? I'll do the dishes, and you guys do the cooking?"

We shake hands on it, but it doesn't take long before the plan backfires. From that moment on, the dishes are done ... not only daily—but several times a day. We're entirely running short of cupboard space since Brett and I banked on the fact that, on average, more than half the plates, pots and pans would be resting in the sink waiting to be cleaned. Not even a single cup is allowed to have a break before it gets polished with water and soap. The kitchen has never been this tormented by detergents, and I am terrified of making anything dirty or leave anything unwashed.

I have created a monster.

10

After Southend-on-Sea and before she moved to Plymouth, Caitlin stayed in Scotland's Aberdeen for four weeks. Even though I promised to visit her, I never did. Aberdeen is almost nine hundred kilometres from London.

On the other hand, Plymouth is closer and, depending on traffic, merely a four or five hours' drive from Ealing. But even there, I no longer visit her every weekend.

"It will only be for two months," I tell her, "and then it's May. We'll be spending three weeks together in South Africa."

Two days ago, Caitlin and I passed our fourth's month anniversary. Still, at times, I think we're only together because none of us noticed we're apart. I wonder how many couples are in a relationship simply because they don't know how to get out. It is as if the fear of the unknown is more menacing than the actual terror of the known.

But I still hope that we can work through our issues. I don't want to give up like I've done so many times in the past. No one will find a soul mate by applying a two-second rule, or even a four month-rule for that matter. After all, there is no reason that two intelligent people like us are unable to make it.

Last weekend, Caitlin came to London and stayed with me in Ealing. We carefully avoided touchy topics, though every time Celine walked into the lounge, the temperature significantly dropped below zero. Caitlin didn't say anything about it, but her frustration with Celine clearly showed on her face. Saturday was still bearable, but Sunday, she refused to leave my bedroom and to avoid ... well ... —conflict, I stayed with her.

"Tell me about that psychic you visited in South Africa?" she asked me out of the blue and perhaps only to kill time. "Hasn't she told you that the girl you'd be with would have a link to Australia?"

"I thought you didn't believe in that kind of nonsense," I object. "The last time, you became pretty angry with me and told me that you were a scientist and on your way to getting your doctorate. You said that I was insulting your intelligence by mentioning twaddle like crystal-ball readings and tarot-hogwash."

"I still think they are twaddle and hogwash," she said, "But tell me anyhow. It's better than having to sit in the same room with that stupid cow."

"I don't know what Celine has ever done to you."

"Never mind," she sighed, "I want to hear about your fortune-teller."

11

Years ago, when I lived in South Africa, I'd arrived at a stage in my life where I didn't know what to do and how to move forward.

I had just broken up with my South African girlfriend, and after she had gone to see a psychic, she came back raving.

"It was truly amazing," she declared, "most of the things the psychic told me were true. You should go," she advised and gave me the woman's phone number.

I was sceptical and believed that all psychics were frauds. Though in a way, I was willing to allow that there could be something out there—something more significant than all of us together. I don't necessarily mean the big G.O.D. or anything else which needs to be translated into an anthropomorphic, omnipotent, supernatural creator. But perhaps there might be a higher level of awareness or consciousness that some people simply could tap into.

Either it was that, or all psychics were indeed frauds.

I decided to give her a call and ended up making an appointment. A week later, I sat in her tiny office and asked her if I could take notes.

"Of course," she replied and smiled, "but it would be better if you'd record it. By taking notes," she explained, "you tend to only filter out what you approve of and end up writing down the things you want to write down. For instance, when you're convinced about my capabilities, you write down what you think I'm correct about. But when you're sceptical, you take note of what you think is not true. Afterwards, when you read through it all, it merely confirms what you'd already set yourself out to believe in the first place. Though when you record the conversation, you might listen to it more objectively."

What she described is what psychologists call 'Information Bias'.

I put my pen and paper away, grabbed my phone and opened the recording app.

"The way I work," she told me, "is that at times I might hold your hands, but if this makes you feel uncomfortable, I'll stop doing it as it will block the connection. Aside from that, I'll be staring into the candle on that little table next to you." She laughed and explained that doctors claimed her eyesight was getting worse because of this, "But then again," she added, "it could just be my age."

A little bit more upbeat, she asked, "Shall we start?" and took my hands while breathing intensely as if she was nervous. She stared into the flame of the yellow candle on my left and began to talk.

Over the many years that followed, I have replayed that recording and also the ones from our follow-up sessions. But that very first time, I was highly sceptical.

She started by revealing things about me; as if she wanted to establish a baseline. The strategy was simple: if she was correct about my past and present, I would easily believe her about my future.

"You feel lost," she began, "and you sense that you're missing a direction in your life."

This was true, but let's face it: would anyone be going to a psychic if things were great?

"You recently broke up with your partner," she continued, "and your feelings of being adrift are related to this. Your mind seems to be very preoccupied with the question of whether you'll meet someone you can finally be happy with."

Again valid, but aren't most people who visit psychics merely interested in issues related to love?

In her book 'Eat, Pray, Love', Elizabeth Gilbert describes how a group of boat refugees were given the aid of psychologists to overcome their traumatic ordeal. The problem was, they were more concerned with talking about whether the guy or the girl in the far end corner of the boat had a crush on them or not.

So, in my case, touching upon matters of the heart would only increase the psychic's chances to be accurate.

"You'll be travelling again," she said and added that she could see white, sandy beaches and waving palm trees. "They remind me of the Caribbean, but it could be anywhere—any place where you can find white sand and waving palm trees. The only reason I mention the Caribbean," she explained, "is because a friend of mine recently sent me a postcard from there. That card simply jumped into mind."

"I can see a boat," she continued, "and I can see you are backpacking together with a group of people going north. About the girl," she concluded and smiled: "You will meet her, but not in South Africa. It might take you years, but it is hard for me to single-out a date and time. However, there seems to be a link with Australia. Have you ever been there?" she asked.

"I haven't," I admitted.

"Well," she started, "I can see someone slender and quite tall. She appears to have brown-blondish hair, but then again; it could be dyed."

When I left, I was more cynical than when I arrived. I felt I'd been ripped off. While I drove home, I went over her predictions. There were a lot of things I was sure I would never do. For one, I never had any desire to go to the Caribbean. It simply didn't sound appealing to me. Secondly, booking a trip on a cruise ship never topped my bucket list. Thirdly, on the subject of travelling in a group, she was wrong again. I've always preferred my independence and like to change my plans whenever I want to. Travelling in a group is a hassle as everyone needs to have their say on what the next direction should be.

Then finally: —about the girl! —

I had no doubts that I'll eventually meet someone. I've never been to Australia; the country simply never appealed to me. I'm truly African, and like Archer in the movie 'Blood Diamonds', I have that continent's red earth in my skin. That's where the psychic really got it wrong. If I was her, I would have told me that I'd end up with a South African girl and not an Australian because I'll never leave this place.

I didn't really think she was purposely trying to con me. She might genuinely believe that she could do what she claimed she could, but she completely missed the ball when it came to me.

I travelled Africa twice before, and picking up my backpack was merely a way for me to stay alive. Not travelling meant I would decompose from the inside out.

Half a year after I'd visited the psychic, I packed all my stuff into boxes and put it in storage. I rented out my house and went up north. I surely didn't see this as any of her predictions coming true.

After someone advised me to check out Mozambique, I crossed the border. I drove until I reached a tiny coastal village called Tofu, close to the city Inhambane. I rented a modest chalet right at the ocean and decided to write, read, and do nothing while drinking beer and looking at the sunset.

But it took me a while before I realised that I was surrounded by white, sandy beaches. I was actually sitting underneath them when I was writing or reading or drinking beer.

It's just a coincidence, I told myself. It has nothing to do with any predictions. You can find this scenery everywhere along the African coastline.

Though a few weeks later, after I'd walked to the top of the dune to buy myself a meal at the local beach bar, a guy with an Irish accent approached me. Before I knew it, we started talking, and he invited me to join him and his friends on a sailing trip to Angoche—all the way to the north of Mozambique.

He told me they needed a minimum of six people to properly manoeuvre the twenty-two-meter steel ketch. The current crew of four was contracted to salvage the wreckage of some sixteen-hundredth' Portuguese merchant ship. The Irish guy introduced me to the boat's two owners, Graham and Alberto, and the following day we set sail.

The boat didn't have a global navigation satellite system, and only a magnetic compass showed our direction. There was no automatic pilot, and since we didn't find a sixth person, we had to team up in pairs of two and take shifts every four hours to operate the vessel. That meant four hours of sleep and two-hour shifts while trying to cover twelve hundred nautical miles on a rough ocean.

After three weeks of hard sailing, we finally reached our destination. I had to leave and hurry back to Inhambane as my visa had expired. At a fine of one million Mozambican Metical per day, it soon added up to six million by the time I could renew it.

After I arrived back at my chalet in Tofu, I spent my days sitting on white, sandy beaches and under waving palm trees. I didn't interpret the boat as one of the psychic's predictions. At the time, I believed that the psychic was talking about a cruise ship sailing the Caribbean islands instead of an ill-equipped yacht.

195

Two months later, Graham phoned. "Are you keen on another sailing trip?" he asked. "We need to get the boat back to Durban for repairs. The yacht can sleep twelve in total. Bring as many as you can," he said and concluded: "The more people, the bigger the party."

I asked around at the bar on top of the sand dune, and before I knew it, I had assembled the required crew. All nine of us left two days later, taking busses and all sorts of local transport to make our way up north.

Only then it hit me … —I was travelling in a group, and I'd spent time on a boat.

This realisation shocked me. It occupied my mind during the entire journey. One of the girls who travelled with us was South African but lived in Australia. Even though she had a boyfriend, I still couldn't suppress the thought that the psychic might have predicted her. I didn't try to find out as I've always believed that people in a relationship are out of bounds. But the idea of the 'Australian-link' was planted. It grew and became more prominent, and I decided that one day I should visit that part of the world.

During my more rational moments, I tried to bring all of this into perspective. After all, the psychic had said that her predictions can vanish the moment someone changes his course. In that way, she incorporated the idea of 'freedom of decision'.

"Fate is not inflexible," she'd told me.

"What's the point then?" I asked her. 'Why would you want to know your future when it keeps changing?"

"Perhaps I should ask you that question?" she smiled.

"But how can the future adjust itself after you've predicted it?"

"Compare it to driving a car on the road," she explained. "In the distance, you can see a traffic light, a woman with a child who's planning to cross the street and a little farther, a motorcyclist who tries to make a u-turn. This information can warn you to be careful. The women and the child might suddenly cross the road, and you should watch out for the abrupt movement of the motorcyclist."

She looked at me and asked, "Would you not want to see that far ahead when you are driving your car?"

"Of course, I would," I nodded.

"But then," she continued, "you, as the driver, take a left turn and by doing so, your future changes. There's no longer a traffic light, no woman, no child and no motorcyclist. Instead, new things have popped up. A dog on the side of the road, a girl on her bicycle and an ice-cream van at the end of the street. You can decide to stop following the path that lies in front of you," she concluded, "but when you make a turn, everything changes."

"Does this mean that the brown-blondish girl with the Australian link could disappear?" I asked.

"That's possible, but don't worry too much about it and let things happen without trying to force them."

"How will I know when I've made a turn?"

"You're the driver," she replied, "but you're blind. Today, I'm your passenger, and I can see."

"You're telling me that I simply have to make a new appointment with you?"

"Only when you want to know what's in front of you," she said.

At times, I tried to convince myself that I have taken a left or right turn and that my future has changed. But subconsciously (and often even consciously), I sifted through girls and compared what I saw with what had been foretold. The one girl was too short to fit the description; the other one was not slim enough. When they didn't have brown-blondish hair, I'd hardly look at them, even though I was told that it could have been dyed.

Time and again, I tried to convince myself not to let this influence me. After all, what if I really had made a turn and my new future had introduced some short, black-haired soul-mate? If that was the case, I'd surely miss out on Plato's assembly.

In the years after, I visited that same psychic on three different occasions. She kept feeding me the same facts: the girl is slender, tall, has brown-blond hair and every time she mentioned the Australia-link.

I no longer think she is a fraud. Not only because she predicted the boat, me travelling in a group and the white sandy beaches, but also because her story never changed. It would be impossible for her to remember what she told me during all those different stages in time. The fact that she keeps repeating the same predictions is, in my opinion, proof on its own.

"When will I finally get to meet that slim, brown-blondish girl with the Australian link?" I asked her one day.

"I don't know," she sighed. "I really wish I could give you a date." She stared into the candle and suddenly asked, "Do you know the story of Rachel in the bible?"

I didn't, and she couldn't remember the specifics either, but she advised me to look it up as it might give me more specifics to my question.

After I told Caitlin my psychic story, she accused me of being gullible. She said, "I don't know how you can believe all of this crap," and doubts whether she can even respect a guy who thinks this kind of nonsense exists.

12

While she was a child, Celine lived in New York, Tokyo, Geneva, Oslo and even in Belgium's ex-colony: DRC's Kinshasa. She doesn't remember much about it, but she claims that we have Africa in common.

Both Celine's parents worked for the United Nations, which explains their constant moving around. They are retired and live in Bordeaux, France. Celine considers this city to be her home.

It is mid-March, and I'm praying for summer to come soon as I'm really starting to get sick of this miserable weather.

The two of us are having a beer outside in the garden. She smokes a cigarette. We talk about living in Africa, and I share Belgium's embarrassing footprint on Africa's third-largest country.

"After its independence," I explain to her, "the Belgian Congo was called Zaire, but at the moment, we know it as the DRC or the Democratic Republic of Congo. About a hundred and thirty years ago, the king of the Belgians, Leopold II, was able to turn Congo into his own private property. In no time, he managed to brutalise the local population into producing rubber. To enforce the quotas, his soldiers often cut off the natives' limbs."

Celine chokes on her beer. "You bastards!" she exclaims.

"I know," I sigh. "That's why we decided to make chocolate: to sweeten our reputation.

"And beer, to get everyone so drunk that we all forget about this?"

"Exactly. But the fact remains that millions of Congolese died of diseases like sleeping sickness and smallpox. A government commission concluded that the population of the Congo had been reduced by half during the rule of Leopold II. Bowing to international pressure, the Belgian parliament took over the king's private property. From then onwards, the country was called the Belgian Congo."

I take a sip from my beer which, by the way, is not Belgian, and Celine inhales the smoke of her cigarette.

"You see," I continue, "we Belgians cannot celebrate many achievements. Perhaps this is the reason why we still rejoice the fact that seven hundred years ago, petite Flanders was able to kick out your big French army in the Battle of the Golden Spurs."

"I have no idea what you're talking about," Celine chuckles: "I've never heard of this Golden Spurs thing."

"Of course not. That's the reason why you started producing wine."

"To forget?" she asks.

"Anyhow, over time, Flanders has been dominated by the Celts, the Germanic's, the Romans, the French, partly by the Normans, the Burgundies, Austria, Spain, the Netherlands and eventually Germany. There is hardly a country in Europe that hasn't rolled over us. But we don't care as we keep reminding ourselves of what Julius Ceasar had said; that out of all the Gauls, the Belgians were the bravest warriors! Did you know that this even got mentioned in your country's comic book 'Asterix and Obelix'? In the volume 'Asterix in Belgium', chief Vitalstatistix learns that Ceasar's soldiers consider being posted outside his village as a period of leave from hard duty in Belgium. He's shocked, and together with a reluctant Asterix and Obelix, he crosses the border to challenge the Belgians to a contest which consists of raiding Roman camps."

"Let me guess," Celine says, "the Belgians won?"

"Don't be silly; 'Asterix and Obelix' is created in France. With all your jacked-up chauvinism, do you really think you French will let tiny Belgium win? At the end of the story, Caesar angrily declared them all crazy, and both tribes laugh the incident off and accept that they are equally as brave."

After I've shared these stories with Celine, I joke and say that the only reason why there are books and movies about the Spartans is because the Greeks never made it to Belgium. "We would have simply kicked them back to Hellas," I jokingly boast.

She warns me to never tell her mum as she is of Greek descent.

"I didn't know you were planning to introduce me to your parents," I flirt.

She laughs nervously. "By this, you are officially invited to come to Bordeaux. It's a beautiful city," she quickly adds, trying to make the invite sound a little less formal, "and I'm sure you'll like it. My Dad owns his own boat, so you and he could take it out for a sail."

I would like that. I haven't sailed since I left South Africa. I tell her that I will think about it. "Though I'm sure Caitlin wouldn't be too impressed if I did," I add.

"Oh yes," she replies while her smile quickly fades, "The 'Caitlin chronicles'. Will you still be going to South Africa with her?"

Celine knows about our issues. Caitlin and I are a month and a half away from flying to Durban, where she will conclude her PhD in Marine Biology. Our relationship is at its lowest, and I no longer visit her every weekend, using the excuse that Plymouth is a little too far away.

"It might be a bit late to cancel," I reply, "and aside from that, it's always good to meet up with my friends over there."

She sighs. She doesn't like Caitlin as much as Caitlin doesn't like her.

"Perhaps I'm still hoping that we can work things out," I say—probably more to myself than to Celine. "I'm waiting for her to come around or rather: for both of us to realise the potential that we have as a couple."

Celine rolls her eyes, "Maybe you are just fooling yourself?"

"There is this little voice deep inside of me whispering to me that you might be correct," I say. "I guess that even Richard and Brett are right when they say that I only fall for the crazy ones. I feel at times that I'm trapped in some Victorian Gothic romance. Perhaps I'm like Heathcliff in Emily Brontë's 'Wuthering Heights' or that Caitlin is the mad woman in the attic in Charlotte Brontë's 'Jane Eyre'. Everyone else: Mary Shelley, George Eliot, Jane Austen and Emily Dickinson, they've all written about Caitlin and me."

"If that's the case," Celine laughs, "then surely you know how your story will end. Do you truly think that love is, as described in those books, eternal punishment? My advice is: give up on that codependent addiction and rather be Rhett Butler in Victor Fleming's 'Gone With the Wind'. Tell your Scarlett that 'frankly, my dear', you don't give a damn?"

This time it's my turn to laugh, but the conversation quickly becomes more pressing. "And what then?" I ask: 'Start all over again? Go back on the internet, key in features like height, distance from London, no children and so on. Again, filtering through hundreds of women who are frantically looking for their other half while they feel they're caught in their own little Victorian Gothic romance? Isn't the main reason behind all those divorces that we give up too easily? Online dating is so convenient. It's a reservoir of potential happiness, a constant promise of love, but we're no virgins any longer. We've all travelled through life, and all of us have picked up our fair amount of baggage—six carloads at times!" I joke. "We've kissed our frogs, but even though a prince or a princess might have appeared, at a certain stage in time, we decided that their hands were too big. Perhaps, I should do what's right and stick it out."

I wait for her to react, but instead, she takes a long drag from her cigarette and watches the smoke climb towards the sky.

"Have you ever heard of Neuro-Linguistic Programming," I ask her?

"Who hasn't," she sighs.

"There's this parable about a person who gets up early in the morning, gazes through his window and decides that the apple tree in his garden looks really impressive. A week later, however, that same person drags himself out of bed, stares through that same window and decides that the tree needs to be chopped down. He suddenly feels it's ugly. The leaves are blocking the sunlight, preventing the bushes underneath to fully reach their potential. But in fact," I continue, "the apple tree hasn't changed at all and only the perception of the person looking at it altered."

"What's your point?" Celine asks while taking another drag from her cigarette. She appears to be irritated.

"My point is that I was madly in love with Caitlin when we met. So, I am asking myself: do I now have to believe that she's a different person? Have her hands suddenly become bigger, or have they always been like that."

"If she's always been like that," Celine replies, "do you expect her to change?"

"That is precisely what I mean," I say. "Maybe it's not Caitlin who needs to change—in the same way as that apple tree cannot suddenly become a pear tree. Perhaps I have to adjust my perception."

"Man," Celine sighs, "you're really a sucker for punishment." She puts out her cigarette and stands up. "Why don't you take a long look at her and tell yourself that the apples on her tree are not rotten to the core."

She turns around and walks into the house.

13

A week after my conversation with Celine, I visit Caitlin in Plymouth. Traffic jams and road-works have lengthened my trip by an additional two hours. I left London at one in the afternoon and only reach the Marine Laboratory after eight in the evening.

Caitlin doesn't run to my car when I arrive and doesn't hug and kiss me when I find my way to her small university room in one of the ugliest buildings I've ever seen. She wears the same clothes as when I drove down here three weeks ago, and it reminds me of the lyrics in Ben Folds' song 'Kate': ' —every day she wears the same thing, I think she smokes pot. She is everything I want; she is everything I am not—"

She doesn't seem to be in a good mood, but I don't care. My attitude has changed. I don't have any patience for her tempers, and I'm no longer sure if she is really everything I want.

Why am I still with her, I wonder? Is it because of the psychic's predictions?

More than once, I have tried to jam Caitlin into that profile. She is slim, tall, and though she has dark brown hair, almost bordering black, she told me on our first date that she always wanted to live in Australia. The Great Barrier Reef was the main reason she started studying coral diseases, so there is definitely an Australian link.

When I shared this theory with Celine, she reacted irritated. She told me that I'd wholly blinded myself with those stupid predictions. But if I am honest, I have to admit that I have tried to squeeze Celine into the same profile. After all, she has brown-blond hair, and though she is not entirely slender, she is certainly not chubby either. On top of that, she was in a relationship with an Australian guy for over five years. If that is not a link, then I don't know what is.

On Saturday, Caitlin and I visit the hundreds of inflated plastic hexagonal and pentagonal cells that form Cornwall's 'Eden Project'. It is situated in a reclaimed clay pit not too far from St Austell and about an hour's drive from Caitlin's dorm.

I have switched my GPS SatNav on, but Caitlin disagrees with any of 'Suzy's' suggestions. It is almost as if she's jealous.

"Why have you given her a woman's name?" she tetchily asks.

I tell her that there was a Flemish band called Noordkaap who'd written a song about a satellite named Suzy.

"But why do you use a female's voice to direct you and not a man's?"

"If a man's voice had to tell me to take a left in three hundred meters," I reply, "I'd probably turn right just to piss him off. But with a woman's voice, it is different. Over the thousands of years of having been nagged by women, most men have learned to immediately react when they're told to do something."

On Sunday, I drive back home and plan to only see her again in about two weeks because she lives too far away. There was a time when I, without hesitation, would have jumped in my car and make the effort that equals interest. But now I feel I've better things to do.

Eighteen days have passed since my last visit, and the Wednesday before my Plymouth's trip, I phone Caitlin to tell her that I won't be able to make it.

She is a bit more quiet than usual and asks me for an explanation, but I am reluctant to tell her that it's Celine's birthday. When I finally do, Caitlin reacts upset. "Is that cow more important than I am?" she asks.

"Caitlin," I say, "please be reasonable. Celine has rented a room above a little pub not far from our house. She's ordered snacks; crisps, cheese, sausages, sandwiches and all kinds of fried stuff." But Caitlin doesn't say anything, which compels me to continue. "About fifty people are coming, and you, of course, are invited as well," I lie, succumbing to the pressure of her silence.

When I put the phone down, I feel bad. I've chosen Celine over Caitlin, and what makes it worse—Caitlin knows.

14

Celine and Peter have broken up again. They've ended their relationship more often than the average English has eggs and bacon for breakfast. If they continue like this, they'll beat Caitlin's and my record.

Celine has never been sure about her feelings for Peter. In a way, both she and I keep holding on for reasons we can't correctly rationalise. While Celine pretends that she is not really in a relationship, I pretend that I am.

Over the next couple of days, Celine rushes through the house like a whirlwind. She dashes from her bedroom through the hallway and into the kitchen, into the living room, into my room, into Brett's room and then back through the hallway. She's constantly on the phone, calling or being called by friends she will see in a couple of days.

She is excited. She says birthdays are important and has invited friends who will be travelling all the way from the south of France.

In total, she has sent sixty-three invitations, and only five have cancelled. Her parents and her brother can't make it. Her brother lives in some exotic country, and her parents are on a cruise ship sailing the Greek islands.

Celine says it doesn't matter because she'll see them when it is her Dad's birthday.

I can tell, however, that she's a little more disappointed than she wants anyone to believe.

Peter, even though they have broken up, is invited too. Brett thinks he's a prick, and of course, I agree. I don't like him simply because he caused Celine to write me that 'I'm sorry' message wherein she wished me all the best in dating, in life and in chasing ducks.

Six of Celine's friends, all extremely pretty, have arrived from France. They flew into Heathrow a day early, and Celine has cooked for them. It's the first time Brett and I are getting to experience her cuisine. It's a massive meal, and far tastier than both of us would have ever been able to dish up.

Her friends have brought wine. We drink and talk. They do their best to keep the conversation in English (as it otherwise would be impossible for Brett to understand). Still, almost once every fifteen minutes, they totter back to French, which forces either Celine or me to translate.

In the kitchen, Brett confides that he really likes one of Celine's friends. Her name is Anaya. She is rather petite, with short black hair and she has a lovely, pretty face.

"Go for it, bro," I encourage him. "Flirt and joke with her in the most obvious way you can."

"Won't she be looking at me as if I'm an idiot?" he asks, "and turn her back at me for the rest of the evening?"

"No," I assure him. "French girls are far more receptive to flirting than anyone else. They even prefer it."

On a few occasions, while Brett, Richard and I went on our usual nights out, girls would gape at us as if we were scum. Even when we didn't try to chat any of them up, they still looked us up and down, rolled their eyes and, with a twitch of their head, turned away. At the same time, their body language shouted, 'Who the hell are you, and how dare you invade our space?'

Richard believes that such behaviour is a 'sorry case of rejecting before being rejected'.

Only much later, when Jessica, Brett's sweet little English secretary, told us about her weekend, we got a better insight into what went on in those pubs. Jessica told us how she spotted this super hot bloke across the dance floor and how it didn't take him long to walk towards her. He tapped her on the shoulder and asked if she'd like to dance with him. She looked him up and down, rolled her eyes, twitched her head and turned away.

But Jessica believed he was adorable. The guy approached her a second time and asked for her name. Again, she pushed him away, and in a condescending tone, she said, "Look fellow, I am here to have a good time with my friends. Can you leave me alone?"

Apparently, he tried a third time and was told off once more.

"Can you believe this guy?" Brett's secretary eventually concluded her story, "He didn't even try a fourth time! If he had, I would have surely spoken to him. He was really super hot, and now I'll never see him again!"

Brett and I looked at each other. We were flabbergasted and told her that we would not have even tried a second time.

"But how can you know that the guy is serious?" she asked, "Because if he has to work hard for something, he'll appreciate it more."

"So, French girls are different then?" Brett asks while we are standing in the kitchen.

"It is much simpler," I reply. "Their yes is a yes, and their no is a no. Be very clear about your intentions. Touch her hand, touch her on the shoulder, look into her eyes and more importantly—don't worry about what her friends might think."

"You can't be serious?" he asks.

"I am," I say. "Her friends will not expect anything less. They're used to guys acting like that. The advantage is that if

Anaya is not interested, she'll be very clear about it, and you can move on to the next girl."

He does as told, walks back to the living room and sits right next to her. At first, she is a bit puzzled, but then I can see she likes his attention. From that moment, they talk. They talk throughout the evening and long into the night, far after all the others have gone to bed.

There are mattresses spread all over the house. They're in Celine's room, in my room and in the living room.

I sleep in Brett's bed, and when he crawls next to me around four in the morning, he tells me he thinks Anaya is lovely and that he doesn't want Sunday to arrive as she'll be flying back to France.

I ask him if he's kissed her, and he tells me not to be stupid.

15

Saturday morning, we give Celine her presents, and she charmingly pretends she loves them all. There're many good things to say about her, but one of them certainly is that everyone she meets immediately likes her. That explains why, out of the sixty-three invited, only five people cancelled. It makes me look at her differently.

I tell Brett my thoughts, and he asks me if I could see her as more than just a friend.

"I don't know," I reply.

"After all, she isn't a bad catch," he comments.

"I know," I say, "but something deep inside of me, in my guts or in my heart, seems to be holding me back. I can't pin down what it is."

"Maybe because she smokes?"

"It could be that. Perhaps I subconsciously think that her smoking is linked to something flawed within her as a person."

"She can always quit," he says.

The pub where Celine has her party gradually fills with guests. Though most of them live in London, they all have different nationalities. Many of them are French; others are from Canada, the US, Brazil, Venezuela, Portugal and even Australia.

Celine is the perfect host. She floats from guest to guest, kisses them on the cheeks, touches their arms or shoulders, and says a few words that make them laugh. Every now and then, she flings a quick look at me, and when she does, I hold my thumb up, letting her know that all is perfect.

I try to help here and there, and haul trays of food around, offer people something to eat or drink. She walks up to me, puts her arms around my neck and kisses me on the cheek. "Thanks," she says, "for lending a hand."

Then the door opens, and when Peter walks in, Celine rushes in his direction. She raises her hands—all happy to see him, and he holds out his arms as they quickly embrace.

I am suddenly aware of every move she makes. When he tries to kiss her on her lips, she turns her head sideward to only find her cheek. She laughs at something he says. She touches his arm, and with one finger, he brushes some hair out of her face.

Brett comes and stands next to me. He looks at her and says, "What about that. I didn't think the prick would show."

"I know," I reply. "It makes me feel a bit—" I hesitate.

"—Jealous?" he jumps in and laughs.

"Don't be stupid," I sigh.

"I've got an idea," he says. "Why don't you walk up to her and pretend that you're her new boyfriend? Just for laughs," he adds.

"That's nasty," I say, but leave him and make my way towards Celine. I gently put my arms around her waist and pull her close. I rub my cheek against hers, and when my mouth reaches her ear, I whisper, "Listen, sweetie, we are running out of wine. Do you want me to go downstairs and get some more?"

She turns to me. At first, she is a little bit surprised, but then she gives me a warm smile. "That would be wonderful," she says.

I softly kiss her on her lips, and while she doesn't evade it, I notice Peter's shocked expression from the corner of my eyes.

"That's my revenge," I say after I've walked back to Brett. "It's payback for that time when the moron took her on a date while it was my turn."

But Peter stays close to her, and she seems to be okay with that. She laughs at his jokes and appears to be fine with him touching her arm. She mingles less with her friends, but when she does, he's always around.

It irritates me. How dare she tell me off about staying with Caitlin when she makes the same mistakes?

But am I being honest with myself? What is this really about? Am I, as Brett implied, jealous?

Don't be stupid.

I try to distract my mind by mingling with the other guest. A German guy with a solid Australian accent swamps my ears with stories from when he lived down-under. I hardly understand what he's saying but offer my obligatory nods every time he looks in my direction. A girl from Brazil tells me she's a corporate lawyer for BP. She wants to know how long I've been living in England and whether I like it here, but even though she looks pretty, I feel bored talking with her.

Every now and then, I look around in search of Celine. Sometimes I see her chatting with one of her friends, but Peter never leaves her side. I become even more aware of my own solitude when Brett walks over and tells me he's having a wonderful time with Anaya. He asks me whether I think she might like him too.

I roll my eyes in disbelieve. "Bro," I say, "if this girl doesn't like you, then you might as well turn gay as no other girl ever will. Of course, she does! It's so obvious that it makes me want to puke."

"What should I do?" he asks.

"You need to kiss her!"

He nervously bites the knuckle of his thumb and tells me that he's scared. "What if you're wrong?" he asks, "What if she rejects me?"

"A girl doesn't spend the whole Friday night, the whole Saturday and Saturday evening chatting to a guy she doesn't like. Especially not when she's French," I add. Again, he chews the knuckle of his thumb. "Let me make you a promise," I say. "If you don't kiss this little French girl in the next hour, then I will."

"You bastard!" he exclaims and sighs, "No need for enemies when I have friends like you."

"Go and kiss your Frog," I say. "And remember: one hour and then it's my turn."

A few minutes later, Richard arrives and slaps me on the shoulder. He points to my empty beer and wants to know if I need a refill. I shake my head, but before he dashes off, I ask him if he has seen where Celine and Peter went to.

He looks at me suspiciously. "What on earth is going on here?" he asks. "Why are you looking for Celine?"

"No reason," I shrug.

"Is it because she invited Peter? Is that what's causing this? I smell some competition in the arena?" he chuckles. "Every time I tell you to go for Celine, you whine about how your heart and guts are telling you differently and that she smokes and all that nonsense. You've had plenty of opportunities before, so why now, Lyam?"

16

I need to think more clearly and decide to phone Caitlin as it might straighten my thoughts. I go outside, and while I search for her number, I notice that I have three missed calls. They're all from her.

It's a quarter past eleven, and after the fourth ring, she answers. "Where the bloody hell were you!?" she angrily asks and yells: "I've been trying to fucking phone you all night!"

"I told you that I'm at Celine's birthday party," I remind her.

"Oh right, that stupid cow. Why don't you go and fuck her!?" she says and ends the call in my ear.

There was a time that I would have phoned her back—that I would have apologised for some unidentified wrong and explained to her that Celine is just a friend, nothing more. But now, I am angry. I can't accept this any longer, and tonight I decide that after South Africa, I will break up with her. I would do it before we go or even phone her now, but we have booked our flights, our hotel rooms and have rented a car for the whole three weeks.

Why are women so complicated, I think?

Before I stroll back into the pub, I see Celine walking towards me. She gives me a warm hug, and when she lets go, I notice that she's been crying.

"Why are men such bastards?" she asks.

"What happened? Has it got anything to do with Peter?"

"Oh," she moans, "let's not worry about it tonight. We better go inside and celebrate my birthday."

She kisses me on my neck, and while we hold hands, we enter the pub and spend the rest of the evening in each other's company. We laugh and tease and flirt. We dance and mingle and listen to Germans with Australian accents and how BP plans to handle the upcoming electric car revolution.

17

On Sunday afternoon, Celine's French friends fly back to France. Brett takes ages to say goodbye to Anaya, who he eventually ended up kissing that Saturday night.

On Monday, Celine shows me her email inbox, which is stacked with messages from friends who rave about her successful party. There is no news from Peter, and she still hasn't told me what happened that evening.

I haven't heard from Caitlin either, and I have not tried to get in touch with her. She was the one who broke off our communication, so it's up to her to re-connect again.

Monday evening, Celine and I are having a beer outside in the garden. Only now (almost two days later), she tells me that Peter harassed her. He wanted them to get back together and kept trying throughout the evening. When she finally said she wished to mingle with her other friends, he told her he felt bad because his mother was ill and that he needed a shoulder to lean on. Immediately after they'd gone outside, he tried to kiss her on her mouth. She stopped him and asked him about his mother. He said that there was nothing wrong with her. When he tried to kiss her again, she slapped him in the face and ran off. That is when she saw me.

"Why are men such bastards?" Celine repeats her question while she takes another sip from her glass of wine.

"Don't you go comparing me with Peter," I laugh, pretending to be wounded by her words. "I'm different."

She looks at me and asks, "Are you really?" and then answers her own question, "Perhaps in some ways, but in other ways, the two of you are just the same."

"How do you mean?"

"It's always wonderful to have some fun, a laugh and a meaningless flirt," she says. "But when you're with the girl, you guys don't give a flip about her feelings. And then, when you realise you can't have her anymore, she all of a sudden becomes game again. Tell me," she asks, "are you really that different?"

I don't reply, but her comment makes me feel bad. Her words feel sharp. They remind me of Richard's words when he asked me if I was trying to find Celine because the competition had shown up.

Do I really just see her as merely a game?

Tuesday morning, I finally receive a text message from Caitlin. She says she is sorry that she reacted so 'out of character'. She asks me if I can wish Celine a happy birthday from her, which I don't as it's two days after the facts.

I send a text back, thanking her for her apology and that I'll phone her later tonight, which I end-up not doing either.

Thursday evening, Brett, Celine, and I plan to go to an Italian restaurant not far from the Ealing Common tube station. But an hour before, Brett cancels and tells me that unexpected things at work have come up.

I'm running late myself and to save time, I ask Celine to meet me at the restaurant. I tell her that I will drive there straight from my meeting and that, if she walks, I can give her a lift back.

The whole of Sunday, Celine and I were inseparable. We joked and laughed and, hardly noticeable to the others, brushed hands or knees under the dining table. We snuggled cosily together on the sofa—pretending there was not enough space because all her French friends were staying over.

This, however, came to an end on Tuesday when she asked me if I was really that different from all the other guys who treat girls as if they're a game.

While waiting outside the Italian restaurant, I see Celine walking towards me and mere seconds after we walk in, my phone rings.

It's Brett.

I apologise to Celine, go outside and answer the call.

"Listen," he starts without even greeting me, "do not, under any circumstances, flirt with Celine."

"Why," I ask.

"While you were at your meeting," he explains, "Celine and I were at the house. She seems quite upset with guys in general. She told me that she thinks everyone is a player. I didn't ask for more details, but I think she was talking about you."

"About me!?" I gasp. "What have I done wrong?"

"I guess you've been flirting a little bit too much, and she might think that you've been playing her. She might have had enough, and I'm sure that if you take that direction tonight, she'll explode. All this shit will hit you in the face, or the fan..., whatever."

"Okay," I sigh, "I understand."

I walk back into the restaurant, and suddenly I become highly aware of every word I utter, every hand movement I make and every laugh I laugh. I consciously avoid any remarks that can be misinterpreted as flirting, and it becomes one of the worst evenings I've ever had.

Chapter 4

What defines me

1

I have never taken Caitlin to the upstairs VIP lounge for two reasons. Firstly, I didn't want to bamboozle anyone any longer by pretending I knew Chelsea football players. And secondly, I felt uncomfortable upholding my lies in front of John, especially after he'd shared one of his biggest secrets with me and told me he'd shot three carjackers in Nigeria.

When we're getting to the end of April, Caitlin and I are two weeks away from flying to South Africa. A couple of days ago, she'd left Plymouth for Eastbourne. It is much closer to London, but still a two-hour drive.

I won't be seeing her this weekend, and instead, I make my way to the trendy bar to finally tell John the truth.

But he is not there.

Another big African guy has grabbed hold of the red cord and hooks it back into the pole when he sees me approaching.

"Where is John?" I ask.

He shrugs his shoulders and tells me he doesn't know anyone named John.

"Champ—?" I try again, but the man only raises his eyebrows. "Chimp?—"I say, "Or perhaps—," and I think hard to remember John's Nigerian name, "Chimwu-something. I believe it means 'God's eyes' or perhaps; 'God has opened his eyes' or something along those lines."

The big muscular man (who resembles John in many ways) looks confused. "I've only been here for three weeks," he finally says, "and I haven't met anyone with all those names."

I walk to the bar and ask one of the barmen who served me my late-night drinks.

"John?" he repeats my question while pouring me a Pimm's: "The big Nigerian chap?"

I nod.

"He committed suicide about a month ago."

I'm shocked. I ask if he's sure and clarify that I'm talking about the big man with the warm smile.

"Yes," he replies. "What I've heard is that John found out his little girlfriend was cheating on him with some French bloke. John had gone over to the guy's house to confront him, but instead, he ended up killing the Frog. After that, he went to his girlfriend's office. He ended up shooting her and her boss, who tried to intervene, in the chest. Both died instantaneously. Then he returned home, and when a police swat-team stormed his house, he'd put a bullet in his head."

I am shaking when I leave the bar.

Outside, it rains violently. Thick droplets gash against my face, and in no time, I am drenched, but I hardly notice it. I stagger over the dark roads with no direction to go. I feel numb, and it is as if everything has become wobbly. My head jiggles up and down, my body sways and what's more—the whole city can't stay still.

How could this have happened, I think? How can such a great guy's life be so filled with murder and death?

A small bus stops, and a guy yells from his wound-down window, "Get out of the rain, mate!" But I want more than that. I want to leave this smothered London. I want to go back to Africa, to the yacht and sail at night while looking at the stars and collide with everything more than me. I feel empty because I realise that my yearning for affection is nothing more than an immature obsession—an illogical extravagance compared to John's suffering.

I don't know how I got home, but Brett is in the living room waiting, and I cry while I tell him about John.

He keeps quiet for a long time, and then, when I've calmed down, he puts his hand on my shoulder and whispers: "It's not what happens to someone that defines him. What defines him is how he deals with it."

2

It's the end of April, and the warm mid-spring temperatures evaporate my feelings of doom. I have been thinking of John almost daily during the last weeks, but I'm determined it should not get me down. On the contrary, I should learn from it and embrace everything positive in life.

Brett, Celine and I've decided to have our first barbeque of the year. However, when Saturday arrives, the weather has changed, and temperatures have dropped to sub-artic degrees. Nonetheless, we all agree to pretend that summer is upon us and carry the foldable tables and camping chairs out into the garden.

Around three in the afternoon, we start building our fire. Brett and I always do it the traditional way; we've never bought charcoal and burn wood instead.

It doesn't take long for the fire to chew into the soft pine, but even though the flames reach high while spreading their heat, I can't seem to get warm. I am already wearing my winter jacket but am forced to walk back to my room to grab some extra layers. I pull another t-shirt over the one I'm already wearing, an extra polo-neck and a shirt over that.

All three of us have invited our friends, and a little after five o'clock they start arriving. Caitlin is not coming. She said she needs to study as we're only a week away from South Africa and doesn't want to arrive there unprepared. She's been in Eastbourne for a little over a week and already got into an argument with three of her flatmates.

All our guests have brought different wines, liqueurs and hard spirits. While they fill their glasses, I stay close to the fire and build it higher and higher. But I continue to be cold. For a second time, I walk back into the house and put on a thick jersey on top of everything I'm already wearing. However, not much time passes before I replicate the whole scenario: I am at the fire, I stand around it for some time, I get cold, I walk back into the house and grab a sweater. I repeat this on another two occasions, and by the time it is eight in the evening, I look like a Michelin-man.

I am still cold.

When the flames settle down and turn the wood into charcoal, I am practically freezing my butt off. I struggle to stay outside. I am already wearing everything I could find in my wardrobe, and when I tell Brett, he says that there's only one option left: "Drink more alcohol."

Richard agrees. "Bring out the funnel," he yells, and Brett disappears into the garage. Minutes later, he comes back with some sort of 'party-kick-starting-device'. It consists of a plastic bottle with a cut-off bottom-end and a tube connected to its neck. The idea is to put the hose into your mouth and drink as fast as you can while others pour all sorts of different concoctions into the halved bottle. It can get someone drunk in no time.

I can't remember when we last used the funnel. It even smells of garage, but I kneel anyhow and put the hose to my mouth.

At first, I taste beer and, seconds later, something more potent. When I finally get up, I see Richard, Brett and a few others holding bottles of vodka, whiskey and Stroh-rum. I can only suspect that this is what I drank, but I don't care.

It doesn't take long for me to feel all cosy and warm. I close my eyes, but when I open them again, I notice that everyone has left. I'm sitting on one of the foldable camping chairs close to a low burning fire, and the only person still around is Celine.

"Where are all the party people?" I ask her.

"They've gone home," she replies.

"What's the time?"

She takes a look at her watch. "A quarter past four."

"Why are you still up?"

"Someone had to take care of you," she laughs. "Aren't you tired?"

I think about her question for a moment. "I'm not. I actually feel quite okay. Did I sleep?"

"I'm not sure. You just sat on this chair with your head in your hands, and on one or two occasions, you simply looked around and stared at everyone. But no matter what we said to you, there was no reaction. Brett even filmed you while he was trying to make you vomit."

"Did he succeed?"

"Yes and no. You eventually ended up throwing up, but by that time, his phone battery died, and he missed it."

"The bastard," I say. "They must have really put some ugly stuff in that funnel."

"I am sure they did," she replies. "It is such a pity. It must have ruined your whole evening. Can you remember anything?"

I shrug my shoulders and sigh, "Not really. I was stupid to drink that much."

Celine is quiet for a moment and then says, "There's another reason why I stayed up."

I look at her.

She hesitates. "There's something I want to talk to you about. I actually wanted to have this conversation a couple of times, but I never found the right moment—or the right words."

"What is it?"

226

"Well—," she sighs but stops talking. There is a long pause, and after that, she giggles. "—I guess I am still struggling to find the right words." For a second time, she pauses, and I patiently wait for her to continue. She takes a deep breath and finally asks, "What is it that really attracts you in a girl?"

"How do you mean?"

"For instance, what would be a reason that you like the one girl and not the other one? What do you look for?"

"If only I knew," I laugh.

But then I realise that this is not random chitchat about my interest in girls: this is actually about her. I try to think hard to come up with a proper answer, but her silence weighs on me, and the pressure turns my mind blank. I repeat her question in my head; I try to concentrate and distil my thoughts, except that there is nothing to focus on. There are no thoughts, or at least— nothing to work with. The only image that pops into my head is the cartoon dog Scooby-Doo. He scarily jumps into the arms of Shaggy because he got spooked by some ghost who later turns out to be the wicked butler at the Duke's castle.

I can't tell Celine that this is all that comes to mind! She might conclude that I'm not taking any of this seriously. She keeps looking at me and waits for me to reply.

Eventually, I succumb to her pressure and say, "The usual, I guess, what everyone is searching for: to be loved, to be respected and to be desired."

When I look at her, it dawns on me that I am Scooby-Doo and that it was Celine's question that spooked me.

"Okay," she says. "Let me rephrase: what don't you want? What would put you off?"

I look at her for a while. Finally, I sigh: "Smoking. When a girl smokes, no matter how pretty or wonderful she is, I'm put off."

227

She's quiet for a long time. Then she nods, "I thought as much." She gets up and grabs some of the bottles that are lying around on the grass. "Shall we go inside? I am getting a bit cold. Not to mention tired."

I look around. The garden is a mess. Greasy pots and pans are all over the place. They lie on the foldable tables we dragged outside for our barbecue and are spread across the grass. There are bottles everywhere, mostly empty, but some still full or half-full. The tables are packed with left-over food, burned meat and half-eaten salads.

I'm not looking forward to cleaning the garden tomorrow morning. Still, when I enter the kitchen, I become even more distressed. There is no single spot left unsoiled, and the floor resembles the muddy garden but without the grass. There are dried-up sludge tracks all the way through the carpeted hallway, and though most of the footprints lead to the bathroom, the rest of the house is not left unvisited.

However, it's the least of my concerns. While Celine and I walk towards our separate bedrooms, I keep thinking of her question and of my reply. Does her smoking really bother me that much? And if it does, why wasn't it a problem for me on our first date? She even chain-smoked two cigarettes, and I thought it was charming. Is there perhaps something else about her that stops me from taking the next step? Could it be the big-hand-syndrome?

On our first date, I'd already decided that I wanted to be impressed with her. I longed for her to make me feel less lonely and just like Brett with his Crawley-girl—I liked Celine even before I'd met her. That's why her smoking didn't bother me, but as the hands, it started growing bigger and bigger until it reached a stage that I could no longer ignore.

What defines me

Or am I lying to myself? Have I learned nothing from big bouncer John? Here's a wonderful girl within arm's reach, and I whine about silly nothings?

3

Caitlin and I have finally reached the day that we fly to South Africa. I pick her up from her tiny flat in Eastbourne, and while she puts her luggage in my car, she eagerly tries to explain to me what her argument with her three flatmates was about. It seems that they'd left the music on at night ... —or perhaps that they'd switched it off while Caitlin wanted it on ... I can't remember because, frankly, my dear, I don't give a damn.

My attitude has changed. Even while we drive from Eastbourne to Gatwick airport, I uphold my zero-tolerance mindset. If Caitlin starts her nonsense again, I tell myself, I'll walk away right here and right now.

Caitlin can feel this. She tiptoes around me—almost as if she is walking on eggshells. She is far too careful to raise touchy subjects and pretends that everything is fine. She puts on her happy face, and I think that I might even start liking her again. However, deep inside, I know that this is only a truce instead of a genuine peace. It wouldn't surprise me if she was simply trying to maintain the harmony to not have to travel to South Africa all by herself. I hold no illusions; the evil will resume the moment I let my guard down.

Or am I wrong?

Could it be that this relationship is more important to her than she's been willing to admit? What if she really wants to make an effort and kick-start 'us' back into passion and love?

Am I then correct to walk around as if I'm a bomb ready to go off under the smallest amount of pressure?

Maybe I should try and tread lightly over those same eggshells and be more careful in what I do or say. Perhaps it could even work. Perhaps this trip to South Africa will turn out to be our long-awaited cure.

Everything goes well at the airport, where we have a nice meal together. She buys a bottle of water to take on the plane, and we laugh and joke and tease each other. We even walk hand in hand when we make our way towards the gates, and I'm ready to fall all over in love again.

But on the plane, while we're waiting for take-off, I ask her if I can have a sip from her water since flight attendants only start serving drinks once we are in the air.

"No!" Caitlin says.

I think she is joking. I take the bottle, which lies in-between the two of us, unscrew the lid and take a sip.

She snatches it out of my hands, and water spills over my trousers. Then she puts it on the other side of her and angrily says, "You should have bought your own when we were still in the shop. You're not getting my water!"

I can't understand this. "It's a full bottle, Caitlin," I argue, "and I would only have drunk a tiny little bit. If you're worried that you might run out during the flight, I can ask the attendants to bring you so many cups that you'll drown in them. We're not in the desert, and even if we were, I would have expected you to let me drink."

She keeps quiet and stares out in front of her. During the remaining eleven hours, we don't speak. The truce is off, and we have entered a stage of cold war.

After we land in Cape Town, we board a local flight to Durban and take a taxi to the Royal Natal Yacht Club. It's the oldest yacht club in Africa and the fifth oldest in the Southern Hemisphere.

Friends of mine, Alberto and Graham, are waiting for me on their twenty-two-meter steel ketch to sail the eighty-seven nautical miles to Richards Bay. It's the first time they get to meet Caitlin, and I prefer to uphold the pretence that she and I are splendid together. That's why I want to patch things up, though; by the time we arrive at the boat, our interaction is still tense.

That same evening, my two friends, their girlfriends and the two of us go out for a meal. After we've eaten, Graham asks if everyone is okay to simply split the bill into six equal shares.

Caitlin objects. "I didn't have dessert," she says, "and it would be unfair towards me if I'd to pay the same as all of you."

"It's okay," I tell my friends, "I'll put in the extra twenty Rands." It is less than two Pounds, and I try to act as if everything is fine, but I'm so highly embarrassed that I feel I could melt and sink straight through my chair, through the floor and through the core of the earth into China.

But Caitlin thinks that I have humiliated her by paying for her dessert. I try to reason with her; make her see my side of the coin. "We're only talking about two pounds, Caitlin," I whisper as I don't want to raise my voice since the walls in our cabin are very thin.

"It's not about the money," she roars, "but about the principle! You should have stood up for me," and adds that she's not sure where my loyalty lies.

"I'm not sure where my loyalty lies either," I reply, and I really wish that by now, I would have reached China.

Throughout our trip, we keep fighting. We break up before we reach the Zululand Yacht Club at Richards Bay Harbour. We break up when we arrive back at Durban's Golden Mile's beachfront; we break up in East London and in Port St Johns. We even return our rental car to an office at the Port Elizabeth airport because we have finally decided to go our separate ways once and for all.

Still, after all these times, it seems impossible for us to follow through on our decisions to stay apart.

It weighs me down, and I feel drained. We've started paying for ourselves when we go to a restaurant or drinks in a pub. Caitlin refuses to add the required ten per cent tip to her bills, and to avoid a crisis, I dig it out of my own pocket.

The money issue is eminent and comes up time and again. "It's because quite a couple of my ex-boyfriends have stolen from me," she justifies.

I ask her to give me more details.

"They always wanted to split the bill even though they ate more than me," she says. "therefore, I prefer to pay for myself."

I am sick of fighting about every little detail. Time and again, I pledge that this is the last straw, but I never keep my promise. I hang onto the fact that when we're good, we're really good and therefore push the bad times aside. I even introduce Caitlin to Brett's family.

When we all go for dinner at my favourite restaurant, I pick up the bill simply to avoid any possible embarrassment. But when we drive back to Byron's house, Caitlin asks if I believe she's a child. "Do you think that I'm unable to pay my own way?"

There is simply no doing right by her.

Why am I still with her? Why do I keep diving head-first into that same brick wall? Perhaps it's true that when we're good, we're good, though I can't remember when last that was. Maybe I'm worried that if I stop believing Caitlin is the girl who has been predicted by the psychic, I might lose everything that has ever been foretold. Perhaps then, I will lose my path and am forced to take a turn to start all over again.

I am sick and tired of starting all over again.

I don't have the energy to return to online dating and take a hundred girls to Covent Garden's little French bistro while having conversations about curling up on sofas. If I force myself to believe that Caitlin is the one who was foreseen, then I don't have to make a right or left turn.

But one question remains: if she's been predicted, then why am I not happy?

Even though Caitlin believes it is all twaddle and crystal-ball tarot-reading hogwash, I think it would help both of us if she visits the psychic. My argument is that if the psychic has envisaged Caitlin for me, will she foresee me for Caitlin?

Caitlin doesn't fight the idea for some strange reason, though I'm not sure if she agrees with my thinking or if she (like me) is just tired of arguing.

I advise her to record the conversation, but her phone's battery is dead, so I hand her mine. I wait for her outside in my car during her one-hour session, and she is visibly upset when she returns.

She hides her face from me, and it appears that she's been crying. She throws my phone onto my lap while yelling that she never wants to be reminded of this load of crap again. Once more, she accuses me of being gullible and raises doubts whether she can ever respect a guy who thinks dragons, leprechauns, sorcerers and psychics exist.

"There's nothing out there," she keeps yelling: "Absolutely nothing! No spirits, no ghosts, no angels and certainly no God! There's only evolution. That's it. I'm a scientist," she repeats, "and no scientist will ever take this crap for truth."

Again, we break up, and by the time we reach Cape Town, we have broken up in Oudtshoorn, in Mosselbay and twice in Stellenbosch.

When we are bad, we are really bad.

4

Two days after Caitlin and I arrived in Cape Town, I fly back to London. She will be in Durban for another three months.

We didn't break up before I left, but there is only one conclusion I can come to: I need to end this torture.

It's twenty past six in the morning when I land at Gatwick airport. I feel exhausted. I didn't sleep on the plane, and while I tried to watch some movies, I was distracted thinking of how to end it with Caitlin.

Brett is waiting for me at Arrivals, and he looks tired too. We give each other a brotherly hug. He asks me how my trip was, and I tell him about my many fights with Caitlin.

"It was one of my worst holidays," I confide.

"Perhaps it's time you do something about this," he says while we climb in his car and make our way back home.

"I know," I sigh.

An hour later, we arrive at the house. Celine is already up and makes breakfast for the three of us: eggs, bacon, sausages and baked beans. We usually only have this on Sunday mornings, but when she gives me a warm hug, she says that it's my welcome-home present.

She smiles, and her eyes twinkle while she fervently tells me a story of how she tried to wash her pair of shorts. She explains that there was grease on her fingers and that instead of cleaning them, she'd only made them dirtier. I'm not really interested, but she continues nonetheless. "Then he there," she shrieks while laughing and pointing at Brett, "he thinks that brown soap is God's gift to mankind."

She talks fast, almost nervously and Brett chuckles. I hardly focus on what she is saying and wait for the ending. "He thinks that when you let something soak and put it for a couple of hours in the sun, all the marks will magically disappear. But you know what happened?" she cries with laughter: "The combination of water, brown soap and sun has bleached my shorts, and now there aren't only grease stains on it, but also faded spots."

"You let it soak too long," I hear Brett laugh. "You should rather have—."

"—but on top of that ..." she interrupts him, and both are now talking simultaneously.

The radio is on. It plays Jack Johnson. The kitchen is dirty, and I think Celine is happy to see me. I believe that this is the reason why she is talking so fast.

I look at the frying pan on the stove, at the eggs and the sausages inside. The microwave beeps, letting us know that the baked beans are cooked, and I just want both of them to leave. I want them to go to work or anywhere but not stay here and crowd my thoughts. I need to think about what to do with Caitlin, but I'm too tired.

Celine loudly lets me know that when, on top of everything else, she tried to scratch the grease out with a knife, she'd cut her finger. "There was blood everywhere!" she snorts, her eyes now filled with tears from laughter: "White stains and grease and blood on my shorts."

I keep quiet, and she stops laughing. "Is everything okay?" she asks while she puts her hand on my arm. She frowns her eyebrows and looks at Brett.

"He just had the worst holiday of his life," Brett says.

"Oh no," she sighs and gives me a hug while whispering, "you must be exhausted. Why don't you eat and then crawl into bed?"

After Celine has left for work, Brett asks, "Tell me your thoughts, Lyam?"

"I am going to break up with Caitlin," I sigh.

5

It is still early in the morning. I take my phone and search for Caitlin's number. I am nervous. There is only a one-hour time difference between the UK and South Africa, so she should be awake. With every ring, I inhale deeply and try to soothe my anxiety.

She finally answers and is surprised to hear it's me. I start by telling her that I had a good flight, that the movies were worthless and that I'm dead tired, but she interrupts my small talk and says, "I can't fight any more."

"We are not fighting," I reply.

"What I mean," she says, "is that we have to stop this."

"Who's fighting, Caitlin?" I irritably ask. "I'm only telling you that the movies on the plane were crap and that I'm tired."

"No," she sighs, "we have to stop this relationship. We can't continue any longer. It's killing me as I'm sure it's killing you."

What the fuck is this!? These should have been my words.

"I'm very sorry," she continues, "but I believe it's for the best. I don't want you to phone me any longer as it only would make things more complicated. We need a clean break from each other."

I keep quiet. I want to tell her that I agree and that our holiday has been the worst in my life. I want to say that I have never met anyone who is as messed-up as her and that she needs to do something about her issues, perhaps even speak to a psychologist. But I realise that I only want to say this, so she feels hurt the way I do.

She ends our conversation by saying that she wouldn't mind us being friends at some point in time, and I mumble that this would be great.

When I put the phone down, I delete her number. I feel fine and even try to make myself believe that I'm relieved. But an hour later, I want to phone her and tell her that we are making a mistake; that we should give it one more go and let the distance between Durban and London make us realise how much we'll miss each other.

I anxiously search for her number, hoping that I have slipped up while trying to delete it, but it is no longer there. I blame myself that I've never attempted to memorise it, though who does nowadays, so I blame technology instead.

When I start breathing normally again, a little voice inside my head whispers: 'it's for the best.' It sounds surprisingly like Brett but seems to be coming from somewhere deep inside of me. It is so hushed that I can barely hear it.

"It's for the best," I say to myself out loud, and I am glad I'm alone in the house.

After that, I fall into a deep and restless sleep.

Two hours later, I wake up feeling even more exhausted than I did before. Again, I panic, but I'm tired. I'm tired of fighting; I'm tired of all of this, and perhaps it is for the best that I deleted her number.

It feels as if there are two different people (two different voices) trapped inside my head. The one is rational and clear and tries to tell me to do the logical thing. The other one seems to be terrified of the loneliness that will torment me over the coming weeks or months. This last voice is loud and screams that I was stupid to delete her number. It tells me that I've ruined everything and that I will never find happiness again. It commands me to find it on my laptop or on Facebook and WhatsApp or whatever programme we used to fight our endless fights. It terrorises my serenity by showing me images of all the plagues that will visit me. It's deafening, and I'm petrified every time it speaks.

But when it finally becomes tired and quietens down, the other one whispers with a tone so soft that I can barely understand it. At times, I don't even know what it's trying to tell me, but when I make an effort to listen, I hear it say that 'it's for the best' and that everything will be okay.

Going back to Caitlin will only be a Pyrrhic victory—I might win the battle, though it will be at great cost, and I will surely lose the war.

It's not what happens to you that defines you, I think, but how you deal with it.

At around ten in the morning, Brett walks into the house to see how I'm doing.

"You know what, brother?" he says, "You might disagree with me now, but in a couple of weeks, you'll see things more clearly. Believe me, a rose grows better on shit, and you'll have to dig your way through all of this to find your soul mate. You will fall in love again, and I'll be at your wedding." He laughs while he jokingly adds, "As your best man."

"She'd better be a rose," I sigh, "because I'm sick and tired of digging through this shit."

"Trust me, you will look back upon this episode in your life and ask yourself, how on earth could I ever had feelings for someone like that."

"The irony," I say, "is that she's broken up with me."

"What!?" he exclaims.

"I know! She didn't even give me a chance and ended it the second she answered the phone."

"What a stupid bitch," he says, "she doesn't know what she's lost."

6

That day I sleep until eight o'clock in the evening. I'm woken by noises coming from the TV, the footsteps through the hallway and whispering voices.

At around eleven at night, Celine's and Brett's finally go to their rooms, and I get up to have a shower. After that, I go to the kitchen, grab something to eat and drink and crawl back into bed.

The rest of the night, I lie awake speculating on what to do and how to make it through the next coming days, weeks and even months. It will be difficult, and I know I will suffer. All the plagues presented to me by my screaming self will rain down. I'm scared of the heartaches and sorrows to come, but I am even more afraid that I'll crack and try to get in touch with Caitlin again.

Over and over, I repeat the sentence 'it's for the best. I whisper it to the ceiling, but it only looks down on me. I tell myself that there have been hundreds of moments where we reached our point of no return, and this break-up was long overdue.

Once more, I have arrived at a stage in my life where I don't know what to do. How to move forward from here? How do I distract myself? Perhaps going back to online dating is the only way?

But it feels I'm blind, and I need to see. I need the advice of a passenger who can warn me of traffic lights, of women with children or of motorcyclists trying to make a U-turn.

Tomorrow morning, I decide, I will phone the psychic in Port Elizabeth. I need her to sit next to me in my car. I don't only want her to tell me what's in front of me, but also (and perhaps even more importantly) what direction I should take. I feel that I've reached a dead-end, and I can't decide whether to turn right or left.

Only around midday, I wake up and even before I shower or have my breakfast, I grab my phone and key in the psychic's number.

She answers after the third ring. I introduce myself, and she tells me she remembers me. It has been three years since we last spoke; seven years since I first visited her. This time there's no candle, and she can't hold my hands.

"Can you do it over the phone?" I ask her.

"I can try," she replies. "I have done it before. Sometimes it works, and other times it doesn't."

"Let's try then," I insist.

After a long pause, she says, "Your love life has been a mess for quite a while."

"That's the least you can say," I remark.

"You need to shake the dust off," she advises, "and change your attitude towards things."

"Can you be a little bit less abstract?" I ask.

"I will try." She sighs and takes another deep breath. "You're not happy where you are. You feel that the city you live in is dragging you down. Maybe not so much the city," she adds, "but certainly the weather. Where are you at the moment?" she asks.

"London."

"Perhaps you need to move to a different country."

"What else can you see?"

"It's difficult. Nothing is clear."

"What about the girl? Has anything changed there?"

She takes her time before she answers: "Very toned, slim, tall and blondish hair. She seems quite pretty."

"I'm still on that same bloody road," I groan. "Any idea when I will meet her because I'm running out of flipping petrol."

She laughs. "I really wish I could tell you when," she says after a long pause. "However, it feels as if it won't be much longer."

"You mean: not much longer in dog years or more in a geological kind of time frame?"

"Hang on!" she abruptly says, "There's something else." She waits a while before she continues. "You need to go travelling again," she finally concludes, "because you won't find her sitting at home on your butt. You need to travel the way you like to."

"Where?" I ask. "Tell me, and I'll buy my ticket the moment I put down the phone."

"I'm not sure," she says. "Australia comes up. I'm not saying that you'll meet her there," she quickly adds, "but I see you going there one day."

She hesitates for a few seconds and then says: "That's it. I can't see any more."

I thank her and put the phone down.

She was right about England, I think. I have been here for a little over three and a half years, and it has been a waste of time. I should have stayed in South Africa. In that way, I would never have met Caitlin, and I would have been spared all this misery.

7

"I need a holiday," I tell Brett the following day before he leaves for work. "I feel it's time for me to claim back my grip on life."

He laughs. "You just came back from one."

"That wasn't a real holiday."

Celine has already left. She leaves around seven. I usually get up at half-past eight, and in those twenty-five minutes before Brett rushes off, we talk while he sits on the toilet. It's almost a ritual. More than anyone else, he loves his morning toilet time and leaves the door open so he can hear me while I make my coffee in the kitchen.

"You need to keep your mind busy," I hear him say, "and distract yourself. What about going back on the dating app?"

"Yes, I thought about that," I shout from the kitchen while pouring hot water over the instant powder in my cup. "But it might not be that fair towards the girls. You know—rebound and that sort of stuff."

"Hmmm," he says and keeps quiet for a while. Then I hear his voice again, "You know that I did?"

"Did what?"

"I went back on that online dating app."

"You did?"

"Yes," he replies. "When you left for South Africa, I was sitting here spending my evenings watching Celine happily tapping on her phone; writing messages to guys, browsing through their profiles and laughing at what they'd written her."

"—Celine is also back on that site?" I interrupt him.

"Yes," he laughs, "We both are."

I feel betrayed.

"I thought she liked me," I say.

"Get over yourself!" he shouts from the toilet, "You're on the rebound and stuff, remember?"

"Yes, but I thought ... I mean—well, that she ... —has she met anyone yet?"

"I don't know," he says, "but anyhow: there's this girl, and I think she's stunning. I'll forward you the link when I'm at the office, so you can have a look and let me know what you think."

"You've met a girl? What is this? I go on the worst holiday in my life, come back to find myself engulfed in this break-up and you bail on me? You're my other leg," I say, "and we're supposed to go out and hunt as bachelors do. You shouldn't leave me limping around on my own."

He chuckles, flushes the toilet, washes his hands and walks into the kitchen. "Not met as in met-met," he says. "We've only started messaging each other."

An hour after Brett has left for work, he phones me. "I can't believe it!" he gasps. 'She's taken her profile off."

"That's silly," I reply. "Do you know of any other way to get in touch with her?"

"I have her email address, but what if she doesn't want me to contact her? I mean, how must I see this? Did she take her profile off because she doesn't want to have anything to do with me?"

"Maybe she's taken it off because she thinks you are 'the one'."

He laughs and says, "Don't be stupid."

8

For the fifth day in a row, I can't motivate myself to do anything. I don't even read the emails my colleagues have sent me, and I don't care if certain things are urgent. But I know I can't keep doing this. I would hate for my Spanish boss Josue to phone and (while lisping his Antonio-Bandera-accent) ask me 'FYI, what's wrong, Rgds, J'.

I need to pull myself out of this swamp before it drags me deeper and deeper. I have to focus, to distract myself, but how do I do that? I'm not one of those people who can drown himself in work, and I don't rummage around in pubs to seek rescue in alcohol or pastime with drunks.

When Friday finally arrives, Brett takes one look at me and says, "We need to go out."

I want to protest; assure him that I'm fine and that I'd prefer pizza and Netflix, but he's already phoning Richard and telling him to come over.

One hour later, I see his Peugeot pulling into our driveway. "We are going to sort you out, Lyam," he says as he walks into the living room.

"I don't need sorting out," I object and try to smile.

I'm still in my pyjamas.

"Get dressed," he orders.

"We'll only have one or two drinks," Brett promises. "I need to work tomorrow morning, and Richard is taking Adele to Brighton."

There are plenty of pubs in and around Ealing, and often we take the tube to go somewhere else, though this time we venture into one of the local joints. We've barely ordered our first drinks when Brett starts interrogating me.

"What do you think?" he asks, "Do you think that you and Caitlin had a fighting chance for happiness?"

The barman puts three pints of Stella in front of us, and I take a sip before I answer. "It depends on what you mean by 'fighting'," I try to joke.

"Look at him; the man's funny," Richard blurts out.

"No, seriously," Brett insists.

"Seriously?" I repeat while shrugging my shoulders: "No, not really."

"Then do you think that breaking up has been the right decision—that you guys should not be together?"

I take another sip from my beer, a bigger one this time and admit, "Being with Caitlin has been the worst time of my life."

"Then why do you torture yourself? Why don't you start realising that only by stepping away from her you can find happiness again?"

"I already know all of this, Dr Phil," I say, "but it isn't that simple. It's like an addiction. The junkie knows in his clear moments that the heroin is bad for him, but when he feels that he needs to shoot up, he can't think of anything else. He lies to his friends, but more importantly, he lies to himself and is convinced that everything is okay. It will take a long time for those chemicals to leave his body."

I pause for a moment and say, "with Caitlin, it was probably a 'codependency thing. Her misery, her issues with her parents, her trouble with her brother and with her friends, dragged me in with her."

"Then pull yourself out of there, man," Brett argues. "Go back online and find yourself another Anna Fatbum", he laughs.

"Man, do you remember her? I still see you going on that one date, thinking you'd found 'the one'. You really thought you could step off that plane and walk into eternal happiness." he jokes. "But you now realise that life doesn't work like that. Reality often makes other plans."

"You know what I think?" Richard asks, "I think this is just all about self-pity."

"What the fuck is this?" I interrupt. "Aren't you guys supposed to make me feel better? Not that I expected Richard to hand me a handkerchief, but come on: self-pity!?"

"Let me explain," he says. "More than once, you've been telling me that you and Caitlin were not going anywhere. You were thinking of breaking up with her, but now that she's beaten you to the punch, you feel rejected. That's what I mean with self-pity. Let's face it, you're unhappy because she kicked you in the butt and not because you lost her."

"He is right, you know," Brett says.

We order another drink and after that, another one. By the time Richard starts telling me that he wishes he was still single, we know we are drunk.

"Women are weird creatures," Richard yells out. "You can't be with them, and you can't be with them."

"You can't be without them, you mean," I try to correct him.

"No, no, no," he mumbles while pointing his finger into the air: "You can't simply be with them. It is impossible." He turns to me and says, "Every time you come over and tell me stories about the girls you've dated or are dating, I want to be you, man."

"And every time I go to your house and I look at your wife and your little kid, I want to be you," I say. "I envy you, Rodney—"

"Richard," he interrupts.

"—I envy you, Richard," I rephrase, "because I want to have a wife and a little family."

"That is such a nice thing to say, bro," he snivels, and we raise our glasses to drink to that.

"Hang on. What about our fifty-year plan?" Brett objects. "We could be sitting on a beach in Bali and drinking beer without being hassled by any woman. Complete freedom!" he exclaims.

We order another round and drink to that as well. By the end of the evening, all three of us are entirely drunk. We struggle to find our way back home, and when we finally do, it is after three in the morning.

9

The following day, I feel ill. My stomach is upset, and I have a massive hangover. It is after eleven in the morning, and Brett must have been at work for a little over three hours. I wonder if Richard is making his way to Brighton, and I hate to think how both of them must feel.

I grab a bottle of lemonade out of the fridge and decide, after nine days, to finally check my emails. There are five-hundred and thirty-two unread messages.

I'm shocked. I don't have the energy, nor do I feel well enough to go through any of them. But the sheer amount makes me realise that I've been avoiding real life for much too long. I need to work, and I need to work hard. I can no longer cancel meetings in the UK with the excuse that I'm tied up in France and vice versa. My job should become my first priority. I cannot afford to lose it. A couple of projects need my immediate attention, and I haven't visited some countries for quite a while.

Suddenly I realise what I need to do. I can combine work with vacation. I could visit friends and family and colleagues and clients all at the same time. I could hold meetings in countries I haven't been in for a long time.

I will go on a road trip.

I roughly outline my itinerary, and Belgium, France, Spain and Portugal are part of it. I can put my bicycle in the back of my car and cycle whenever I have time. That will undoubtedly clear my head.

On Sunday morning, I start leafing through my emails. I don't read the ones where I have merely been put in cc. Only a few messages are essential and need an immediate reply, but luckily, none of them are urgent.

On Monday I phone people in the different countries I want to travel through. There is a lot that needs to be organised, and closer to Thursday, everything starts falling into place. By the time Friday arrives, I'm all set to go.

When I kiss Celine goodbye, she appears to be sad and asks, "Why are you leaving again?"

"This time, it is for work," I lie.

Brett grabs my hand (thumb to thumb) and pulls me closer to give me a brotherly hug. "Good luck, Lyam," he says.

"The same to you," I reply. "Good luck with your date next Tuesday. I told you that she'd taken her profile off because she thinks you're 'the one'."

He rolls his eyes. "Don't be ridiculous."

"I have to be honest and say that I'm afraid you will be wasting your time going on a date with that girl."

"Why do you say that?"

"Because you'll be too scared to kiss her. It'll be French Anaya all over again: "Oooh, my hands are sweaty, and I'm too nervous," I imitate him, "I can't kiss her. What if she doesn't like me?" I laugh and say, "But this time, I won't be there to hold your hands, and you'll end up not kissing her at all. This will make her think that you don't like her, and she won't get back in touch with you again. You see: a waste of time."

"You bastard," he says. "I will kiss her."

10

It's a six and a half hours drive from Ealing to my mum's place in the north of Belgium. It feels weird to say such a thing. Belgium is so tiny that north, south, east or west, don't seem to willingly fit its size. When you are in the centre of Belgium and travel more or less two hundred kilometres in any direction, you will have left the country.

My mum is happy to see me, and it feels good to be home. It is mid-spring, still far from summer, but it's a beautiful sunny day.

I take my laptop and walk outside to the veranda. I look around. There's a big garden behind the house with chickens, geese, ducks and a few rabbits that have spread their network of warrens throughout the field. The little pond, which is so muddy you'd think nothing could survive in it, holds fish.

The next day, I cycle together with some of my childhood friends through the vast forest that surrounds the small village.

Suddenly the thought that I could come back and live here jumps to mind.

When I arrive back at my mum's, I wonder: could I really live here? Could I return to Belgium after all those years and leave England behind — not even go back to South Africa?

My boss would not mind me staying in Belgium, though I'm sure he would disagree with me moving to South Africa. Eighty per cent of our company's turnover is achieved in Europe. Even though part of my responsibilities stretches far into Africa, flying the eleven hours up and down would be pointless.

For a moment, I think of resigning, but I know that I can't afford it. My house in Port Elisabeth needs the extra cash, and selling it in today's market would only mean I have to accept far less than I paid for it. I need another year—at least another year to create a buffer that keeps me floating in case dire straits knock.

One more year in London?

A feeling of uneasiness tightens my chest. It's clear to me that I'm struggling with this concept. But what about Belgium? I could stay at my mum's and save as much money as possible and then resign. At least it gives me something to think about.

My mum has joined me on the veranda. I look at her and see her lighting another cigarette. She's been diagnosed with lung cancer but still smokes a lot. The doctors told her ten years ago that she had six months to live, but my mum is very stubborn, and eight years later, she (though very skinny) is still alive.

As much as I love to cycle in our village's forest, and as much as I love rabbits, the ducks and the little pond, I might not be able to live here. For one, I hate the climate—which is pretty much the same as in the UK. But most importantly, my mum still thinks I'm a child.

When I mow the lawn, she often yells things like: "Be careful not to put your fingers underneath the machine, or they'll get chopped off." And then I shout back: "Mum, I'm thirty-four; I've mowed the lawn a thousand times!" And then she'll yell something illogical like: "Yes, but this machine is different."

It infuriates me. It makes me feel I want to jump on a plane and move to South Africa or London, or anywhere but back to where I grew up.

I have introduced Caitlin to my mum, and it was clear that she disapproved of her. But then again, my mum never approves of any of the girls I've brought home. Most of the time, I don't tell her that I have a new girlfriend and most of the time, she doesn't ask.

I shouldn't have told her about Caitlin, but for some reason, I thought she was worth mentioning.

My mum is not an easy woman, but I admire her toughness. She truly believes that she can do anything, and when I was younger, I used to call her Rambo.

Rambo can do anything. He goes to a machine-gun fight with a knife and decides that he will not die, just like my mum decided that the doctors were wrong.

She has not asked me about Caitlin. Instead, she has told me off for putting the glasses on the top rack in the dishwasher, not on the bottom one. I've apparently made the mistake of putting the spoons in the same tray as the forks.

I cannot live in Belgium.

11

On Monday morning, I officially start my road trip. While I drive eighty kilometres from my mum's place to the Belgian head-office, I think of Caitlin. I can't help but wonder if she's missing me.

When I arrive at the office, I meet up with three of the salespeople. One of our international customers has an issue and keeps pushing for a solution. Still, all he has received from us is a description of how tricky the situation is.

My three colleagues explain to me what the predicaments are. They keep repeating the difficulties involved and how messy everything has become. Almost endlessly, they try to justify why this or that solution cannot work, and eventually, I explode.

"I know what the problem is!" I yell at them. "I've known it already for a couple of months. The international buyer phoned me a week ago. He knows what the problem is. He was even able to describe it to me in a better way than you guys have been doing. I don't want him to embarrass us by coming up with a solution that the three of you haven't been able to think of because you have been too busy finding reasons why things can't work!"

They all keep quiet, and the rest of the meeting continues with an edgy feel.

When I am in my car driving towards Paris, I regret my outburst. My colleagues have never seen me like this as I'm usually calm and composed. I realise that it was not them I was angry with. My three colleagues were only a mirror, and it was me I was shouting at.

There is truth in what they say: that what you dislike about yourself, you hate in others.

Later that evening, I arrive in Paris, and my GPS SatNav guides me through all kinds of little backstreets. It's bizarre how French driving differs so much from English driving. While the English stay politely in their lanes, certainly won't jump queues, keep their distance and even let others pull in front of them ... — the French seem to be on a mission to take you down. Officially, the traffic code is the same in both countries, but the interpretation differs. In France, the informal road regulations are often as complicated as their movies.

When I was a child, there weren't many channels on Belgian TV. At times, the choice was only between a German Krimi (like the police detective series 'Tatort' and 'Derek') or a French movie. On rare occasions, my parents selected the French option. Still, by the time it had ended, we all stared at each other, thinking—what on earth happened; can anyone perhaps explain the plot?

In traffic, it's pretty much the same. When, for example, you leave only one centimetre between yourself and the car in front of you, other drivers consider this an invite to pull in. There is no room for error. If you do something wrong, drivers hoot and make gestures with their fingers or even try to push you off the road, leaving you thinking—what on earth just happened.

But when you visit a company, it all changes. In England, people who are not direct colleagues of yours will not greet you. They won't shake your hand or even recognise the bare essence of your being. In France, however, everyone wants to kiss you. Even the people you've never met before will stop and exchange a few words—asking you what you're doing or where you're from. Regardless of their status, from the director to the person who sweeps the floor, everyone acknowledges that you exist.

Perhaps it is because they merely want to take a break, but, aside from the kissing, I prefer the attention.

I check myself into a hotel close to the French head office, and the following day I get up early. On average, it takes me about an hour to wrestle my way through my French colleagues' greeting ceremonies. All the women want their two kisses, and even the men, at times, insist on it.

By the end of my meeting with the French sales team, my brain feels slightly overcooked. It is mainly because of the lack of practice that I still don't fully understand the Parisian-French. I have to constantly focus not to miss vital info. At times I found myself nodding yes while it should have been no. And when I ask them to repeat themselves, they look at me surprised and say, "but you are Belgian? Non?"

12

I have always liked Paris. I love the look of the Sacré-Coeur, the fact that its stones remain white (despite weather and pollution). I certainly enjoy the Champs-Élysées, the Arc de Triomphe, and of course Montmartre.

Throughout the centuries, Montmartre has been famous for its bohemian types, its painters and its sculptors. Van Gogh, Picasso, Utrillo, Pissaro and Toulouse-Lautrec all lived and worked here. There are still a few houses and studios left where some of the most famous paintings in the world have been created.

For a second time, the thought that I could live here jumps to mind. I could rent a cheap room above a cosy bistro and become one of those artists. Not necessarily become a painter and cut my ear off, but I could write a book. I could stroll among them and walk the stairway towards the timeless white Basilica of Jesus' Sacred Heart. I could have my little coffee, my pains-au-chocolate, my croissant or even my éclair. I could dress like them—wear a black smock and a beret—though I would probably skip that part. I might just stick to jeans and a t-shirt (and in this way become an eccentric among eccentrics).

I would not allow myself to have a car, but I don't see this as a disadvantage. Once, while driving through Paris, I searched for a car without a dent and couldn't find it. They had all been wounded on the Parisian battlefield.

The idea that I could live in France is growing on me. Moving back to Belgium and staying at my mum's place, after having lived on my own for so many years, might not be the right choice.

On the other hand, it doesn't necessarily have to be Paris. The winters here are almost as wet as in London, but there's the south of France which certainly would be a better idea.

Two days later, I arrive at Montauban, a city about fifty kilometres from Toulouse. My two French colleagues, both chemical engineers, have invited me for dinner. We drink lots of wine and order seafood cocktails for starters, a calamari steak for mains, and cheese dessert. My Colleagues advise me not to have the hotel's breakfast and insist on taking me to a lovely little café where the bread is extra crispy.

France is indeed a country where I could live.

I think of Caitlin and tell myself that I am glad she hasn't tried to message me.

I continue my trip to Narbonne. I planned to stay the night in that small city. Though eager to make it to the Mediterranean, I continue my journey over the limestone massif 'Montagne de la Clape' until I reach Narbonne-Plage.

In the afternoon, I take my bicycle out of my car and cycle to a couple of real estate agents. They are all more than happy to show me their two-bedroom properties. They overload me with brochures, and I take their business cards and tell them that I could come to a decision in less than two weeks. They assure me that Narbonne-Plage is an excellent place to live.

I visit the petite cafés, drink coffees and talk to the locals. There's a good vibe, and everybody is friendly. I haven't felt this peaceful for a long time.

In the morning, I leave for Barcelona, but I have decided not to rush. I follow the coastal route over Perpignan, avoiding the concrete ribbons of the French super-highway. I drive onto the foothills of the Pyrenees, and the scenery is breathtaking. I stop at the lovely seaside village of Collioure, and only after that, I cross the border into Spain.

After Girona, I continue the remaining hundred kilometres till I reach Barcelona.

13

Around eight in the evening, I get a call from Josue. "Have you checked into the hotel?" he asks and enquires whether I enjoyed my journey.

He doesn't know that Caitlin and I have broken up, and though he shows patience, he is not sure why I have undertaken this road trip.

"Shall we meet for dinner?" he suggests.

An hour and a half later, he picks me up. I am starving, and the glass of Mojito (author Ernest Hemingway's favourite drink) doesn't befriend the meagre content of my stomach. Only after a quarter past ten, we start eating.

"How was South Africa?" he wants to know while he grabs some of the tapas and puts them on his plate.

"Wonderful," I lie.

He likes to believe that we are friends (and in many ways we are), though I wonder how his friendship would uphold when he needs to cut back and offer me a redundancy.

I update him on my fall-out with my Belgian colleagues. He knows about the issues we're having and tells me not to worry about them. "Someone had to wake them up," he says, "and I'm glad it was you. They respect you, and I'm sure that they'll come up with a solution."

"I blame the human resources department," I say. "They tell us how much someone is allowed to earn or what car they can drive, but they don't care if we struggle to find good people.

When you pay peanuts," I add, "you can only employ monkeys. I can understand that HR needs to show their own spreadsheets with savings. Still, at the same time, they should understand that their salaries are generated by the good salespeople and not by the bad ones."

Josue starts laughing. "What's wrong?" he asks. "Are you sure your holiday in South Africa was all wonderful? You sound a little stressed."

I sigh. "I'm thinking about leaving London and moving to France," I suddenly throw in, "and I would like to know how you feel about this."

He is taken aback for a moment but quickly recovers and says that the team in Paris would be happy for me to join them.

"I wasn't necessarily thinking of living in Paris," I confess.

He raises his eyebrows.

"I've been taking a closer look at Narbonne-Plage. It's very close to Barcelona, and I could easily take internal flights to Paris." I hesitate for a moment. "London depresses me. The only difference between winter and summer is felt in the temperature of the rain. It drives me mad. I need the sun!"

He takes a sip from his wine and wipes his mouth. The waiter brings another dish with Spanish canapés, but both of us are getting full.

Finally, he looks up and asks, "Why not Barcelona?"

I take a moment to think about it. "It's a possibility," I eventually say.

Though I already know it isn't. I feel more comfortable having some kilometres between Josue and myself. Even though he is a nice guy and I like him, I don't want to see him every day at the office. I prefer him to phone me and arrange a meeting. I still want to have the autonomy to look in my diary and lie that I'm all booked up for the next ten days.

The following day at the Spanish head office, Josue and I spend the whole day in meetings. We discuss marketing plans, forecasts for the coming year, and he asks me what my main projects are at the moment.

Again, I lie. I exaggerate and tell him that I've been busy while I have hardly done anything.

14

I love Barcelona, but I'm still not entirely sure what to think of Antoni Gaudi's distinctive architecture. He tried to steer clear of the constant repetition used in Gothic designs and preferred to stay closer to more natural forms. I like his Casa Vicens, the Casa Batlló, the Casa Calvet, and I especially enjoy walking around the Park Güell. But most impressive, of course, is his unfinished masterpiece: the Sagrada Família's crypt.

I have seen these buildings more than once, but I plan to revisit them. I leave my bicycle in my car and hop on and off the red sightseeing busses as this is the easiest way to get around. I walk over the golden sandy beaches, which are not more than ten minutes away from the city's centre. I take my sandals off, and while I let the water touch my feet, I stare at the sunbathing girls. Some of them are topless, others are wearing tops, but none of them are ugly.

Do I perhaps have to move to Barcelona?

Out of the blue, I decide to phone Brett.

"Finally, bro," he roars, "we thought you'd jumped off a bridge or something. Why don't you reply to your emails?"

"Emails? I haven't checked my inbox for about a week. Why didn't you WhatApp me?"

"Never mind," he says and wants to know how the road trip is going.

I don't tell him that I'm considering leaving London and moving to the south of France. He doesn't need that information right now.

"Where are you?" he asks.

"Barcelona. And man," I gasp, "you won't believe how good-looking the girls are over here. Even the ugly ones are beautiful compared to what we've been looking at in England. You need to resign, leave the ugly village behind and move to Barcelona as soon as you can."

He hesitates for a moment and then enquires, "but do you think you could be happy in the pretty village?"

Some months ago, I'd asked him to imagine what it would be like if he'd grown up in a village where only ugly girls lived. But, if he'd never travelled to any other place, I prolonged my hypothetical subject, he would not perceive the girls as ugly. The reason is that he would not be able to compare them to the prettier ones in other villages.

"Say now," I concluded, "that you married the prettiest girl in that ugly village; do you think you could be happy?"

"Yes," he agreed. "If I didn't know better, I'm sure I could."

"Does that mean that happiness lies in ignorance?"

"Perhaps it does," he replied. "But imagine now that the ugliest girl in the pretty village is prettier than the prettiest girl in the ugly village. And let's assume that you can decide to live anywhere; where do you think you'd be the happiest?"

"I might decide to move to the ugly village," I told him, "because there, at least compared to the others, I will be with the prettiest girl."

"Then that means," he concluded, "that unhappiness is influenced by comparison."

"How was your date?" I ask, suddenly remembering that he must have met with the girl about a week ago.

"If you'd read your email," he replies, "you would have known." He waits a moment and then sighs, "It was cancelled."

"Why?"

"I don't know. I wasn't the one who cancelled it. Perhaps she met someone else. She can do whatever she wants for all I care."

"How did she cancel?"

"She wrote me an email saying that something had come up. She asked if we could postpone to a later date."

"Perhaps something had come up," I tell him. "Why don't you try to set up another date, and if she ditches you again, well … then stuff her. How's Celine?" I ask, changing the subject.

"I think she's sad because you're not here, Lyam," he says. "But you know what happened? She stopped smoking. I haven't seen her touch one single cigarette since you left. How about that? Maybe she did it for you? What do you think about that?"

"Rubbish," I reply.

"She's sent you an email as well, and you haven't replied. She asked me the other day if you were upset with her."

"Why would I be upset with her?"

"I have no clue," he says. "You know what women are like."

I sigh. "Tell her to use WhatsApp. What's wrong with you people. You might as well have sent me a fax."

He chuckles and then asks, "So how are things?"

"I keep myself distracted," I answer.

"No place better for that than in the pretty village of Barcelona," he laughs.

That same evening, I finally check my emails. There's one from Brett and one from Celine, wherein she simply updates me on what's happening in London and lets me know that she is okay.

'Hi queen of swans,' I reply, reminding her of our date in the park where we kissed, but delete it the moment I've written it. I start again with 'Hi sweetie,' and delete that as well. Finally, I write, 'Hi C,' keeping it concise and formal and tell her that I had a wonderful time in the south of France but don't share with her that I plan to move there. 'In three weeks, after Madrid and Portugal, I'll be home,' I write and end my email by saying that I miss our little tripod. I don't close it off with three kisses in the form of x's like I usually do.

Rereading it, I realise it sounds very reserved, but I don't want to make it too familiar.

Celine replies immediately. It means that she's in front of her computer. She writes that she is thrilled to finally hear from me and is glad the Caitlin-shit is not troubling me too much. She says she misses me and ends her email with no less than six kisses.

I feel guilty that I can't return her affection.

15

The following day, Josue phones and asks me if I'm still in Barcelona. I finally tell him that Caitlin and I have broken up.

"I thought as much," he says after listening to my story and adds, "that's why I don't mind you taking days off here and there."

He is not a bad guy at all, and perhaps living in Barcelona wouldn't be too terrible.

"Do you want to have dinner tonight?" he asks. Before I can reply, he continues, "Yesterday, I had a conversation with our human resources manager and this morning, he's sent me a couple of attachments. I would like to share them with you."

When we are in the restaurant, Josue pulls out a file. It shows a spreadsheet of most European countries. It mentions gross salaries, minimum and maximum country tax and other benefits like company car and bonuses. Belgium, France, Spain and Portugal are on it and so is Germany.

The gross salaries in Portugal are only sixty per cent of the ones in Belgium and Germany. But the Portuguese taxes are about half compared to the ones in Belgium. Spain is somewhere in the middle, and I'm surprised to see France ranging closer to the bottom end. No wonder everyone strikes there all the time.

"Impressive," I say.

"I assume you don't want to live in Germany," he laughs. "I left it in as a comparison., but take a look at Spain," he continues while browsing his finger over the list, "you can see that it doesn't compare too badly with the UK. That is if you take taxes and all that into account. You also need to consider that most senior managers live here, which seems to have turned Barcelona into our company's unofficial headquarters."

"I really appreciate this, Josue," I say.

"No pressure, but please think of Barcelona. It will certainly help you with your Spanish."

"They speak Catalan here," I throw back, and he laughs.

"Yes, they do. But it's still better than German."

16

Two days later, I continue my journey to Madrid. Twelve people are waiting for me to share our new system, which identifies microbial issues in food-producing companies. It's a two-day course, but already after a few hours, I realise that most of them hardly speak English.

While driving through Spain, the thought crosses my mind that I might not really be looking for a place to live, then that I am looking for a reason to leave England. Again, I think about resigning and moving back to South Africa and have to remind myself that I need another year to reach dry ground.

"Stick to the plan, Stan," I say out loud and let the rhyme, like a mantra, echo through my head.

When I leave Madrid, I don't take the direct route to Lisbon but head for Porto first. After I've arrived and checked into a hotel, I check my emails.

There's one from Caitlin.

She lets me know that all is well. She writes that she has been hanging out with some German students she met at Durban's Oceanographic Research Institute. Most of the time, she admits, she strolls around the city by herself. She has been asking herself whether it was the right decision to break up with me and acknowledges that she feels lonely.

She ends her message by saying that it was the right thing to break up and that we should not get back together.

What on earth is this all about? It sounds a bit like Paul Simon's song 'Graceland', where he sings: 'she comes back to tell me she's gone'.

Caitlin doesn't have to tell me that she has doubts and then say that she is convinced she did the right thing!

I'm irritated. I forward the email to Richard and ask him what he thinks she's actually trying to tell me? Does she perhaps want me back?

His reply comes the next day, 'No, she means precisely what she's written: that it was the right decision to break up.'

I don't believe him and forward the email to Brett, but he replies in a similar and writes: 'Move forward, Lyam, not backwards.'

Then why did she write to me? Why couldn't she just have left me alone? I was doing fine, and she didn't have to come back to tell me she's gone.

During my four-hour drive from Porto to Lisbon, I think about whether I should reply or not. I decided against it but can't resist the temptation after I have checked into my room. I open my computer and angrily type that she should not have contacted me. I tell her that I'm fully aware that we've broken up and that she didn't have to repeat it.

An hour later, her reply falls in my inbox. She is furious. She calls me a bastard and writes that she should have known that I would have no consideration for how miserable she feels. She reminds me that she's all alone in a strange city while I have the benefit of surrounding myself with friends.

'I'm sure you are glad we've broken up,' she concludes, 'because now you can finally get together with that French slut who's had an eye on you from the beginning.'

This infuriates me even more. I start my reply by saying that I wish I was in Durban instead of miserable London, but that there's no point for her to be in England as she doesn't have friends anyhow. 'And as for Celine,' I angrily tap on my keyboard and lie, 'yes, we are together, and I'm far happier than I ever was with you.'

I reread it and start laughing. Caitlin and I have been apart for a little over three weeks, and there are about ten thousand kilometres between the two of us, but we can't stop fighting.

I can't believe it. I delete the email, close my computer and think: move forward, Stan and not backwards.

17

I like Portugal and adore its people. Portuguese girls are stunning. There is something casual about them—something nonchalant which certainly appeals to me.

I like its Latin-based language. Perhaps it is because it reminds me of my days in Mozambique. The Portuguese almost appear to chew it, which seems to make it all a little more digestible. On top of that, many English words simply need to be tied to the suffix 'ção' to make them sound Portuguese. Informação is an example, and so is complicação.

I am in Lisbon for no official reason, and I enjoy the sun, the strong ocean wind and the salty Portuguese food. Almost every morning, I take my mountain bike and cycle alongside the windswept sandy beaches of Estoril. The rugged Atlantic coastline is magnificent. The ocean's violent water crashes over the edged rocks, and its wildness reminds me of South Africa.

In the meantime, I'm getting nicely tanned.

Cascais is a suburb about thirty kilometres west of the Portuguese capital. Its microclimate (with almost Mediterranean-like features) has become a popular vacation spot for local and foreign tourists.

I love Cascais. It is absolutely stunning. Its pine-tree forests remind me of Belgium, and I could be happy here. I no longer think of moving to either Barcelona or Narbonne-Plage. Once more, I spend my afternoons gazing through some of the real-estate agents' windows.

When I walk in, they besiege me with brochures, leaflets and business cards. Some of them even show me their vacant properties, and I tell them I should be able to decide in less than two weeks. They assure me that Cascais is an excellent place to live.

That evening in the hotel, I search the Portuguese outlet of the same online dating app I've subscribed to in the UK. I key in the usual features: pictures, height, twenty kilometres from Cascais and no children. But there's something extra I need to let the app know: she has to speak English.

Only sixteen girls pop up.

I do another search. This time, I leave the distance to Cascais open and select English again as the preferred language. More girls show, though only two of them excite me.

The first one is beautiful. She has bleached-blond hair and writes in her profile that she lives in Faro. That's about two-hundred and eighty kilometres from Lisbon! The second one is a brunette with an adorable smile. She is in Porto: three-hundred and twenty kilometres away from here!

I message them both, and though they reply, the conversations don't flow.

I cancel my Portuguese subscription and browse the United Kingdom's version. In addition to the regular features, I select the language Portuguese. I figure that a girl who lives in England can speak English. Perhaps she will consider moving back to the country she was born in, and we could even live in Mozambique at some stage. Wouldn't that be life? Being surrounded by white, sandy beaches while sitting underneath waving palm trees? It could be my private adaptation to Brett and my fifty-year plan.

I wink at three of the girls whose profile pop-up, and a day later, my inbox shows that two of them have replied.

The first one, a girl with big Bambi-eyes and dark hair in a ponytail, lets me know that her father has a holiday home in Cascais. She tells me that she loves it there and that she wouldn't mind leaving England. Her name is Carla, and I respond that I'll return to the UK in a week. She agrees to meet me at Covent Garden the Saturday after I've arrived.

The other girl looks beautiful. She has long, curly brown hair and an incredible smile. However, her messages are dull, and because of this, I don't ask her on a date.

It's complicação.

18

I plan to leave Lisbon over the weekend. It will be a long drive to London, but it shouldn't take me more than two days. I am used to driving long distances. When I lived in South Africa, a friend and I once drove twenty-four hours to buy a Mitsubishi Pajero four-wheel drive we'd seen advertised on the internet.

I haven't heard from Caitlin since I stopped myself from replying to her last email. She hasn't been on my mind ever since those two London-based Portuguese girls reacted to my wink.

When I open my phone, I see a WhatsApp message from Celine blinking on my screen. It asks: 'Are you online?', but was sent an hour ago.

'Yes, I am,' I type.

It takes her a while to reply, but her message arrives: 'Good. Where are you now?'

'Close to Lisbon in Portugal. It's really lovely here.'

'Are you having fun?' her following message asks.

'I am. How is Brett? Has he been on his date?"

'He has, and it's hilarious,' she writes, 'but you need to ask him about it.'

We touch on some meaningless topics, and she tells me that travelling to Zurich is becoming really tiresome. 'The customer wants me to visit him more often,' she complains, 'but my company whinges that it's costing them too much on airfares. That's why I seldom spend the night in Zurich, which means that I leave extremely early in the morning and only arrive back home late at night.'

'What's the alternative?' I ask.

'I don't know,' she replies, 'perhaps moving to Switzerland?'

While I chat with Celine, I check my dating inbox. There is one from the pretty Portuguese girl with long, curly brown hair and dull messages. She writes that she has quit her job and has applied to become a police officer. She needs to go for a one-day assessment. If she gets denied, she says, she will try and join the Metropolitan Special Constabulary and explains that this a part-time volunteer police force in London.

It makes her sound even more boring.

'Listen,' Celine's WhatsApp message shows.

It is strange to see someone writing 'listen' while the only thing you do is read. Unless we select the 'talk' mode, though, at this stage, I prefer the shelter offered by the written word.

'What?' I reply.

'I'm not sure when you plan to drive back to the UK, but I will fly to my parents' place on Thursday. It seems that you have to pass Bordeaux when you drive to Calais, so how about coming over for the weekend? I promise that you'll have a wonderful time.'

I'm not sure, but I don't write that to her.

On the one hand, I wouldn't mind meeting up with Celine, but I feel uncomfortable being introduced to her parents. Will they think that I am just a friend, or will Celine leave them with a different impression?

While similar thoughts enter my mind, Celine becomes impatient. 'So, what about it,' her message insists.

'I was thinking of staying close to Lisbon during the weekend and start heading towards the UK around Monday.'

'Oh,' she writes, and it is as if all of her disappointment hides in that one word.

I feel guilty. 'On the other hand,' I continue, 'driving over Bordeaux might not be a bad idea. When do you expect me there?'

'Yippee!' she exclaims. 'As soon as you can: Thursday evening, Friday morning, Friday afternoon. Whenever you feel like it.'

'Friday afternoon?' I reply, and she answers by sending me a yellow smiley face.

'Good. Looking forward to that. I need to go now and do some more cycling,' I write. 'Just send me your parents' address, and I'll put it in my GPS SatNav so I won't get lost.'

19

Friday morning, I leave Lisbon and drive over Guarda and Covilhã into Spain. I gradually enter the Western Pyrenees around Balboa, and only the French toll-stops slightly slow me down. It's a thirteen-hour drive. I left at five in the morning and anticipate arriving around six in the afternoon.

Everything goes well until my GPS SatNav tells me to leave Bordeaux' ring and proceed in the direction of Eysines. It further advises me to continue toward Blanquefort, and that is where it goes wrong.

My GPS SatNav doesn't seem to have a clue. The smaller farm-roads are not on its map, and 'Suzy' decides to merely guess! She leads me left, right and straight to constantly make me detour through lovely countryside sceneries I can no longer appreciate. I leave small villages behind, drive through vineyards and sunflower fields. I stop, turn around and again steer my way through sunflower fields, vineyards and into small villages. I ask pedestrians and cyclists for directions. I take their rights and lefts and end up asking the same person the same question half an hour later. I phone Celine about fifteen times to help me find my way. She keeps asking me where I am, and the only answer I can give her is: in my car.

I'm irritated. I don't know where I am!

"But what do you see?" she asks. "Is there a church close by? Did you pass a big pink house? Have you seen a little chapel with a blue roof aside of the road?"

When you rely on a GPS SatNav, you don't look for those things. You only focus on the arrow showing you to go left, right or straight. You know exactly how many kilometres you still have to drive and at what time you are expected to arrive.

I'm ashamed to admit this, but I've been living in England for over three and a half years and wouldn't even know how to get to my office in Northampton without 'Suzy's help.

"But what do you see now? What is around you?" Celine insists.

"Vineyards," I reply, "and farmland, and more vineyards. Wait, there's a tall pole standing in one of the fields. It almost looks like a cross, but it has some sort of a basket on top of it."

I hear her speaking French to some other people. She is asking them if they are familiar with this. After a while, she says, "My dad seems to know where you might be. You're close, so sit still and don't go anywhere. I'll come and get you."

Ten minutes later, a red Volvo arrives. Celine jumps out, runs towards me and gives me a warm hug.

"Man, you're lousy with directions," she laughs. "Throw that rubbish out of your car and buy yourself a proper one."

20

Her parent's three-storey house is painted white. Her dad designed it.

Celine grabs my hand and leads me through the rest of the house. It's big, though it feels kind of upside-down as the top floor contains the living room and the kitchen. The middle floor is practically empty, and the ground floor holds the bedrooms and the bathrooms.

"The living room is there because of the views," Celine explains. "And it's cooler in the bedrooms when they're not directly under the roof."

"But the second floor seems to be a bit of a waste," I remark.

"It's there in case my brother or I decide to come back and live here." She rolls her eyes and smiles, "Probably more for me than for him," and quickly adds: "Not that I'll ever consider it."

There is certainly enough space for two families. The whole top floor and middle floor are entirely surrounded by a balcony. Her dad intended it this way so they can have their petit déjeuner, their déjeuner, their diner and their souper while moving around the balcony to avoid the blistering sun.

It makes me question how people can live in a place like London, where the only sun they see is streamed on TV.

Suddenly and without any warning, a thought jumps into my mind. I can hit myself for even thinking it. How can I consider moving here and living together with Celine on the second floor? That's plainly ridiculous.

'She isn't a bad catch,' the little voice whispers.

I haven't heard it since I left London, but I immediately tell it to shut up and that the idea on its own is utterly stupid.

But could I live here?

I look at the balcony. In the morning, I could work at the east-side, I think. Around lunchtime, I could move to the south side, and during the evenings, I could watch the sunset or read a book on the west side. In that way, I follow the sun and indulge in something I've been deprived of for years.

Perhaps Celine is in my life for a reason. Could this be fate? She did, after all, quit smoking.

"Come on," she says while grabbing my hand for a second time, "I'll introduce you to my parents."

They are lovely. Her mother is a delightful, sweet Greek woman. She is curvy, has a tiny waist, a full backside, brown wavy hair and an almost olive colour skin.

"How wonderful to meet you," she says and walks up to me with her arms spread wide like an eagle ready to land. She gives me a hug, then grabs hold of my face and smacks two wet kisses on my cheeks.

I can easily see where Celine got her good nature from.

With his bronzed face and grey hair, her father resembles Marlon Brando in Francis Ford Coppola's 'The Godfather'. But unlike Vito Corleone, who keeps the corners of his mouth turned downwards, he seems to always laugh. He is the family's patriarch and copies his Greek wife by placing two kisses on my cheeks. I immediately like him (but not the kisses).

He is into making his own wine and asks: "What do you think?" after he's poured me a glass of red and puts it in my hands.

I swirl it, sip, swish and have a sincere taste, but who am I kidding; I'm not a connoisseur. I know that it's not beer; I want to joke, but keep quiet. "Hmmm," I say: "Yes, it's excellent."

Both of Celine's parents speak English. Her dad is practically flawless, but her mum stubbornly clings onto some undecisive accent. She insists I speak French to her. "After all," she claims, "you're Belgian. Non?"

I suppose I am. Even though only thirty per cent of all Belgians grew up in the French-speaking region Wallonia, the vast majority is, like me, Flemish.

There are still differences between the French and Walloon-Belgian language. For instance: the French say that they can or cannot do something, like, 'Je ne peux pas dormir' (if they can't fall asleep). Walloon or Belgian-French relies heavily on the verb savoir, or 'to know'. In this way, we say that we don't know to sleep or, 'Je ne sais pas dormir'. This might come across as trivial, but the French always crack up laughing every time they hear it. When they're trying to be polite, they say something like, "Oh, that's so interesting," but disappear into the kitchen and crack up laughing anyhow.

Belgians hate to be patronised.

It is painful to see how both Walloon and Flemish's uniqueness is slowly fading. Walloon is little by little soaked-up by French in much the same way as Flemish is by Dutch.

Yes, we are Belgians, but only on two occasions. Firstly, when we have to defend the origin of our French Fries, which we vigorously claim was invented by us. And secondly, when the Belgian football team plays well in the world cup.

They have played exceptionally well over the last few years and currently rank first place, coming from sixty-sixth in 2009 and number five in 2015. So yes, we are Belgian.

Sometimes.

We've let her know

21

While we sit outside on the eastern section of the balcony, Celine unexpectedly leans over and whispers in my ear, "Are you hungry?"

I'm happy, she asks. I am starving. The French have their dinner much earlier than the Spanish, and because I arrived later than I hoped, I've missed out on a meal.

In France, there is still something called souper, which is often served late at night. It's usually a light meal, consisting mainly of some bread and soup. But it was getting later and later, and perhaps Celine's parents only stick to three meals instead of the usual four.

"I am," I whisper back.

She starts laughing, and her parents look confused. "He's too 'timide' to say that he's hungry," she blurts out.

Her mum looks at me, and a sequence of expressions reel over her face. Shock is first, quickly followed by concern and, finally, embarrassment. "O mon Dieu!" she cries out, "how could I have been so rude. Of course, you're hungry."

She rushes out of her comfortable futon, waves her hands next to her ears as if she has done something terribly wrong and dashes off into the kitchen.

It doesn't take long for her to return. One by one, trays with food land onto the dining table, holding sliced pork, beef, baked lamb with potatoes, Greek dishes like Moussaka and Souvlaki and others that I cannot identify. Every time I tell her to stop, that it is more than enough. Still, she doesn't listen and brings out a variety of cheeses: Camembert, Brie, Roquefort, Boursin, Reblochon and Chèvre. And those are only the ones I can identify.

I pinch Celine on her thigh as a punishment for shouting out what I'd only whispered in her ear. I thought she would simply make me a sandwich, but now that her mum is involved, there's enough food to feed the complete French bloody Foreign Legion.

I reluctantly move to the dining table and start eating. They all gather around and watch me. I feel embarrassed.

That night I fall into a deep, dreamless sleep only to be woken by clattering pots in the kitchen.

When I walk downstairs, I see Celine's mum preparing even more dishes. The entire counter is filled with food. There are baskets with tiny little pieces of bread and baguettes. There's a wooden plank carrying a big Pain Poilane. There're pots with Andouillettes and plates with all different Quiches and pâtés. I believe a vegetable stew, called Ratatouille, is laden with aubergines, courgettes, peppers, and tomatoes. A big clay bowl on the kitchen table contains lamb-feet with little tripe-parcels in a savoury sauce. Celine's mum is busy stirring a wooden spoon into a big pot of Coq au vin. In the living room, there's even more. The dining table is stuffed with different desserts: 'mousse au chocolat', various 'choux pastries', little fruit cakes, caramelised apple tart and a big 'gâteaux', which is soaked in 'crème au beurre'.

I'm shocked. Is this all for me? What on earth has Celine told them?

"Where is monsieur LeFevre?" I ask, trying my best to make it come across nonchalantly.

"Oh," Celine's mum smiles and walks over; her arms spread out: "I didn't see you." She kisses me on my cheeks and says, "He's in the garden spit-roasting a pig."

"A whole pig?" I ask, shocked.

"Non, non," she laughs, "only a little suckling one. Why don't you go and have a look," she says. "He's been up since five this morning."

Celine's dad stands next to a charcoal rig holding a big shovel in his hands. "Good morning," he smiles and kisses me on the cheeks.

I look at the piggy's cute little eyelashes, at its cute little snout, its cute little ears and its slit throat. Mr LeFevre has stuffed the animal with vegetables and apples for moisture.

"Would you mind taking over for half an hour?" he unexpectedly asks. "I need to go into the village and get the Jambon Sec. Just turn it every five to ten minutes into the same direction," he instructs, "and keep the charcoal lit."

Then he's off.

"Where's my dad?" I hear Celine ask. I turn around and see her walking down the balcony stairway. "Did you sleep well?" she inquires and kisses me on the cheeks. I don't mind them coming from her.

"He's getting even more food," I sigh.

"Hmmm, dad is always worried that there isn't enough. Have you eaten yet?"

"What is this? A 'getting-the-visitor-fat' contest?"

She giggles.

I see her dad pulling into the driveway. He steps out of the car and walks towards the two of us while carrying a big ham on his shoulders. After he's dropped it onto a wooden table, he kisses his daughter and—again— kisses me!

Minutes later, a van, with the word 'boulangerie' written across its doors, stops. The driver gets out and starts carrying more bread and patisseries into the house.

"What is actually happening here, Celine?" I ask. "Don't tell me this is all for me?"

"Oh no," she casually says, "It's my dad's birthday today."

"What!"

She shrugs her shoulders and laughs.

"Why didn't you tell me?"

"I just did," she replies.

"Celine!" I gasp, "Seriously, you should've told me."

"I didn't want you to go out of your way and look for presents or even worse: you might have decided not to come."

"Of course, I need to buy your dad a present," I protest, "and yes, I would have decided not to come."

When we're back in the kitchen, Celine turns to her parents and laughs: "You know what Lyam thought?" She laughs louder, and tears fill her eyes. "He thought that all this food was for him."

22

An hour later, I arrive back from the nearest village. I have bought Mr LeFevre an excellent bottle of Cognac and her mum a big bouquet of flowers.

In the meantime, the guests start arriving. Celine grabs my arm and tows me around while introducing me to almost everyone.

"This is 'Le Maire' of the village," she says while the mayor smiles and shakes my hand. This is Monsieur 'le Général' and this is 'Maître' Piccard. His title informs me that he is a lawyer.

Most of them have high ranking jobs within either the United Nations or other governmental organisations. Some have travelled from different countries to wish her father a happy birthday.

When some guests politely enquire what my relation to Celine is, she replies, "Il est mon ami," and explains that we live together in London.

But it is only when people suddenly start looking at me differently, saying things like, "Oh la la," and clapping me on my shoulders, that I pick up on it.

In the French language, saying 'he is my friend' means that you are the boyfriend. Instead of 'mon', Celine should have told them, "Il est un ami," which means that I am 'just' a friend.

I point this out, but she simply shrugs it off and tells me not to worry about it. Only when some of her parent's friends ask if we would like to have children one day, she decides to rephrase it.

By the time it is six o'clock, over a hundred people have arrived. Everyone seems to enjoy themselves. Celine's dad entertains his friends while her mum potters around in the kitchen. But every time some Greek music echoes through the house, she takes her apron off, leaps out of the kitchen and into the living room. She then slowly twirls around, shouting 'hoppa', while raising her arms, shaking her hands and lifting her legs. The whole place is quickly converted into a Big Fat Greek Wedding.

I watch Celine encouraging her mum by clapping her hands to the rhythm of a song. Then I see her getting up. She grabs her phone out of her trousers' pocket and briefly looks at the screen. A big smile appears on her face, and she runs outside.

The 'hoppa'-shouting women and men take advantage of my distraction to pull me onto the dance floor. They force me to twirl around, to raise my arms and kick my legs. Too self-conscious to even enjoy myself, I try to imitate some of the men who alternate between leaping and shuffle-dragging their feet. More than once, I try to flee, but every time someone grabs my hand and pulls me back onto the floor.

Half an hour later, when Celine arrives back into the room, I am drenched with sweat, and she bursts out laughing. When finally the last guests have left, the two of us sit outside in the garden.

"This was really great, Celine," I say. "I'm happy you invited me."

She gives me a warm kiss on my cheek and smiles, "It was wonderful to have you here."

"I noticed you got a late call tonight."

"Yes," she gasps, "I still can't believe he phoned me."

"Who did?"

"This guy I met," she replies.

It feels like she just threw a bucket with ice-cold water in my face.

"What guy?" I cautiously ask, but think: what on earth is wrong with me? Why do I react this way? I've known Celine for over a year, and all this time, I have kept her at a distance. Why do I feel shocked about some guy phoning her? Have I changed, or am I that bastard again who only pursues a girl when she is not available?

"It just happened on the tube from work to home," she explains. "A guy was standing a bit away from me, and it was clear that we were both checking each other out. And then," she giggles, "just before I jumped off at Ealing Common, I walked up to him and gave him my phone number."

"You gave a random guy on the tube your phone number!? You don't even know who he is, Celine," I say. "For all you know, he could be a serial killer."

"Oh, come on, dad," she laughs, "don't be silly. It's not that different from meeting someone in a pub. Everyone could be a serial killer if you look at it that way. I didn't even expect him to phone."

"And what now?" I ask.

"I don't know," she sighs. "He sounded really great. He was witty, charming and funny, and he wants to meet up."

"So soon? After one phone call?"

"Yes," she laughs. "We're not going to WhatsApp each other for the next three weeks. I've already seen him in real life, remember."

"I don't know, Celine," I say. "It all sounds a bit weird."

"Weirder than online dating?"

23

The following day, the house looks like a battlefield. Celine is still asleep, and her mum doesn't allow me to help with the cleaning-up.

She puts all kinds of cheeses and tiny pieces of bread in front of me and orders: "Now eat."

After that, she grabs a chair and leans close to my ear. I almost expect her to whisper like Michelle, the local French Resistance leader in the British sitcom 'Allo "Allo!': 'listen very carefully, I shall say this only once'. But instead, she asks, "Is Celine happy in London?"

I think about it for a moment, and I say, "Yes, I believe she is." I tell her about our little tripod family and how we go to the supermarket and take turns cooking.

She quickly looks around and says, "I think Celine likes you."

"I like Celine too," I reply.

"But do you?" she asks, "Do you really like her?"

Later that afternoon, while driving the nine-hundred kilometres to the Chunnel in Calais, slowly making my way back to London, I think about her mum's question. Hasn't it become time for me to finally answer this for myself and stop being the bastard? I'm carefully evading the hooting, zigzagging, queue-jumping and finger-gesturing French drivers. Still, I can't help but wonder what the hell happened? Why did I feel jealous when I learned Celine had given her phone number to some random guy on the tube?

Do I want to be that guy?

I spin the question in my mind and roll it from one side to the other. It wouldn't be too bad an idea to be with Celine. We could live in the south of France (in that beautiful house on the second floor) and of course, her parents are lovely.

Could I live there? Could I see Celine as more than 'just a friend? Could I perhaps see her as 'mon amie'?

What would Richard say about it?

Richard would say that I invent this wannabe life, that I even tell myself I truly want it, but that the moment it comes closer, I run.

And Brett?

Even Brett would say that I need to stop clutching onto those predictions made by a candle-staring phoney. While Celine is not from Australia, she is, more importantly, a fantastic person. He would say that this is what happiness is all about. I should simply convert Joe Jackson's lyrics and tell myself that if I can't be with the one who has been foretold, I should be with the one who is standing right next to me.

But if that is the choice I have to make, is love then all about compromising? Do I have to surrender, to mollify myself into... —into— into what exactly?

Would it be better to be with someone like Caitlin and getting torn apart when I am not with her and torn apart when I am? Or would it be better to be with someone like Celine, who is already a truly unique friend and with whom I can easily get along?

If that is the choice, then am I simply choosing between rationality and feelings—between head and heart? Both voices in my head shout: 'pick me, pick me'; one a bit louder than the other, but I still don't know what to do.

Perhaps some of those early philosophers were right, and love is a tool created by the gods to make humankind suffer. Maybe we are only fooled into thinking that, as Plato believed, we have to search for our other half. What if I decide to step away from this torture and focus a bit more on the fifty-year plan? Would that make me happy? What if even our search for happiness is a scam, an immature obsession, or rather—an illogical extravagance?

Perhaps the machine I should be looking for is not the one that erases your memory but ends your pursuit for idiocies like happiness and purpose and love.

Then again, love could be overrated, and maybe it has nothing to do with a happy marriage.

While I am driving closer and closer towards Calais, a thought occurs to me; perhaps I should bungee-jump this decision.

When I stood on top of Zimbabwe's Victoria Waterfall Bridge, I was very nervous before my jump. I thought, how will I ever be able to do this? Then the answer came to me: I simply needed to take one more step forward. That step would automatically result in me jumping!

So, if I take steps forward, perhaps I could fall in love with Celine. I could take little steps like kissing her. I could take her to the movies, to restaurants, and perhaps we should chase those ducks again. The more steps I take, the more closer we will become, and one day I could simply ask her to marry me. Just by taking tiny little steps and by letting the fall be the fall, I could find my eternal sunshine.

Though this is not bungee-jumping. There is no elastic. Celine is an excellent friend, and we could be great together. But something is missing.

I don't really—... couch her.

What defines me

Chapter 5

A new morning

1

I have been away for close to four weeks, and it feels weird to walk through the empty house in Ealing. I stroll from the living room into the kitchen, where I make myself a coffee.

After that, I return to the living room and look around. My eye falls on the shelf above the unused open-fire place. It holds a picture of our little tripod, showing Celine, Brett and me sitting closely together in some central London pub.

We do look like a family.

A WhatsApp message from Celine makes my phone's screen lit up. She lets me know that we don't have to wait for her for dinner. When she lands in Heathrow, she writes, she will take a tube to Hammersmith to meet with the guy she'd met on her way back from work.

It reminds me of my very first date with Anna and how I'd left South Africa thinking that all the pieces of the puzzle would simply tumble into place. I would meet her, fall in love, get married, have children and live happily ever after.

What a flipping joke!

How stupid was I to think about such things and, more importantly—to leave South Africa.

For a moment, I wonder how Anna is and whether online dating has introduced her to someone she is happy with. Her ex-colleague's name is still on my Skype, and perhaps I should write Anna a short message. But my next thought is: don't be an idiot; you need to move forward and not backwards.

I need to focus on my new plan: one more year of saving money, and then I will ditch London.

It is close to six in the evening, and before Brett is about to leave his office, I phone him and ask, "Pizza tonight?"

"You bet," he replies.

After he arrives, we take our seats on our sofas and place the Domino boxes on our laps.

"How was your weekend at Celine's parents' place?" he enquires and laughs, "I heard you're quite the Zorba-the-Greek, kicking your legs up in the air and stuff."

"Oh man, she told you about that? What else has she said?"

"Only that." He waits a moment, chews his pizza and says, "You know that she's gone on a date tonight?"

I nod.

"You need to make a decision, Lyam," he sighs. "She even stopped smoking for you, and you can't keep her on a string."

"I have," I say. "I've finally decided to move on. I can't do it, Brett, I don't feel what I need to feel, and it would be better for the both of us if she likes the guy she's meeting tonight."

"Well," he moans and points to his heart, "if it isn't there, it isn't there."

"What about your date?" I ask.

He starts laughing loudly. "Dates," he corrects.

I raise my eyebrows. "Two dates?"

"I went on a third one last night. By the way, her name is Julia."

"Three dates in a mere ten days? A while ago, you thought she might not like you because she'd postponed, and now you're practically moving in with her."

He laughs even louder, almost choking on his pizza. "Let me tell you what happened on our second date," he says. "We got into an argument."

"You never get into arguments with anyone."

"I know." He rolls his eyes. "Our first date was only an after-hours drink. It went very well; all sweet and stuff, good conversations and feeling comfortable—that sort of thing. Then, a couple of days later, I phoned her and asked if she'd be okay coming over to Ealing so I could cook for her."

"That's risky!" I throw in, "To invite a girl to your place on the second date. She could have thought you only wanted her there for sex."

He laughs. "Wait until you hear the rest," he says and continues, "so I went to Tesco's and bought a big lemon meringue pie for dessert, and of course I made her my famous lasagne. She was especially impressed that I could bake such a lovely meringue pie, and I let her believe that I had. I even told her how I struggled to get the egg-white right, whisking it between each addition without overheating, adding the cornflour, the sugar, and so on. She completely bought it. The rest of the evening went well, and by the time we moved from the table to the sofa, I told her that I quickly had to go and change into something more comfortable.

"You're not serious," I say.

"I was still in my suit-trousers and shirt," he protests, his voice leaping to high tones. "I'd come straight from the office and hadn't had time to change. But, listen—when I arrived back into the living room and sat next to her on the sofa, things changed. She suddenly became all tense. Whenever I moved closer, she moved farther away until she was all squashed against the sofa's arm.

"Exactly what outfit did you slip into, Brett?" I slowly ask.

"The usual. What I always wear."

"You are flipping kidding me?"

"Okay," he says, "you're getting me worried, and I'm starting to sweat now."

"Don't tell me that you were wearing your t-shirt and underpants."

"They are not underpants," he objects. "They are boxer-shorts!"

"Boxer-shorts, underpants. What's the difference? I can well imagine what that poor girl must have been thinking when you showed up in your undies."

He starts laughing again, and this time tears crop in his eyes.

"Oh no," I say and look at him in horror, "you didn't wear the ones with the holes in."

"I might have," he replies while laughing even louder.

"You do realise that everything is on display when you lift your leg up in those pants? Ask Celine! I can't believe that you let a girl on your second date have a direct view of your balls," I gasp. "Was it your plan to make her feel comfortable, or did you think that she might as well check out the merchandise straight away and make a decision then and there? No wonder she got all tense!"

He is completely in tears with laughter. His whole body shakes, and the slice of pizza in his left hand quakes up and down.

"But she didn't say anything," he finally manages to verbalise.

"Of course not. The poor girl was trying to be polite."

"That's not all," he says, still crying with laughter. "We ended up arguing."

"Oh, yes, I forgot about that. What did you end up arguing about?"

"We were talking about internet dating, the good and the bad, and somewhere down the line, I mentioned that I generally try to avoid dating English girls. You know," he adds, "because of what my secretary Jessica told us: that they look at you all condescending and play that game of telling you off while they want you to keep trying and trying? All those rules and stuff. You have to wait so many days before you phone her, so many days before you see her again. And then the confusion about whether you are 'dating' or 'just seeing each other'."

"This girl, Julia, she's English, right?"

"Yes, but I immediately told her that she's different. That she's not a typical English girl. Then she suddenly became furious, and everything went wrong."

"Let me summarise this, so I can better understand it," I say. "You invite a girl to your house. You take off your clothes, only wearing a t-shirt and undies with holes in them. You show her your balls and make her think you only want sex, and finally, you tell her that she's not like all the other English girls because ... —she's easy?"

"Oh my goodness," he whines, "if you put it like that."

302

He places his slice of pizza back in the cardboard box and starts rubbing his hands. "They're all sweaty now," he says.

"But how on earth did you manage to convince her to go with you on a third date? I thought that by now, she would have written a formal harassment complaint to that dating site."

"I kissed her."

I am flabbergasted. "She let you kiss her?"

"When she left, and I walked her down the stairs to the door, I suddenly remembered our conversation. You know, before you went on your road trip, you joked and said that I would never kiss her. That it would be a French Anaya story all over again."

"Yes," I smile, "I do remember that."

"Back then, I swore that I would kiss her, no matter what. And when I walked down those stairs, it popped into my head. I knew that if I didn't do it, you'd be laughing and mocking me about it for weeks. When we stood outside, she thanked me for the pizza and the pie, and I was sweating, man. I could feel it dribbling down my back and building upon my forehead. I was very nervous," he says, "but I finally leaned in and kissed her."

When, a week later, I get to meet Brett's Julia, I am very impressed. She is lovely and has a beautiful smile. Of course, I immediately told her that he'd bought that lemon meringue at Tesco, which sort of got him in trouble.

There was a moment I feared that a couple who argues on their second date might, like Caitlin and me, argue their way to a break-up. But this is not true for Brett and Julia: they are exceptionally well suited and in such harmony with each other that it amazes us all. It didn't take long for them to merge into one being and become inseparable. Wherever you see Brett, you see Julia and vice versa. Richard and I even started calling them 'the twins'.

2

Though I am pleased for him, Brett's happiness contrasts my desolation. I haven't heard from Caitlin since our last email argument.

My subscription to the dating app is reaching the end of its thirty days, and I am unsure if I want to extend it. I have never taken the six-month option, even though it is much cheaper. The reason, I guess, is that I never thought I'd be on it for longer than a month. But now, four years later, I should finally decide to stop this nonsense.

I still have two dates lined up with those Portuguese girls I winked at while I was in Lisbon.

When I phone Carla (the girl whose dad has a holiday home in Cascais), I immediately notice that she sounds very English: almost without a Portuguese accent. She lets me know that she can't make it this Saturday. Something has come up, she explains, but promises to make it up to me. She asks me if I wouldn't mind coming to her flat in Kensington two weeks from now. She can cook me her country's national dish, 'bacalhau', which is basically dried salted cod.

Celine has been on a couple of dates with her tube guy, but she doesn't sound too excited when I ask her about it. I am not sure if she is trying to play it down or that she really doesn't feel he is 'the one'.

As for Brett, he is barely home. He spends most of his evenings and even his nights at Julia's. On Saturdays, he plays rugby and hardly even joins Richard and me when we decide to go out for a drink.

During one of those evenings, Richard tells me that he and Adele are seriously considering moving back to South Africa.

"I thought you'd wait until your second child is born, so it has an English nationality?" I ask.

"Not since we are on the verge of bankruptcy," he says. "We've built up a tremendous amount of debt."

"How did you manage that?"

"Using many different credit cards," he explains. "It's easy to get new credit cards. You just need to lie on your application form."

He further tells me that the house they have bought as an investment has lost over thirty per cent of its value. Their deposit is completely gulped up. "We're left with nothing," he sighs. "Do you have any idea what you could do with that deposit in South Africa? You can practically buy a whole bloody house with it!"

"What are you going to do?"

"I've applied for a couple more credit cards, and after they're maxed out, we'll do a runner. I've spoken to a solicitor," he explains, "and he told me exactly what the next step is. From the airport, I'll make a single phone call and tell him to file for bankruptcy. He will push all the paperwork, and I'll get a completely new start back home."

"I can't believe this, Richard," I say. "How did this happen? You and Adele came to London so you could save money and have a head start, but now you've ended up worse than where you were when you arrived."

"I know," he says. "I've been working my arse off, but there's no escape. This place is a swamp, and it has dragged us so deep that it's impossible to get out. At least when you're trying to do it the honest way," he adds.

"But what about the thief story you once told me. Didn't you say that whether you steal a loaf of bread or a million pounds, you're still a thief?"

"Yes," he replies with a strained smile. "There's a big difference in what you would like to do and what you have to do to survive. So, when you're forced to steal, you better do it big and take the million pounds. I'm left with no choice, Lyam," he finally sighs.

3

Almost three weeks after my return to London, I take the tube to Kensington to meet Carla. When she opens the door, she is wearing her apron and has her dark hair tied in a ponytail. Her big eyes are endearing, but she isn't as attractive as she looked in her pictures.

I don't mind. I no longer need to be with the prettiest girl in the ugly village.

She gives me a kiss on each cheek and invites me in.

Her apartment looks posh. A massive flat-screen TV is joined-up with an expensive Dolby Digital surround system. It turns her nice sized living room almost into a movie theatre.

She grabs some crystal glasses to pour out the expensive two-thousand and five Chryseia red wine. She tells me she hopes I am not too hungry as she only started cooking ten minutes ago.

I join her in the kitchen. Over the next hour, I learn that she hasn't only lived in Amsterdam, Stockholm, Miami and Singapore, but even in Brussels for one year. She explains it was all Rotary-club related. She asks me if I know this or that senator and tells me she used to be friends with the Dutch prime minister's daughter. She doesn't work, but instead, her dad sends her a cheque each month to cover her costs of 'studying English'.

I carry plates, cutlery and glasses into the living area and set the table. It almost feels natural. I open another bottle of

Chryseia red and top up our glasses. She turns the TV on and browses through some Spotify songs.

Carla is silent for a moment, but while I pluck on the cod (a fish I never learned to appreciate), she suddenly starts laughing. I ask her what's funny, and she makes me promise that I will never tell Elana if I eventually end up meeting her.

"Who's Elana?"

She laughs even louder. "The other Portuguese girl you messaged," she finally says.

"What other gi … —," I want to ask, but then it dawns on me. "— … The police constable?"

"She told you about that?" she asks, visibly irritated. "I can't understand why this girl wants to walk around with a baton and hit people on the head!" Carla looks at me for a moment, starts smiling again and teasingly says, "You wrote us more or less the same messages."

"Oh no," I say, "I'm so sorry."

"Don't be," she giggles. "We all laughed about it."

"All?"

"All of my friends."

The temperature in the room has unquestionably increased by another ten degrees. I feel stupid, and Carla must surely see the deadened look upon my face as she laughs, "Don't worry, it was funny. Aside from that, Elana knows I'm meeting you today."

There goes the backup plan, I think.

But despite the embarrassment, I am actually having a good time. Though perhaps the wine is to blame for that.

When she gets up, I help her clear the table, and we move everything into the kitchen sink. She says that she will do the dishes tomorrow, and while she is facing one of the cupboards, I gently brush my fingers over the backside of her neck. She turns around, and we kiss. It feels good, but again, it could be the wine.

When I pull away from her, she has a big smile on her face. She playfully slaps me on my bum and says, "You go back to the living room and relax. I'm just going to slip into something more comfortable and will be there in a sec."

When she comes back, she wears a beautiful yellow summery dress that stops slightly above her knees. She walks up to me and tenderly pushes me down onto the sofa. She puts one leg across and sits on top of me. We start kissing again.

Spotify plays in the background, and I hear Alanis Morissette sing that she is looking for liberation or, to a certain extent, some patience. She claims that she is consumed by the chill of solitary and humbled by the humble nature of the spiritual man. But what she really wants is to find a soulmate, someone else to catch her drift.

Carla moves her body to the rhythm of the song and unties her ponytail. She swings her head forward. Her half long black hair falls next to her face, and I think, shit, she looks like Michael Jackson. Here I am in the living room of a girl who looks like a dead rock star, and I am about to have sex with her.

I need to stop this!

I can no longer do this. I genuinely need to stop pursuing girls I don't really want to be with. I should get up and go home! But the wine disagrees. She tops up my glass for the fourth time, and I think she might become my soulmate if I drink a little more.

I smile at her and pretend I like to see her moving her body to the beats of the song, but my previous thought (that she looks like Michael Jackson) reappears. It takes the form of a voice which faintly whispers in my head: 'You can no longer do this.' I can hardly hear it, but it is there. 'You need to follow your heart,' it says.

"I need to go," I quietly say to Carla, and she looks confused. "Thanks for the wonderful meal and lovely evening. I really enjoyed talking with you."

She is silent. She doesn't know what to say.

I don't want to lie to her. I don't want to use some flattened excuse that I need to get up early tomorrow morning or some fabrication that can make my getaway easier. Instead, I tell her that I wish we could be friends, but I don't feel there is 'anything more'.

"Sorry," I whisper.

I wish I could tell her other things. I wish I could say that it could have been different if I had met her in a pub. I have met almost all my dates over the online dating app. I am well aware that my profile doesn't reveal my true self. I grabbed the opportunity of anonymity to paint a different image, but so has everyone else. I could have looked in other places: in pubs, bars or even on the tube. But I seem to have convinced myself that one cannot find dates in pubs, bars or on tubes. I even made myself believe that I only want to have a good time with my mates when I go out and that I can't be bothered playing magic tricks to chat up girls.

I wish that everything was different. I wish that people who go to pubs and bars would not pretend that they only want to have a good time with their mates. I wish that they wouldn't put so much effort into acting as if they can no longer be amused by magic tricks.

In big cities like London, millions of singletons tell themselves every day that they are happy with being single. That we just want to have fun. We browse our dating apps but ignore that, amid all the pictures and the lyrical flights of imagination, we cannot check-box chemistry, or the level of connection two people could share.

I grab my jacket, and though Carla hasn't spoken a word, she follows me to the door. Just before I walk out, she touches my arm and says, "Thanks for not lying to me."

4

While I sit on the tube, making my way back to Ealing, a man with a guitar walks in. He has long, greasy hair and is shabbily dressed. He unzips his guitar from its black bag and starts test-playing his harmonica. There are only six people in the compartment, and some of the other passengers tautly look away.

The man starts singing Gerry Rafferty's 'Baker Street'.

At first, I don't listen, but I start paying more attention when I pick up some of the words.

'Another year, and then you'll be happy,' the man sings. 'Just one more year, and then you'll be happy. But you're crying, you're crying now.'

I am shocked. Wasn't that what I have been thinking all this time ... —one more year in London? One more year of saving money so I can finally leave? I have done that for the last four years, and in the meantime, I was crying.

By the time I realise that this message is for me, the man has finished the song and makes his way to the few passengers to start begging for money. When he stands in front of me, I ask him if he can sing it again. This puzzles him, and a few of the other passengers look up and uneasily stare at me.

"Please," I say, "I will give you twenty pounds."

"You're fucking on," he replies and immediately apologises for swearing. He pulls out his guitar and starts singing the song for a second time.

I listen closely. There is no uncertainty: this message is intended for me. The man, dressed in ragged clothes, waves his guitar in front of me, and I try to soak up the significance of his words. 'This city desert makes you feel so cold,' he sings, 'It's got so many people, but it's got no soul, and it's taking you so long, to find out you were wrong when you thought it held everything.'

He doesn't look at any of the other passengers, which makes his message even more personal. I shiver. The man must surely see the tears in my eyes. There is no denying it. I have been telling myself that this city holds everything, but I have never been so lonely in my life, and though it is a desert, it makes me feel cold.

But there is hope, the song promises. It tells me that when I wake up, there will be a new morning. The sun will be shining, and I will be going home.

I cannot believe it, I have finally woken up.

5

It is getting closer towards the end of summer, and things are moving fast.

Half a year after the tube-busker sang Gerry Rafferty's 'Baker Street', Richard, Adele, and their little kid leave the UK. He makes his phone call from the airport and files for bankruptcy.

Barely a week later, Celine returns from Zurich and says her client has offered her a job. She will be doing what she was doing before, but she will work directly for them instead of being outsourced. She half-heartedly laughs when she tells us there will be no more flying up and down.

As it didn't work out between her and her tube guy, she feels she is ready for a change and ready to leave London. Even though she still needs to work her notice, her company has agreed she can go a month earlier. This means she will be moving out by the end of November.

I hate to see her go. I feel sad, but I have no words on offer that may stop her from leaving.

Around mid-October (five weeks after Celine has told us she will be moving out and six weeks after Richard has left), Brett phones me from his office and says we need to talk. When, in the evening, he arrives at the flat, he has brought two Domino's pizzas for the occasion. It makes me realise it is serious.

"You know," he hesitantly starts while ripping the barbecue-sauced pizza into slices, "things have been going really great between Julia and me."

"I noticed," I laugh. "I hardly see you anymore."

"That's actually what we need to talk about," he sighs and pauses. He takes a couple of breaths. Then he says, "Julia was wondering if it would be a good idea for the two of us to move in together, and I guess I would like to hear your opinion."

"But the two of us have already moved in together," I joke.

He nervously laughs and says, "You know what I mean."

"What are you trying to tell me?" I ask, "Are you breaking up with me?"

"You know it's not like that, baby," he replies.

"Don't give me the 'it's-not-you—it's-me' bullshit," I say while acting hurt. "Fine, leave me. See if I care."

He waits for a moment and then asks, "So what do you think?"

I bite a big chunk of my pizza. Chewing it stops me from being able to speak. He waits patiently. Eventually, I reply, "I think it's a good idea. You're great together and living in the same flat will show if you're completely compatible. But there's one thing that jumps to mind, and that is: what about the 'South Africa factor'? With her being English and all, are you still planning to move back?"

"Definitely," he says. "Julia and I have talked about it, and she's more than keen. We're planning to pack up in a year, and I guess that the sooner we move in together, the sooner we can spot the cracks. That is if there are any."

"When are you planning to move out of the Ealing house?" I ask.

"With Celine leaving in November, I think the end of the year is good timing."

We eat our pizza, and the only sound that fills the room is us chomping on sliced crusts.

What now, I think? All this time, I have been telling myself that I need to leave this flat, that I need to leave London and the United Kingdom, but I have been unable to make the decision. But now, with Richard gone and Celine and Brett leaving, there is nothing left for me.

Is this perhaps providence taking charge? Am I being forced out like some lazy couch potato who would otherwise not get up by himself? There I was, going on and on about how I want to leave, but I don't bloody jump until I am finally pushed off the cliff. Am I now the victim, or should I embrace it as a gift—as a helping hand?

I am scared. I am not ready to leave. Something is holding me back, and I don't know what. I tell myself that I need more time to save more money, but on the other hand, it could simply be fear paralysing me. I am worried about replacing the known with the unknown. No matter how I dislike the known.

From that moment on, I tumble into indecisiveness. It is almost as if I expect providence (which has forced me out of my lazy couch-potato stance) to clean up the mess it has created in the first place. If it tells me to leave the Ealing house, it should at least present me with a clear and open direction that I can embark upon.

I am waiting for that.

And I wait.

October comes to an end, and so does November. Celine moves out, and we all cry while saying our goodbyes. We promise each other to write, phone and visit.

By the time it is mid-December, I am still waiting. That same providence fails to offer me a solution to my desolation.

Brett urges me to make a decision. He says I could stay in the house, but I have only a couple of days to decide as they need to put it on the market and find a tenant.

I don't want new flatmates. On top of that, paying rent for a three-bedroom house would interfere with my saving plan. So, after months of dithering around, I finally make my first decision. I let Brett know I won't be staying in Ealing any longer.

Closer to the end of December, Brett flies to South Africa to visit his family, and I drive to Belgium to spend Christmas and New Year with my mum. The only action I take is walking. I walk for miles and miles. I walk through the immense forests surrounding the village I grew up in. I walk over the heath-covered moorlands, and I walk through winter's frosty weather.

By the time January arrives, I am still unclear about my next steps. Only after an English colleague asks to meet up, the situation dawns on me: I am not in London and can't stay at my mum's place forever. I need to go back to the UK.

But there I am, homeless. Providence has done squat-all to help me out of this predicament, and I am irritated. The psychic made her predictions, and the hobo sang his Baker Street, but no one told me what to do next. I am left on my bloody own!

I finally phone Brett and ask him if his rental department can find me a place to live. A couple of days later, he comes up with two options: one flat entirely for me or another one I will have to share with its Jamaican owner. The latter has the advantage that the lease is on a month-to-month basis. It gives me the freedom to move out whenever I want.

I finally drive back to the UK and learn that the Jamaican owner is a girl. She is thirty-something, twice my size, not pretty at all, and completely sticks to herself. She is friendly, though disappears into her room every day after work, where she stays the entire evening. We hardly talk.

I miss the tripod.

Brett and I phone each other regularly, and Celine let me know that things are going well in Switzerland. We write wall messages on Facebook, but nothing feels the same any longer. I can't cook my dinners together with them, I can't flirt with Celine, and I can't chat to Brett in the morning when he sits on the toilet while leaving the door open. There is no curling-up on the sofa, no watching Netflix and no Italian restaurants on Wednesday evenings.

I have become what I was most scared of ... —... lonely.

Everything depresses me: the English weather, my flatmate's aloofness and the fact that my life endlessly seems to be going around in circles. It feels like I am trapped in space, and I can't get out. I have even forgotten to cancel my subscription on the dating app, and every month it deducts its fee from my bank account. I don't have the energy to go to the settings and correct it. I don't have the energy to check profiles from women over their fifty's or sixty's who wink from Canada, Columbia or Ukraine. A few messages from some pretty girls pop up every now and then, but I can't be bothered. I don't even read them, and I don't browse through their pictures. Instead, I delete them the moment they come in.

I haven't felt this low for ages. I have sunken so deep that I don't know how to get out.

I force myself to phone Celine in Zurich, but the only thing I do is moan about trivial things. She listens, and at the end of our conversation, she tells me that she misses me. I tell her the same. It only makes me feel worse.

I phone Richard in South Africa and Brett in Twickenham. They both tell me how wonderful life is and how excellent their decisions worked out for them. That makes me feel even worse.

There is no one else left to talk to.

It is as if a leather belt has tightened itself around my chest. I can't breathe. I am suffocating from my own indecisiveness. I wake up at night: hyperventilating, drenched with sweat and gasping for air. I know that I can't go on like this and that I need to do something. I make attempts to bend my mind into thinking positive thoughts, but I cannot hold on to them. I try to exhaust my body to awaken my soul and go on lengthy cycle trips. At times I disappear for over five or six hours per day. My usual route leads me over Staines and into the English countryside, though most of the times, I merely do laps around Richmond Park. It makes me feel better that same day, but my inner darkness quickly swallows it up by the time the evening arrives.

Where is the beggar on the tube who sang me a promise for change? I need to cash in on the twenty pounds I gave him. I cannot live like this! I cannot cry for yet another year. I need to wake up and find my sun. But where must I look?

6

One day, while chatting over WhatsApp, Celine tells me that her brother has quit his job and left to cycle from Argentina to Alaska.

It feels to me that it is all uphill as he needs to start from the bottom of the globe. But at the same time, I think: I could do this. I should take a year off or even resign and cycle from the north of Norway all the way—downhill—to Cape Town in South Africa.

The more I think about it, the more excited I become. I create an Excel spreadsheet on my computer. In one column, I take note of the things I already have: my bike, a rainproof jacket, a sleeping bag, back-wheel panniers, bike repair tools, thermal clothing, shoes, sunglasses, my e-reader and so on. Next to it, I write down the things I still need to buy: new tires, a tent, waterproof trousers, better panniers, a better D-lock, cooking pots, a sleeping mattress, a lightweight notebook, sandals, e-books from the internet and so on.

I estimate how much money I would need and check my bank account to see how much is already there and how many months I still have to save. I return to the list of things I need and delete the new tires, the waterproof trousers, the better panniers and even a better D-lock. I can do without them, I tell myself. I can travel light and buy cheap clothes along the way—the shorter I can make my stay in London, the better.

I google the distance from the North Cape in Norway to Cape Town in South Africa. Cycling over Gibraltar and entering Africa through Morocco is shorter than taking the longer route across the Middle East. After I've received my bonus in April, I can go. In that way, I can cycle through Scandinavia during spring and summer to leave Europe and enter Africa by the end of autumn. I don't need to stay another year to save more money. I will worry about the future when the future arrives.

I phone Richard and Brett and ask them for their opinion. They both think I am mad. I am sure Brett's dad will only say that this is another example of my addiction to pain, so I decide not to call him.

This plan lifts me up. I cycle even more, following the route over Staines and stay away for seven or even eight hours per day.

When I am lazy, I merely do laps around Richmond Park. Even then, I aim to clock forty kilometres a day during the week and around a hundred per day during the weekends.

I feel much better and try to add to my positive spirit by finding extra redemption in work. I fly to China's Shanghai for a two-week seminar and, after that, to Kenya's Nairobi. I visit Beijing and Mombasa in my own spare time. Almost immediately after I've returned to the UK, I leave for California in the USA.

I have been away from London for about six weeks. When I finally arrive back at the flat in Osterley, my Jamaican landlord complains that I haven't cleaned for over a month. "It was your turn, and I did it instead," she moans.

That Saturday afternoon, I feel misery sucking me back into emptiness. The leather belt is tightening its grip around my chest.

I know I need to fight this. I can't sit here and wait for the darkness to surround me again.

I quickly change into my cycle gear, grab my bike in the hallway and leave the house. I cycle six kilometres from Osterley and enter Richmond Park from Richmond Hill into Sawyer's Hill. I do a full lap around the park (eleven and a half kilometres), but I feel lazy and lethargic.

Winter is on the verge of redecorating towards spring, and it is getting warmer.

I stop for a drink close to the end of Queen's Road. I lean my bike against one of the benches, sit down and look at the people running, cycling, or simply having a relaxing stroll with friends or family.

It is pleasant to sit on a bench and watch people.

But then I notice two girls and a guy arriving on their mountain bikes. They stop, park their bicycles against a bench a couple of meters farther and sit down.

One of the girls is quite pretty, but it is not her that I am fascinated with. Instead, the guy draws my attention as his sturdy bike is mounted with four fully loaded panniers. Two of them hang next to his back wheel and the other two next to his front wheel.

The guy seems to have a good-natured, gentle face, but he doesn't look like a die-hard cyclist. Still, judging from the way his bike is set up, he appears to be either on some long-distance cycling trip or preparing for one. The coincidence of me meeting him here while my mind has been overloaded with planning my Norway-Africa journey is vast. For some weird reason, I feel I want to connect this to my Baker Street's tube message.

While I walk towards the guy and the two girls, I feel nervous and excited at the same time. He gives me a warm, friendly smile when I ask him why he is carrying panniers on his bike. He opens his mouth to reply, but the nice-looking girl is faster.

"He's getting ready to cycle from London to Budapest," she responds.

"That's amazing," I say and ask him when he will be leaving.

"Next week," the girl replies.

"Are the three of you going?"

"No," the guy finally says, seemingly annoyed with his friend answering for him. He introduces himself as Anthony. "No, these two are not," he says, "but I will be teaming up with another guy and a girl in Harwich before we take the ferry to Hook of Holland, close to Rotterdam. The plan is to first follow the Rhine and, after that, the Danube."

"I'm impressed," I say and tell him that I once cycled from London to my mum's in Belgium. Brett and I took the ferry from Calais to Dunkerque in France. We completed the four-hundred and fifty kilometres in four days.

"I'm actually busy planning a trip from Norway to South Africa," I add.

He looks surprised, though this information lures both of us into a technical conversation about advantages or disadvantages around tyre-types, ceramic wheels, aluminium or alloy frames, front suspension, pannier brands, how many spare parts to take and whether to carry additional spokes or not.

I am about to wish him good luck with his adventure and cycle another lap around the park when he suddenly asks, "Why don't you join us?"

I am taken aback and hesitate before I answer. "I certainly would like to, but—"

"—But what?" he laughs.

"Well, for one, there is my job, and secondly, you and your friends have been planning this for weeks, if not months, and I certainly don't want to impose."

"You're not imposing at all. And yes, I've been planning this for a while, but simply because I like it. Aside from that, I've only met the others once."

I think about it a little longer. "I can't, really," I eventually sigh. "I wish I could, though."

"Well, think about it," he replies. "We take the ferry this coming Sunday, so you still have a couple of days to make up your mind."

I am about to leave and take my bicycle to do one more lap around the park and then go home.

Then the girl says, "I'll give you my email address in case you decide to cycle with Anthony to Budapest. I'll make sure he gets it." She smiles and writes it down on a small piece of paper.

I start my last lap, thinking that I can't possibly go. The main issue is my job, but aside from this, I'm not sure what it would be like to team up with a guy I just met and another couple who he's only seen once.

After four kilometres, I seem to change my mind. What if, I think? What if I do go? It doesn't have to be all the way to Budapest. I could cycle with them as far as Cologne in Germany. There, I could simply make a right turn to my mum's place, which is not far from the Dutch-German-Belgian border. But then, of course, there is still my job.

By the time I have clocked eight kilometres on my speedometer, I wonder what distances we have to cover. From London to Harwich should be around a hundred and sixty kilometres. From Hook of Holland to Cologne is more or less three-hundred kilometres. And finally, from Cologne to my mum's place would be around a hundred and forty. Anthony didn't look like he was planning to break any world records, but if the couple, who's joining us, is not too slow, I could be at my mum's in about seven or eight days.

Hang on; did I just say 'us'?

324

Different schemes enter my mind. I could reply to emails from my phone or, at worst, link it to my laptop and sneakily pretend I am sitting in front of my computer at home. If I regularly stop and answer emails and phone calls, no one would notice. It would be deceitful, but I could fake work for a week.

I am excited and start cycling faster. I am on Sawyer's Hill and have only one kilometre to go before I reach the place where I left Anthony and the two girls.

By the time I arrive, I have done the eleven-point-five kilometres in seventeen minutes, but they are no longer there. I return to my flat in Osterley and write the girl an email. I ask her if she can let Anthony know that I am keen to join.

In the early evening, I receive a reply. She tells me that she has forwarded it to his address.

And then I wait.

7

Sunday comes and goes. So does Monday and Tuesday. By the time it is Wednesday, I am becoming worried. How stupid was I to think that Anthony's offer was genuine—that he was actually inviting me on their cycle trip and not merely making polite conversation. Would anyone ask a random stranger he'd just met in a park on a trip he'd been planning for months?

No! Of course not.

I am irritated. I'm annoyed with myself for letting him fool me. What did George Bush say again: fool me once—shame on you, and fool me twice ... —shame on you too!

On the other hand, he probably never expected me to say yes.

But then, when Wednesday evening arrives, a message from Anthony appears in my inbox. He apologises for his late reply, though he explains that he first wanted to confirm it with the others. 'In Harwich, there is a pub with a small campsite,' I read, 'and we'll meet you there Sunday evening.'

Friday, I double-check my bike and pack my two panniers. I reckon that a hundred and sixty kilometres on a mountain bike loaded with twenty-five kilograms of luggage will take me two days.

Saturday early morning, I start cycling. It doesn't rain, but it pours and buckets of water gush over me. After an hour of cycling, I am thoroughly saturated.

"Mental note to myself," I say out loud, "add a new waterproof jacket and re-add rain trousers to the Norway-Africa Excell list."

By the time it is five in the afternoon, I knock on the door of a tiny Bed-and-Breakfast in Maldon and hang all my clothes out to dry. In the morning, everything is still wet. I am about thirty-five kilometres away from our meeting point, but it rains relentlessly.

Early afternoon, I arrive in Harwich. I prefer not to spend the night in a soaked tent while wearing damp clothes, and for a second time, I check into a Bed-and-Breakfast.

After a warm shower, I climb back on my bicycle. I quickly find the pub with the tiny campsite, but there is no one there. I return to my room, wait a couple of hours and cycle back to the campsite.

Still no-one.

Only after my third visit, I see, from a distance, three people erecting their tents. When I get closer, I recognise Anthony.

He waves and laughs. "I guess you've had your fair share of rain."

"Yes," I sigh. "That's why I've checked into a B&B. All my stuff got soaked."

The other guy introduces himself as Colin. He looks rough in an unpolished kind of way. He carries a heavy 'Scouse' accent typical for people who live in and around Liverpool. More than once, I have to ask him to repeat himself, which is embarrassing for me as I am sure it is for him.

"You must be the Richmond Park guy," he mumbles, and again I can barely understand him.

After that, I walk to the girl to greet her. She is busy reading her tent's instruction booklet while standing next to a pile of aluminium poles, fly-sheet and ropes. I see her picking up a stake, studying the booklet and putting it back. She is clearly struggling to work out what the required steps are in pitching a tent.

When she sees me, she smiles amicably, shakes my hand and tells me her name is Jenny.

I immediately like her. She is pretty, tall, slim and has shoulder-length brown-blondish hair. For a moment, I contemplate lending a hand, but the other guys might think that I am merely trying to impress her. Instead, I turn around and talk to Anthony.

Colin and Jenny are surely not a couple, I think. She wouldn't be pitching her own tent if they were.

That evening, we have a meal in the local pub, and one of the regulars makes it his mission to try and guess where our different accents come from. Without hesitation, he identifies Colin's and also Anthony's. He is uncertain about mine. He reckons it to be a mixture of South African with something else, but he can't distinguish where that 'something else is from.

When he finally concentrates on Jenny's, he listens long and hard. "I'm not sure," he eventually says. "Your accent is clearly English. And you might have been living in London for quite a while, but there's an underlying tone that makes me think you were born in—" he hesitates and finally asks, "—in New Zealand perhaps?"

"Australia," she smiles.

8

At night, while I lie in my bed, I'm trying hard not to let what I heard in the pub sum up into something ludicrous. I make an effort to keep the faintly whispering voice inside my head quiet. Still, the moment I let myself be distracted, it murmurs, 'hang on: slender and tall with brown-blondish hair and linked to Australia!'

No, I command myself.

No, no, no.

Even if there is a link, I will not listen. I have been bitten too many times. Over and over, I managed to tell myself that quite a few of the girls I'd met were in a way tall, even when they stared me in the belly button while standing up. I convinced myself that they were slender in a miss-elephant-contest kind of way. And I swore that their hair, although black now, was most likely brown-blondish when they were about three years old. At one stage, I even made myself believe that everyone coming from anywhere in the world below London had an indirect link with the word 'Australia'. It is, after all, derived from the Latin *australis*, meaning … —'The south'.

It is time for me to stop tricking myself into accepting some fictitious, candle-wax twaddle that has been haunting me for far too long. Keep your feet on the ground, I remind myself. There is no higher cause or cryptic meaning. Everything is pure coincidence.

'Coincidence?' the voice asks. 'Let's talk about that for a moment. Didn't the psychic say that you would meet her while travelling the way you like to travel? You like to cycle, and isn't that the way you met Anthony? What about the singer in the tube or Celine telling you her brother is cycling the America's or all the other little things that lead you here?'

No! Absolutely not, nothing, zero! I don't want to listen to it. I can't afford to.

But the following day, on the ferry, Jenny and I tie our bikes together to an iron pole, and I find some deeper meaning in that. In the lounge, she comes and sits next to me, and I feel my heart accelerating. I can't believe how pretty she is. When she smiles, her face brightens, and so does everything around her; the clouds disappear, birds come out and chirp. It even stops raining. Every time she looks at me, I sweat and choke and cannot think. Her hair is half-long and curls towards her neck. She looks sophisticated, intelligent. She is tall and lean, slender and fit. She is very athletically built, with the most beautiful backside I've seen in a long time. It makes me want to pull in my stomach muscles. It annoys me that Brett and I stopped going to the gym because now all hope (that I will ever be able to impress her) is lost.

I like her. I like her a lot.

But I mustn't allow myself to get carried away by those silly predictions. If it is true that life is about learning lessons, I have learned squat-all.

It takes the ferry seven and a half hours to reach Hook of Holland, and even the Netherlands are tormented with rain. We don't cycle too far that day and pitch our tents at a campsite southeast of Rotterdam. Jenny gets her instruction booklet out, but this time I decide to help her.

"I've actually never seen anyone needing a manual to build a tent," I joke.

She points at the cheap and shoddy one I bought for next to nothing at Halfords' and strikes back: "We'll see who has the last laugh tomorrow morning when I'm still dry, and you're soaking wet."

9

That morning, while rain bashes against my tent's fly-sheet, I have my first phone conference. I have connected my phone to my laptop; I open the Zoom app but disable my camera. While on the call, I simultaneously check my emails to see if the others sent documents through.

But it doesn't feel relaxing. I am aware of all the noises surrounding me; the rain against my tent, the voices of fellow campers, the children yelling and laughing while splashing each other wet in the puddles of water. I am worried that either Colin, Anthony or Jenny will call out my name to ask me where I am and that I am forced to yell back: 'I'm here in my tent!'

An hour later, the phone conference ends and my colleagues say their goodbyes. I am relieved I've made it this far, but then suddenly my phone rings: It is Josue!

"Are you okay?" he immediately asks when I answer. There is no point in greeting each other as we have just spent an hour on Zoom.

I am nervous. Is it possible that he suspects something?

"Yes," I wearily answer. "Why?"

"You sounded different," he says: "you were very quiet. I thought that something might be bothering you. Anyhow," he sighs and then he gives me a list of things to do. Shortly after the call, my inbox shows his FYIs, including attachments with Excel sheets and reports for me to go through.

I spend the next hour and forty-five minutes in my tent working and pretending to be in some UK office. I repeatedly encourage Colin, Anthony and Jenny to start cycling without me and assure them that I will catch up. Still, all three patiently wait until I finish work, pack my laptop, fold my tent and mount my bike.

Around eleven in the morning, we eventually leave the campsite and follow the Rhine even though it is not always clear which small rivers can claim this mighty name. During the rest of the day, I regularly have to stop to answer my phone and return missed calls. The next few days are not that much different. While we cycle through IJselstein and continue over Arnhem into the direction of Germany's Duisburg, I stop in cosy Dutch café's to catch up on work and write or reply to emails.

Colin and Anthony have discovered their mutual interest in World War II relics. They halt at every little village which has something on display from that era and are drawn to the old military tanks that often embellish a city centre. They let themselves be lured into the most insignificant museums, which are seldom larger than the size of a small living room. Every old black-and-white picture, every newspaper article and every rifle, bullet, helmet, jacket, grenade or even combat boots suffers their meticulous scrutiny.

Jenny and I can't be bothered. At first, we politely tagged along, but now we spend our time sitting on park benches or drinking coffee in the many café's while waiting for them to return. This allows me to get to know her a little bit better. However, I constantly remind myself not to make assumptions and get carried away.

Jenny worked in corporate finance but decided to take a career break. She lived a few months in France, where she took a language course. She spent long days and evenings meditating and doing yoga in an ashram in the Bahamas to qualify as a yoga teacher.

"This cycle trip is part of that extended sabbatical," she tells me, "but I have to get myself into the 'financial' market again or else they'll forget about me."

I feel relaxed around her. In the early evenings, after we've pitched our tents, we stroll along the riverside and just talk. At times, we walk so closely to each other that our arms touch. It would be easy for me to simply grab her hand and walk as if we've been together for years.

But I am nervous.

What if she rejects me? The 'I-don't-give-a-fuck'-attitude doesn't work when you like the girl (when you actually give a fuck). Then everything becomes loaded. You start to worry. You grow tense and slip up. The hunter turns into some feeble prey, and whatever you do to impress her will only push her further and further away.

Even if she does like me, I can't allow myself to do this. We will reach Cologne in a couple of days, and that is where I will leave her. I can't let myself think anything else. I can't get distracted. Not this time; I cannot stay any longer in London and need to keep that in mind.

"What do you think about London?" I ask her.

"I have been living there for twelve years. What further is there to think?"

"Do you like it?"

"I do," but she hesitates before she continues. "I'm actually trying to decide whether I will stay in the UK or move back to Australia. I hope that this cycle trip will help me make up my mind."

"And, is it helping?"

"Not really," she sighs. "The one day, when it's all sunny and bright, I feel like staying, but on other days when the weather is miserable, I want to leave."

"It's the same with me," I admit. "I don't like it in London. It's probably weather-related. For the last four years, I've been telling myself that I need to move back to South Africa. Or some other warm climate country," I quickly add. "I've been checking out other European cities like Narbonne-Plage in the south of France, Lisbon and even Barcelona."

"I like the south of France," she injects and says that she wouldn't mind living there.

When on the road, I often cycle behind her. She's got the cutest backside, which looks extra adorable in her tight latex cycle shorts. When there is a strong head-wind, I tell her to cycle behind me to save her energy. We cycle as a team and fast— faster than Colin and Anthony. On many occasions, we even leave them behind.

"You know what he plans to do?" Anthony asks Jenny one day while pointing at me. "He wants to cycle all the way from Norway to Africa."

"Is that so," she requests and looks surprised.

I nod.

"Just by yourself?"

"That's the plan," I casually reply, "but you can always join me."

She gives me a warm smile and says: "Let me think about it."

10

"Have you ever heard of Reiki healing?" Jenny asks one evening when we stroll along the riverside. "I took a course some years ago," she lets me know and explains that it is a spiritual practice developed by a Japanese Buddhist. It focuses mainly on stress reduction, relaxation and healing by transferring energy through the palms of one's hands.

I tell her that I have heard of it.

"Do you believe it works?" she wants to know.

I shrug my shoulders. "Perhaps it does, but more in the way placebos work."

"Let me try it on you," she suggests and tells me that she managed to help a friend get rid of his back issues.

She stands behind me and floats her right hand over my back. She doesn't touch me, but I can feel the warmth it conveys. More than the Reiki itself, I want her to come closer and hold me. I want to turn around and kiss her, but I can't allow myself to get sidetracked. I will head for Belgium the day after tomorrow, and starting something now will only make things complicated. After she has finished her Budapest trip, I could give her a call, and we could meet up in Covent Garden. I can take her to my favourite little French bistro not too far from the tube station. We could drink a coffee or a glass of wine and even have a meal, but tonight I need to keep my feet on the ground.

The next day, while still following the Rhine, we cross the Dutch-German border and cycle farther towards Duisburg.

Before the rain sets in, we pitch our tents in Meerbusch, and the four of us seek refuge in a rustic German beer house.

Colin takes a seat on my left while Anthony and Jenny sit opposite us. We order food and four large German wheat Weißbiers.

While Colin is quiet and reserved (abiding by the typical stereotype of a northerner), Anthony, on the other hand, adequately compensates for his new friend's silence. He talks for two and keeps mentioning the many different girls who seemingly form a big part of his life.

After our food arrives, we ask the waitress to bring another four beers.

My muscles ache. I have been pushing myself more than usual and probably only to impress Jenny. While I stretch my legs, I accidentally touch hers, but she doesn't move away. For a moment, I am inclined to shift a little more to the right and break contact, but I decide to leave them where they are and wait for her to react.

She doesn't do anything, and our legs keep touching. It's almost childish and silly in ways, but I push mine slightly harder against hers, and she pushes back. I look at her, stare into her eyes, and she warmly smiles back. I stretch my other leg, and so does she. With our feet, we embrace under the table and with our eyes, we flirt.

I struggle to follow the conversation between Colin and Anthony. Both Jenny and I try hard to pretend towards the others that nothing is going on, but suddenly, Colin lifts up the table cloth and quickly peeks underneath. He doesn't say anything and continues talking to Anthony as if he hasn't noticed our entangled legs.

When we leave the beer house, it is still raining. Colin and Anthony hastily march to their tents, but I linger and quasi indifferently wait for Jenny to catch up. When I feel her hand touching my arm, I stop. Her body leans closer to mine, and she gives me a tender kiss on my neck.

"Meet me at the washing area after you've showered," she whispers and starts walking towards her tent.

While the downpour drums onto the tin roof, I wait for her under a shelter close to the washing area. Dim light reflects in the rain that sheets down from the dark and cloud-covered skies. I am not sure what to expect and even feel nervous. Then I see her running towards the washing area (all careful not to slip and fall in the mud), and my concerns disappear. She looks adorable. The rain has glued her brown-blond hair against her cheeks. Droplets of waters skid over her face towards her chin and fall onto her rain jacket.

Without hesitation, without saying anything, she walks up to me, and we kiss. We both laugh when we stop for a brief moment, and then we kiss again.

I hold her in my arms and press her body close to mine. The rain on her jacket drenches my t-shirt, but I don't care. A harsh voice inside my head says, 'You fool, I thought you were going to wait until Covent Garden,' but I ignore it.

11

While we cycle, Jenny and I stay close together. We deliberately loiter and fall behind or cycle ahead so we can briefly touch or hurriedly kiss before the guys have caught up. More than ever, we are pleased with their interest in war stuff. Every German village offers its fair share of military tanks and tiny museums. During those moments, we hold hands, talk, and kiss as if we were teenagers.

I still remind myself that I should take it slow. I am not ready to fall and to get hurt. I vehemently try to push any thoughts of predictions out of my head because I can't allow myself to get carried away.

The day before we reach Cologne, it rains relentlessly. By the time the evening falls, everything is wet; our jackets, clothes, tents, and even sleeping bags. All of us agree that it is impossible to camp under these conditions.

I am the only one who speaks German, so I translate to the others what the friendly lady at a Bed-and-Breakfast tells us. Except for the part where she explains that she had only one twin room left. The other one is a double.

I let the lady know that this is perfect and hand the keys for the twin room to Colin and Anthony while I keep the double one for Jenny and myself.

The others haven't noticed anything. When Colin wants to be sure that he and Anthony will be sleeping in separate beds, I can happily confirm this to be the case.

Jenny giggles when she sees the double bed. "You are very sneaky," she says.

We don't waste time. We kiss and wrestle each other onto the bed. Our clothes are ripped off in no time, and we play-fight and laugh like two adolescents on their first night out. It all feels so natural: as if I've known her all of my life.

We don't rush to put our clothes back on. It doesn't feel awkward in any way. Instead, it feels comfortable. We walk around naked as if we have nothing to hide and have been married for twenty years.

After we've showered, we still don't get dressed and lay on the bed while holding each other tightly. I feel close to her. She is a friend and at the same time already so much more than that.

Then there is a knock on the door. Faintly voiced, I yell that I will be right there. Jenny grabs her clothes and disappears towards the shower. I dive into my shorts and t-shirt.

When I finally open the door, I see Colin and Anthony. They want to know where we'll be having dinner tonight. I let them in and watch their surprised look when they realise Jenny and I sleep in a double bed. The sheets are still messed up, and I clumsily kick Jenny's pink underpants under the bed.

I am sweating and notice how Anthony and Colin exchange looks. I am pretty sure I hear them suppressing a chuckle. However, they pretend they haven't seen anything. I am grateful for that.

Over the following days, Jenny and I are careful not to display our affection for each other too publicly, but we don't try to hide it either.

On Friday, when we finally arrive at a campsite six kilometres from Cologne's city centre, we put both our tents up. But only use Jenny's for our bags and mine to sleep in.

Today, we visit Cologne's Dom and tomorrow, I will cycle my remaining hundred and forty kilometres to my mum's place.

I dread to leave her. I have been exhausting my mind with weighing up potential scenario's that all include me staying longer. Could I pretend for another week that I am sitting in front of a computer in a company's office?

But Sunday morning, I load my bags onto my bicycle. Jenny and I kiss, and before we say goodbye, she says: "I've been thinking about your Norway-South Africa cycle trip, and you might have found yourself a teammate."

12

"What are the chances of anything like that happening?" Brett gasps when we meet for lunch close to his office in Ealing. "I mean: even when we leave out the fact that your psychic predicted the whole Australia factor. There's still the fluke that you met that guy in Richmond Park, that he invited you and on top of it all: that you went! If you ask me: that is pretty impossible."

"It doesn't have to mean anything," I object.

"Bullshit!' he reacts. "If this doesn't mean anything, then nothing does."

"I'm just trying to pace myself. I can't let this go to my head."

"But what if it is all meant to be?" he asks. "What if she is 'the one'? What if, after all these years in London, you've finally met her? What are you going to do then? Are you leaving London or are you moving to Australia? And what about South Africa?"

"Stop this," I tell him, "don't ask all those questions. As far as I'm concerned, Jenny and I had a good time in Holland and Germany. When she finishes her Budapest trip, we might even meet up somewhere in London, and only if we do, we'll decide then what the next steps are. Perhaps I won't hear from her ever again."

"Bullshit again!" he says.

What if Brett is right, I ask myself after I climb on my bike and cycle back to Osterley. What if this is all meant to be? I certainly like her but is it too soon to say something as trivial as that. After all, this might just be another one of those silly infatuations. I need to remind myself that 'love-at-first-sight' is often confused with 'lust-at-first-sight'. Or even worse: a fabrication of your own mind.

When you see someone you like, you most likely start creating an image that is not really there. You want her to be a little bit more like this and a little bit less than that. So you add characteristic simply because you hope they will be there. You tie all the good things together and leave all else out, and before you know it, a completely different person is standing in front of you. You have actively wishfully thought her into existence and allowed yourself to fall in love with an illusion. This is where things go wrong; you've actually wilfully made her hands look smaller.

But after some weeks, or worse, after some months, you start asking yourself who that person sitting in front of you is. How can she have changed so much in such a short time? When the drug of infatuation wears down, you will start seeing her hands' real size. That is the actual explanation for the big-hand syndrome.

But what if it is her, I wonder. What if Jenny is predicted by this psychic in South Africa?

Hold on for a moment. Let me ask myself one question first: 'what exactly was predicted'?

13

I open my computer and browse to a folder I named 'Fortune_Telling_RSA'. Every time I recorded one of the psychic's sessions, I dragged it into that folder. The last file even shows the phone conversation I had with the psychic after Caitlin and I'd broken up.

I double click the file and start listening to it. I fast-forward through the boring parts, and then I hear myself ask, 'What about the girl? Has anything changed there?'

I listen carefully. 'Very toned, slim, tall and blondish hair,' I hear the psychic say.

Then it's my voice again: 'Any idea when I'll meet her because I'm running out of flipping petrol?'

The psychic laughs but says it shouldn't be much longer.

I inattentively hear myself asking her a question about dog years and geological time frames. Then I remember that during one of our sessions, when I asked her about timings, she'd made some reference to a story in the bible. I can't remember what exactly she'd said, and if I want to find it, I'll have to listen to all the files in that folder. That could take hours!

I decide to do it.

I patiently playback the recording. While I do, I learn that some predictions are incredibly accurate, while others never happened.

When I lived in South Africa, I worked on a project that (for many reasons) never materialised. On one of the recordings, I hear the psychic say that a guy named Ronald appears to be playing some double game. A Ronald worked in my team, and later I found out that he tried to cut himself a deal with the sellers without me knowing about it. It reminds me of how correct the psychic can be.

The folder also includes a file that doesn't have a name. I click it open and immediately realise it is Caitlin's session. During her session, she had used my phone to record it. I remember her saying that everything the psychic had said was nonsense. I remember dragging the file onto my laptop, but I never listened to it.

I fast-forward through the usual greetings, and then I hear the psychic ask if Caitlin ever had an abortion.

She answers, 'Yes'.

I never knew this.

Other things come up as well. The psychic tells her that she sees a big building that reminds her of a university and asks if she is perhaps studying or doing research. Caitlin lies and says she isn't. The psychic asks if she is a doctor, which is funny as Caitlin often claims she is while she hasn't even finished her PhD. 'No,' Caitlin replies.

'Strange,' I hear the psychic reply, 'perhaps you will become one someday.'

It feels weird listening to this. It is almost as if I am eavesdropping on something I am not supposed to hear. It is as if I have opened her diary and sneakily started reading it. I should not be listening to this, but I can't stop myself. It is strange to hear her voice again, though it only reminds me of how terrible our relationship was.

While the recording plays through the tiny speakers on my desk, my mind slowly drifts towards memories of Caitlin and me. I hardly listen any longer, but then suddenly, something grabs my attention. I am not sure if I heard it correctly. I rewind the recording and play it again. I hear the psychic hesitate before she asks, 'Was there perhaps a rape in your family?'

Caitlin answers, 'No', but the psychic continues, 'I see a little child, and there was a molestation by someone she was close to, perhaps a friend of the family or a relative.' She is quiet for a while and then asks, 'Could this be you?'

After that, I hear the noise of chair-legs scraping over a tiled floor and Caitlin shouting: 'Stop it. What a load of crap this is!' She sounds upset. I hear her say something about money, and then the recording ends.

I rewind and listen to that last bit again. 'Was there perhaps a rape in your family?' and Caitlin answers, 'No'.

I stop the recording and stare out in front of me. How much of this could be true, I wonder. The psychic was right about a couple of things but was she right about the rape? Could that girl have been Caitlin? It surely would explain a lot. This is the type of baggage that would be too heavy for anyone to carry. Perhaps it clarifies why she has issues with her mother, her father and her brother.

I suddenly feel sorry for her, and I want to write her an email to let her know that I have listened to the tape and that I know. But what if the psychic was wrong?

Move forwards, not backwards, I remind myself. I should simply leave everything the way it is.

While I search through the other files, I mainly press the fast-forward button. Eventually, after a couple of hours, I am rewarded.

'When will I finally get to meet her?' I hear myself ask. 'I don't know,' the psychic sighs, 'I really wish I could give you a date.' And then, there it is: 'Do you know the story of Rachel in the bible?'

Rachel in the bible!?

I decide to google it, and three-million nine-hundred and thirty-thousand results promise to give me more information. I click on the link that takes me to the free Wikipedia encyclopaedia. I've often been warned not to trust its info, but how wrong can it be when it comes to bible stories?

When I start reading, I learn how Jacob, one of the Biblical Patriarchs, falls in love with Rachel when he sees her watering her lamb. He speaks to her father, Laban, and to marry her, Jacob agrees to work for him for seven years. But on the wedding night, the bride is veiled, and Jacob only finds out afterwards that he was tricked. Laban has not given him Rachel but her older sister Leah. Of course, Jacob confronts his deceiving father-in-law, who assures Jacob that he can take Rachel as his wife if he works for him for another seven years.

There are other incidents mentioned. One is about Jacob and his wives fleeing. Another one is about some misunderstanding and how Jacob accidentally cursed Rachel. The online encyclopaedia also says that she initially struggled to give birth, but I don't seek any meaning in them. After all, I have asked a question about timing and not about honesty or even pregnancies.

It is, however, the 'seven years' I concentrate on. Jacob had to wait for Rachel for all this time, and though he got tricked into being with the wrong girl, he was finally able to marry the one he truly loved.

It has been seven years since my first visit to the psychic. Perhaps it is the right time, and maybe I have been tricked into believing that Caitlin (like Leah) was the one.

In a way, some veil had blinded me too, but could this mean that I have finally met my Rachel?

14

My phone rings. It is Jenny. We speak every day, and by doing so, I keep track of their cycling progress. After they left Cologne, they progressed over Bonn, Koblenz and Mainz. They average a steady eighty kilometres per day, and I expect them to be somewhere around Mannheim closer to the weekend.

While we speak, I get an idea. Our German head office is in Mannheim, though I can't claim I know the area well (only 'Suzy' does). Perhaps I could surprise-visit her and pretend towards Josue this trip is work-related.

I don't tell Jenny, but after we end our conversation, I phone Anthony and tell him about my plan. He declares me crazy, though he promises to keep it a surprise. Every now and then, he updates me on where he believes they might spend Saturday night. On Friday morning, I drive the six and a half hours from Osterley to my mum's in Belgium, where I stay the night. Saturday morning, I head for Mannheim.

Anthony lets me know that they'll be pitching their tents at a small campsite in Sankt Leon-Rot, not too far from the French-German border. I estimate that I'll arrive there a little after three in the afternoon.

In the meantime, Jenny and I have been sending each other text messages. In my last one, I write that I am at my mum's place watching TV, but I wish I was there with her. By the time I receive her reply (that she misses me and wish I was there), I arrive at the campsite.

She has her back turned toward me, and I quietly sneak up behind her. With my hands, I hold her eyes closed and ask: "Guess who?"

She jumps up and throws her arms around my neck. "I can't believe this," she cries with laughter. "I only sent that text a minute ago, and now you're here!" She looks at me. "Is it truly you?" she asks and pinches my arm.

"Aiii," I laugh. "You're supposed to pinch yourself if you think you're dreaming, not me!"

"Oops," she says.

I stay the night in her little tent. Being with her feels natural. We lay close in each other's arms and talk.

The following day, I return to the UK with a warm fuzzy feeling of togetherness. It is as if our relationship has become deeper … —more solid. I find it weird to think this as I haven't spent more than ten whole days with her, but it feels like I've known her for months, or perhaps even years.

When I reach the Osterley flat on Monday evening, I have covered a little over two thousand kilometres just to see her. Even Brett thinks I have lost my sanity and doesn't weigh his words when he phones me: "You're barking mad!"

But it's the interest that generates the effort, I think.

15

My Jamaican landlord is hiding in her room again. I have only seen her once since I returned from Germany a week ago. It makes me feel lonelier than I already am, and I miss Jenny. I feel ridiculous admitting this, and a voice inside my head says, 'get a grip, you hardly know her.'

I try to motivate myself to cycle my forty or eighty-kilometre laps in Richmond Park. I often can't be bothered to gear up in cycle clothes, take my bicycle out, and carry it down the stairs, let alone cycle. Just like before, I stay at the flat and seek distraction by browsing Netflix.

Then, almost sneakily, a thought enters my mind. It starts off small but snowballs rapidly, and like a locust plague, it quickly becomes uncontrollable. It forces me to put the TV remote on the table next to me, get up, and walk to my laptop. It compels me to open my Google calendar and look up how many holidays I have left. And, it finally makes me write an email to my boss and ask his permission to take seven days leave. With both weekends added, it means that I can spend an additional eleven days with Jenny.

Might I actually be barking mad?

I surf to Google Maps, and, based on Jenny's, Colin's and Anthony's progress, I try to estimate where they will be in a little over eight days. It should not be too far from Munich, I conclude.

The following day, Josue replies to my request for leave: 'Not a problem,' and asks, 'South Africa again?'

'No,' I write back, 'cycling from Munich to Budapest.'

'Can you ever be normal?' he wants to know.

Jenny is thrilled when I tell her of my plans. "You're not kidding me, are you," she asks. "Tell me you're serious."

She wants to know when, where, for how long and if I will bring a bigger tent this time. We discuss the route the three of them have been following. In a couple of days, they will pass Hohentengen-am-Hochrhein and will be well on their way to Lake Constance, which glues Germany, Switzerland and Austria together.

Though the Rhine is believed to source at Tomasee in Switzerland, Jenny, Colin and Anthony will turn into a south-easterly direction and cycle seventy kilometres to catch up with the Danube in Donaueschingen. This river empties into the Black Sea, but they plan to only follow it for another thousand five hundred kilometres until they reach Budapest.

Both Anthony and Jenny believe that Ulm, about a hundred and sixty kilometres west of Munich, could be our meeting point.

16

It feels strange to see Jenny again, but at the same time, it is as if I've never left.

I leave my car at the Bed-and-Breakfast's garage in Ehingen close to Ulm, and the four of us mount our bicycles.

Same as from Harwich to Colone, Jenny and I stay close together. She cycles behind me when it is windy and in front of me when I seek inspiration by looking at her cute backside.

Anthony has lost quite a bit of weight, and his pace has increased compared to Colin, who seems to be troubled by an injured knee.

It still rains a lot, and though there are days that the sun breaks through, the dreadful weather bothers Anthony. He expresses his displeasure by using colourful vocabulary. Colin, as one would expect from northerners, soldiers on with stoicism. He remains reserved and hardly complains about the weather or his knee. The only way we can recognise any form of agony is when he avoids our company and stays on his own.

We all agree that cycling the first part of the Rhine was magical, but following the Danube feels in ways wetter. Jenny mentions Johann Straus' waltz, 'An der schönen blauen Donau' ('at the beautiful blue Danube'), and points out that the river's colour is not blue—but brown.

We meet other cyclists. More and more people have packed panniers on their bikes and cruise the gently sloped downhill ·ds their individual destinations.

After Dillingen-an-der-Donau, Neuburg-an-der-Donau, Ingolstadt and Regensburg, we cross the German-Austrian border at Passau. Up till now, the landscape has been beautiful, but only after we've entered Austria, it becomes breathtaking. We cycle through gorgeous stone villages, pass the many homely café's and can't believe the outstanding cycle paths and the incredible cleanliness.

The rain has almost become unbearable, but Jenny and I hardly notice it. We don't care that we are getting wet and reside in our own little, waterless bliss.

One evening, when Colin and Anthony return from their walk to Passau's centre, Anthony says we need to talk. The rain has shifted into a drizzle. While Colin disappears into his tent, the three of us gather around.

"Colin really struggles to keep the pace," Anthony starts, "his knee is swollen, and it's getting worse. He's suffering more and more each day he cycles, and he doesn't want to damage something that might turn out to be irreparable at a later stage."

"Does this mean that Colin won't continue to Budapest?" Jenny asks.

"It means that both of us will stop here," Anthony sighs.

We are surprised. "You as well?" I ask. "Why?"

"I'm sick and tired of the weather. I can't do this any longer. None of my stuff gets the chance to dry properly. In the morning, I drag myself out of bed and put my damp clothes on just to get wetter during the day. I need sunshine, and I need it soon."

"It might get better," I try.

"No," he says. "I've had it."

He pulls out his phone and shows the weather forecast. The whole of Austria is covered in rain clouds. The map predicts that bad weather will follow us until we reach Budapest.

"What will we do," Jenny asks after we cosily snug up in my little tent. "Pack-up like the others, or do you think we could finish the trip?"

The rain bashes against the cheap fly-sheet, and there have been nights where the water managed to soak our sleeping bags. As long as we can keep each other warm, we don't mind.

"It's another seven-hundred kilometres," I say. "If you cycle by yourself, you will have plenty of time, but I only have six days left before I have to go back to work."

"At least it's six days," she says.

I look at her and nod. "Six days. And if we get up early in the mornings, we could do roughly a hundred and twenty kilometres per day. It might be tough, but it is manageable. I'm more than happy to give it a go."

"Okay," she smiles, "let's do it?"

17

There is no time for sightseeing and hardly a moment to enjoy the scenic villages, the food, the café's and Austria's incredible cleanliness. We are in a rush. We hurry past Linz and Krems-an-der-Donau and can maintain our daily kilometre ratio. Only Vienna, Austria's capital (which hosts about twenty-five per cent of the country's population), stubbornly insists that we need to stop end sightsee. And so we do, though not longer than half a day. We only have time to visit its Schönbrunn Palace, a former imperial summer residence. After that, we continue our trip.

We do appreciate the excellent cycle paths. I also realise that, though my mountain bike performs well on rough down and up hills, it's not built for long-distance cycling. My back and shoulder muscles ache, but more agonising is—my arse. My saddle digs deep into my backside's flesh, and it has long past the stage where only red inflammation is showing. I now sit on open wounds and wear two cycle-shorts on top of each other. Even that doesn't offer much release.

It is maddening to see Jenny effortlessly breeze through all of this. Her yoga guards her against muscle aches, and she is too light to even consider something trivial as saddle pain. However, she does get tired and wants to retreat into our tiny tent earlier and earlier each evening. It only makes me love her more.

Stop!

'Did you just say: 'love her'? You can't be serious! Have you completely lost your mind?'

I guess I have.

'What about the Norway-Africa trip or your fifty-year plan?' the bullying voice insists. 'What about not letting yourself get hurt anymore? Surely, you're setting yourself up for heartache again. But don't come crying to me when you do. I'm tired of your stupidity and your lack of common sense.'

It's for the best, I reply, and I feel at peace … —as if nothing bad can happen to me.

When we cross the border into Slovakia, we only look at Bratislava from a distance since we have no time to even briefly stop. While cycling, I turn to Jenny and ask, "Have you seen the city?"

"Yep," she shouts back. "We can now say we've seen Bratislava and check-mark that box."

It quickly becomes clear how Austria has spoiled us. The excellent and separate cycle paths have disappeared, and traffic-burdened roads are what we are left with. The scenery is monotonous and almost grey, like in the old Eastern European movies.

Still, even though the Slovakians are poor, they are certainly friendly. One shop owner refuses to take our money and insists that the watermelon we tried to buy is his gift.

We cycle a hundred and fifty kilometres and stay at the Slovakian side until we cross the Danube and, with it, the Slovakian-Hungarian border. We pitch our tents at a campsite next to the river.

The many rains have made the land soggy and wet; however, that is not what bothers us. What bothers us are the billions of mosquitoes who've all declared war. We're unable to reach our tent without being bitten a thousand times, and even ⌐dily closing our mosquito net lets hundreds of them in. The following day we are covered in red, itchy tiny dots. Jenny and I take revenge by rolling the remaining blood-sucking insects in our tent to never open it again.

When finally we reach the Hungarian capital Budapest, we've run out of time to explore it. We only briefly look at its neo-Gothic Parliament from across the river, and we don't even visit its basilica's, its concert halls and its many beautiful churches.

Instead, we are entertained by a little old lady who rents us an exquisitely, delightful room. In perfect French, she lets us know all the house rules, though only mentions what is forbidden: which is, about everything. She amuses us with stories about when Hungary was one of the Soviet Union's communist satellite states. Her husband had sneakily named his dog 'Democracy', but one day, the dog had run away, and she, her husband and their son were all forced to go into the streets and call out for 'democracy'.

Now, her son studies at Paris' La Sorbonne, and she says she's happy that times have changed.

18

The next day, Jenny and I take the early five o'clock train from Keleti pályaudvar or Budapest's central train station. We travel over Győr, and from there, we take the train which briefly passes through Slovakia and over Austria's Vienna to halt at Germany's Munich. A third train takes us to Ulm and a final one to Ehingen, where my car waits for us at the Bed-and-Breakfast's garage. After another day of driving, and at about two in the morning, we finally reach my mum's place. We sleep for a couple of hours, and before we continue our trip to London, I hurriedly introduce Jenny to her.

It feels strange.

I want to let my mum know that, this time, it is different and that Jenny is not like the others I've brought home. But I am sure my mum (by now) will roll her eyes and thinks: whatever!

On top of that, there is still that bullying voice shouting, 'Are you a complete idiot!? You shouldn't have even introduced her and have simply said that Jenny is just a friend. After all: you haven't even had the 'exclusivity conversation yet!

When we are alone, my mum wants to know if Jenny is a doctor, just like Caitlin, and I explain to her that Caitlin wasn't a real doctor. Not like the ones who can sew fingers back on when they've been chopped off by the lawnmower. Or like the ones who made a mistake and underestimated my mum's stubbornness when they told her that she had only had six to live.

"So, what is it then that Jenny does?" she asks, and her interest surprises me.

I want to say that she is in finance, but instead, I reply: "Jenny makes me happy."

"I guess that's all that counts," she sighs.

I look at her, surprised to see that she has softened up, and it makes me realise that one day Rambo will die.

I wish we weren't this rushed and had more time to spend with my mum and in the house I grew up in. I want to show Jenny the garden, the chickens, the geese, the ducks and the few rabbits that have tormented the field by digging their burrows. I want to show her the muddy pond and the extensive forest that surround the village, but it's already Monday, and I can't steal more days from work.

19

Before we even realise it, we're back on the road, travelling the six and a half hours to London. Later that afternoon, I drop Jenny off at her place in Wimbledon.

I haven't felt this tired for a long time, and when I arrive at the flat in Osterley, I plan to have a shower and hit the sack as soon as I can. But then my phone rings and when I answer, I hear it is Jenny.

"What a nice surprise," I say.

She hesitates for a moment, then says: "There is something strange happening here—."

My heart stops beating. This is it, I think; this is where she will tell me that we can't continue any longer and that we need to end our relationship for whatever reason. In my mind, I hear her say we need a clean break because dragging it on would only make things more complicated. I keep quiet; I have stopped breathing altogether and merely wait for her to say that she is sorry and that she's met someone else.

"—I just opened Skype," she continues, "and planned to chat to a friend in the US, but then I noticed your name in my contact list. How is this possible as I'm sure I've never met you before we went on our cycle trip? I certainly didn't add you while we were rushing through Europe as I only use Skype to chat with friends overseas."

"Did you click on 'history' to find out what we might have
˥ about?"

"I never save my conversations."

"Hang on," I say, "let me check my Skype."

I click on 'contacts' and search the list of names for Jenny's details. At first, I can't find it, but one name jumps out when I go over it again.

"Is your name Jennifer Caldwell?" I ask.

"Of course, it is." She giggles.

"I'm pleased to finally meet you," I joke. "I've only known you as Jenny, but I knew of your existence for about four and a half years. Do you happen to know someone named Anna? I don't know her surname. I think she was a colleague of yours."

"Anna?"

"Before I was relocated to London, I was on this dating app ... —,"

"— ... Are you talking about my former personal assistant who stayed at my place for a couple of weeks?" she interrupts. "But how do you ... oh no, you were on that dating app ... you're not that guy who ... yes you are: ... —you've lived in South Africa. My goodness," she finally utters, "Anna went on a date with you! I can't believe this. That is ... it is so long ago. But why is your name on my Skype?"

"I think Anna' phone got damaged, or something like that, so she couldn't go on WhatsApp, and therefore she used your Skype."

"Of course. But it seems that she almost used more than just my Skype," Jenny laughs and then she exclaims: "Oh nooooo! I feel ill,... —this is not real."

"What is not real?"

"The coincidence! Do you realise that we could have met four years earlier? Anna had told me about your first date. She liked you, but she didn't think you were her type. She suggested that you and I should meet and even planned this whole scheme of inviting you to a barbecue, but she never heard back from you.

Imagine that you had shown up," Jenny gasps, "we would have met four years earlier!"

"If only I had known," I say. "I thought she wanted to ... I mean ... I cannot believe this ... —I cannot believe the amount of time I have wasted."

The End

Author note

Thank you for reading this book. You might have gathered that it is based on my life while in London. However, 'biographical fiction' means that not everything is authentic, and some parts have been coloured in and are actually fictitious.

Writing this book has been on my mind for quite some time, and Covid lockdowns allowed me to get it materialised.

There is something magical about being a writer, and though I would love to do it full time, leaving a full-time job isn't an option. I have two young boys and, therefore, all the responsibilities that go along with it.

I'm always reading and writing, and my laptop is stockpiled with ideas and half-written novels that one day need to spread their wings and get into the world.
Many readers have asked me if there will be a sequel since Jenny was only introduced at the end of this novel. I can assure you that there will be a second part and hopefully the third one.

Filling out your email address while downloading the bonus section (see next page) will guarantee I'll let you know when the second book ⁀ublished.

I hope you enjoyed 'We've Let Her Know', and please leave a review on either <u>Goodreads</u> or the platform you bought it from. In the case of Amazon, find the URL below:

Goodreads reviews:
https://www.goodreads.com/book/show/57586108-we-ve-let-her-know

Amazon reviews:
- USA - <u>https://www.Amazon.com/review/create-review?&asin=B09188Y5FT</u>
- UK - <u>https://www.Amazon.co.uk/review/create-review?&asin=B09188Y5FT</u>
- Australia - <u>https://www.Amazon.com.au/review/create-review?&asin=B09188Y5FT</u>

For other Amazon market places, simply click on the Amazon US link and replace the .com with the market place you are in (.de, .fr, .es, .it, .nl, .jp, .br., .ca, .mx, .in)

Bonus section

'We've let her know' has a short section which has not been included in this book.
Find out what happens to Lyam and Jenny next.
Please download the bonus section.

Simply download it from:

<u>https://we-let-her-know.gr8.com/</u>

Other books by this Author

The Flying Man

Buy at Amazon:
getbook.at/Flying-Man

L eon finds himself lying on the bathroom floor. To understand why he is unable to move (is it the drugs, is he asleep and dreaming?), his thoughts need to progress through different times, places, and events in his life.

On his journey, he meets a beggar who talks about humbleness and Beatrice, who reminds him of his wife and asks him if he thinks he exists.

Only when the identity of The Flying Man is revealed, is Leon allowed to accept the impact that choice and doubt have made on his life.

The Flying Man is a must-read. (…) it touches on the evolution of the soul through the human mind and explores questions around existence, reality and immortality.'
J.M. Edwards, The Chronicles

'… this is an intriguing and thought-provoking'
Ed Peters, The Reviewer

'… It is a shining example of good craftsmanship…'
Writer's